Harrowed

Haunts and Hoaxes Episode 2

IRENE PRESTON

LIV RANCOURT

IrenePreston.com
LivRancourt.com

PrescourtBooks.com

This is a work of fiction. Names, characters, places, businesses and incidents either are the product of the author's imagination or are used fictitiously. Any resemblance to actual persons, living or dead, events, or locales is entirely coincidental.

Harrowed
© 2020 by Sharon Stoker Laurent and Amy Dunn Caldwell

Cover Art: Kanaxa
Editor: Linda Ingmanson

ISBN: 978-1-7358404-0-6

To seekers of truth and freedom....

Chapter One

I shouldn't be allowed to work in an office. Shaking his head at yet another (un)pleasant encounter with the (un)charming front receptionist, Noel hung up his phone and closed his laptop. With the exception of Porter Bergeron and maybe one or two others, there wasn't a soul in the place he would want to survive the apocalypse.

On the other hand, insurance hours were a helluva lot more predictable than his job with the LAPD had been. He still hadn't gotten used to walking out on Friday afternoon, secure in the knowledge they couldn't get at him until Monday.

Even so, he didn't let the door hit him on the way out.

One frustrating rush-hour drive across town later, he eased his Lexus into a spot in the alley. When he first talked about moving to New Orleans, his mother insisted on calling a friend, which was how he ended up with half of a double gallery duplex in the Uptown district. *Because yes, I'm a spoiled trust fund baby.* It was more house than he needed, but the bar down the block had a chair with his name on it, ergo he didn't complain.

Tonight, though, he denied himself the pleasure of a

visit, choosing to make his own after-work cocktail. He had plans; maybe not a date, but close enough.

He and Adam had been together some two months, long enough for a walk outside to feel like taking a cool bath to taking a slightly warmer bath. Long enough for Adam to be running out of excuses to keep *Haunts and Hoaxes* paying the rent for his Garden District apartment.

Long enough to surprise Noel that they were still fucking like dogs. Must be some truth to the old *opposites attract* thing.

Gin and tonic in hand, Noel settled into a chair. Netflix carried four seasons of *Haunts and Hoaxes*. Sixteen episodes a season. Noel knew this because he'd watched them all. Adam Morales didn't appear in every episode…but the ones he did, Noel watched twice.

Not that he'd admit it. Ever.

The episode ended, but rather than watch another, he switched to *Drag Race*. Adam had spent the week up in Natchitoches where the crew was doing a show on the Magnolia Plantation, and he was due in any time. Better he think Noel was getting his Blair St. Clair fix than know he was parsing another of Adam's forays into the supernatural.

A shiver chased down the back of Noel's neck. Yeah, he'd lived through enough unexplained phenomena on his own time.

His chair was strategically close to the open front window, and not just to catch the occasional errant breeze. Smart money would have kept the window closed, but the AC's refrigerated air didn't smell like magnolias. A car stopped, and he glanced up in time to see Adam climb out of his VW Bug. At almost six feet of dark-haired Cuban brawn, Adam looked tired and rumpled and hot as shit.

"You're late," Noel called through the conveniently open window.

Adam snorted, hoisting his bag on his shoulder. "I came straight here."

That made Noel smile. *He has it as bad as me.* Striding up the front walk, Adam's tweed jacket—because yeah, he took his professorial image seriously—flopped open to show a white button-down and a single gold chain. Jeans and biker boots finished his "academic with an edge" persona, and while Noel liked the wardrobe, his priority was getting Adam undressed.

Noel met him at the door with a beer.

"You're a bitch," Adam said, raising the bottle in toast. They had an ongoing debate about whether Noel was trying to make him fat.

Noel rubbed up against his hard, not-fat body. "You've been in the car for what? Five hours? It's not like I'm going to pour you a Diet Coke."

"Truth." Adam wrapped his free arm around Noel's waist, and they walked into the front room. "Closer to six hours, really. Between an accident in Alexandria and the overturned truck outside Opelousas, I got to sit in rush-hour traffic pretty much solid from Baton Rouge to here."

"Jesus." Noel led him to the couch. The remains of his gin and tonic made a puddle on the coffee table, and the ceiling fan clicked and whirled, doing its best to keep the heavy air moving. "You hungry?"

Adam took a solid swallow of beer, his gaze sliding in Noel's direction. "In a manner of speaking."

Oh hell yes. Noel reached up and tugged at his jacket collar. Adam shifted and Noel pulled the tweed off his shoulders. Leaning into the couch, Adam chuckled when Noel went to work on his shirt buttons. From the flat screen, RuPaul told the girls not to fuck it up, and then went silent.

While Noel had been busy with the buttons, Adam had grabbed the remote and shut off the TV. "You can watch it later."

Noel barely bothered to respond, too busy tugging shirttails out of his pants. Black curls peeked out of the neckline of Adam's white undershirt. Crawling up into his lap, Noel lifted the beer bottle and reached around to set it next to the glass on the coffee table.

"Now wait a minute." Adam wrapped his hands around Noel's wrists, and just that little bit of control sent a zing to his cock. "Before we get too distracted, I want to talk to you about something."

Noel gave him a raised-eyebrow glare.

"Don't—" Adam said.

Noel cut him off with a kiss. It took a couple of beats, but Adam's lips softened, and he kissed Noel back. Adam still held his wrists, and he rocked his hips against the bulge in Adam's jeans.

Adam pulled away, dropping Noel's wrists to grasp his hips, and Noel folded against him. "Save it." His lover smelled good, spicy and a little sweaty, like he'd had a shower but then spent hours in a car. Noel licked a stripe across his throat. "We can talk later."

Adam tipped his head against the couch. "You dog."

"Mmhmm." Noel grinned and kept licking. *I win.* His dick was hard, and Adam's was getting there. Adam pulled him closer, and, turned on by the gesture, Noel ground down onto him. From the very beginning, Adam's strength had drawn Noel in, until now he was like a drug Noel couldn't go without. "You were gone"— Noel nipped the bristled skin under his jaw—"too long."

Adam grunted, fingertips digging into Noel's back.

"This is going to bug me."

"What?" Noel blew in Adam's ear until he shivered and rolled his hips. "Your mouth is saying one thing, but your body's got something else going on." Smirking at his own joke, Noel nibbled his way down Adam's neck, shutting down a quiver of anxiety. Whatever he wanted to talk about could wait. *Right?*

Noel latched onto one of Adam's nipples through the thin cotton of his tee, working up some spit to make the fabric wet. Adam held his hips down, and Noel thrust against him, gripping his shoulders to gain traction.

Until Adam went still.

"Noel." His voice had a growl in it. "I want to tell you something, and I can't relax, or won't relax, or whatever, until I do."

Sighing, Noel cupped Adam's face in his hands. "My dude"—he couldn't stop a few baby thrusts—"your timing is shitty."

"Just..." Again, Adam grasped his wrists, which pretty much guaranteed Noel would do whatever he wanted. "Hang on."

Noel slid off his lap and flopped beside him. "Fine. Get to the point."

"So"—Adam pressed a kiss to Noel's temple—"last night, right before we knocked off, a thing happened."

Shit. Noel bumped his head against the back of the couch. "Hey, Buzz Killington, a thing's happening right now, or it was."

"I know, chulo, but just let me get this out." He patted Noel's softening cock. "You know how the crew sets up all their fancy recording equipment?"

Noel shrugged, aiming for halfway between *yes, I know* and *do we really need to do this now?*

"We were filming in one of the outbuildings. It was pitch-fucking-dark, and Jim and Brittany were doing their whispered schtick, when the recorders picked up something…"

His shiver scared Noel more than anything he'd said.

"Something I couldn't honestly explain. It was like, a sound? But not one of the usual static surges the team gets all excited about. This…" He worried his lower lip with his teeth. "This shut them right up."

All that lovely heat in Noel's belly turned to dread. "Damn."

"Yeah." Adam rubbed his thigh. "So I'm wondering if you'd go back there with me."

Dread turned to stone in the pit of Noel's belly. "Why?"

"Because." Adam shifted restlessly. "Don't you want to know?"

Noel flashed back to waking up on the cemetery path, his eyes watering like he'd never seen the sun before. "You're crazy." Reaching for his glass, Noel downed the rest of the melted ice, wishing it was straight gin.

"Yeah, I might be." Adam's fingers dug into Noel's quadriceps. "If I'm not now, I'll get there if I don't figure this out."

Blinking up into the ceiling fan, Noel thought about sending him on his way. He was asking a lot, maybe too much.

Adam shivered again.

"Fuck, all right. When do you want to do this?"

Tomorrow. Next week. Never. It all depended on what part of his brain you asked. Adam snuck a look at the man next to him, trying to figure out which answer would be most acceptable. Okay, *never* wasn't really an option except to his dick, which would pick anything to end this conversation and get Noel back in his lap.

The researcher in him wanted to go tomorrow. After ten years of telling ghost stories to subsidize his fascination with history, two months ago, he had been blindsided by evidence that ghosts were real. Or at least that everyone who claimed to see one wasn't faking it or crazy. He was *itching* to figure out exactly how Noel's abilities worked and what they could learn with them.

On the other hand... He gave Noel's thigh a final reassuring rub, then shifted to wrap an arm around him instead and pull him in close. Noel resisted for a second, then allowed himself to be cuddled. Prickly little bastard.

Adam took it as a good sign. At least he hadn't been summarily evicted from the premises, which was a win on any day, really. Noel Chandler was rich, vain, spoiled, and more than a little high-maintenance. Adam might be the TV personality, but Noel, with his California golden-boy image, was the one who drew looks when he walked into a room. And in case that wasn't enough, the sun-streaked-blond hair, golden tan, and wicked hazel eyes hid a sharp mind that had fast-tracked him to detective on the LAPD in his past life. In short, Noel was way out of Adam's league.

So far, he hadn't seemed to notice, but Adam knew he was on borrowed time. It made bringing up the anomaly in Natchitoches particularly hard. Noel got squirrely when the subject of his supposed psychic abilities came up. He'd been putting Adam off about a trip to check out a haunt in Georgia for the entire two months they'd been together.

Adam had figured Natchitoches for a hard no and wasn't sure what to do with acquiescence. Bottom line, he wanted to keep Noel safe. He just wasn't sure if *safe* meant testing Noel's abilities or keeping him far, far away from anything that might trigger them. It seemed at least some controlled exposure to find out what they were up against was called for.

He hoped that was Adam-the-boyfriend logic and not an Adam-the-researcher rationalization.

"Don't suppose you could take off work next week?" he finally offered. Noel had weekends free, but frankly, Adam wasn't up for spending another day in the car tomorrow with what was sure to be an irritable companion.

"Not Monday. Got some kind of staff thing."

Adam waited. Pushing Noel worked about as well as tossing a cat in a bath. The results weren't generally what you were hoping for.

Noel's foot started the little jittery thing it did when he was keyed up about something. The sight of it upped Adam's own tension. About half a second before he caved and called the whole thing off, the foot suddenly went still. "I could probably skip out early next Friday."

"Sure." Adam kept his voice level. "Whatever works for you."

Noel twisted out of his arms to glare at him. "Just us,

right? You don't have a crew waiting up there?"

"Of course not. We've been over this. I haven't discussed you with anybody. I just think it would be better to run some experiments where we're in control rather than wait for you to get blindsided again."

Noel chewed on his lip for a minute. "Fine. Next Friday. And we're taking my car."

Adam suppressed a grin. Noel was an unholy snob about some things. His Lexus was one of them. "Bug gets better gas mileage."

"My car or we stay home."

"If you insist." He didn't really care which car they took, but it was better to let Noel think he'd won something at this point. Adam supposed it was too much to hope he was still getting laid. He'd been gone a full week, but obviously, he should have let nature take its course before he ruffled Noel's feathers. Moral integrity sucked. "You have something in mind for supper?"

"Whatever you want to order in later." Noel lunged, and Adam let out a little *oomph* as he caught him. "After you make up for shutting me down over this bullshit."

Okay. Maybe the night wasn't a lost cause after all. Noel fused their lips together like it was his personal mission to keep Adam from ever speaking again. Apparently, his libido was willing to overcome the buzzkill of a proposed psychic adventure.

Adam approved. Mostly. Except the seduction seemed a little more frantic than usual. He twisted his mouth away. "Noel."

"Christ. What now?"

He rested his hands on Noel's hips, holding him carefully as he searched his gaze. "We okay?"

He caught the hesitation, that moment when Noel

rolled his eyes ceilingward and considered telling Adam to fuck the hell off if he didn't want to have a good time. But when he answered, his voice was serious. "Yeah, we're good. Anything *else*?"

Adam let his body relax. Well, most of it. There was a noticeable exception pressed against the front of his jeans. "Yeah, one more thing."

The look on Noel's face was priceless. Adam hooked one finger in Noel's collar. "How much did you overpay for this shirt?"

Noel sputtered.

Adam let his voice drop into a deeper register, almost a growl. It felt hokey, but he knew it revved Noel's engine. "Get it off, or I won't be responsible for damages."

The shirt came off with gratifying speed and minimal huffing over whatever blah-blah designer needed some respect. Everything else followed in short order until they were both naked and sweaty and Adam was feeling his way through a little game they played.

Noel lay stretched out underneath him, arms over his head where Adam used one hand to anchor his wrists down. His other hand was exploring territory farther south that had Noel squirming and cursing, but not squirming *too* much, because Adam's weight on him kept him pinned, while he used one leg to keep him spread open.

"Fuck you, Adam. I'm going to fucking choke you on my cum when you finally get your mouth where it belongs."

Adam responded with the barest whisper of a finger over the little pucker he'd been circling. "Thought maybe we'd wind up with my dick in your ass instead."

"Hell yeah, do *that*, then, but move it along, Professor. You need a map?"

Noel was bossy as fuck and generally needed to be In Control at all times. So it had taken Adam a little while to figure out the same rules didn't apply in the bedroom. Except, of course, it couldn't be that simple.

He sucked on the side of Noel's neck and pressed down against his wrists a little harder, just as a reminder.

"*Adam*." This time, it was less a demand and more a plea.

"Patience, chulo, we'll get there. I've been thinking of this all week. I want to enjoy it."

He wasn't under any illusion he was really in control. Adam might be bigger, but Noel had been a cop and a competitive athlete before that. If he wanted up, he was getting up.

Adam walked a fine line in not triggering that response. If the dominance got too overt, if he accidentally stepped on his ego or masculinity, Noel would retreat in a heartbeat and Adam would be nursing his blue balls back in his own apartment.

Noel didn't want to be controlled. He just wanted a place where he didn't have to be *in control*. And he didn't want to admit it.

So Noel got to issue orders, and while he bossed and begged, Adam got to pin him to the sofa and play with his trim body until neither of them was in control anymore. He considered it an honor.

And despite his words, he had been gone a *week*. He wasn't going to last. He fumbled around in the drawer in the occasional table until he found the little packet of lube and condoms he knew Noel would have stashed there.

Then he got serious with the southern hand, opening Noel up and getting him nice and slick.

Noel's wrists flexed, pushing back a little. "I swear,

Adam, if you don't..."

Adam shoved his tongue down Noel's throat at the same time he plunged his fingers deeper. Noel made a choked sound in the back of his throat and *melted*. God, Adam did love shutting the man up.

Five minutes later, he had Noel's legs over his shoulders and neither one of them was capable of coherent words. Looking down at Noel under him, eyes half closed in pleasure, body trembling, Adam had no words. There was only the bright shimmer of impending orgasm and a sense of completeness that made him stave it off as long as possible. He rode that shimmer, denying himself release to bask in the glory of shared pleasure until Noel's face went taut and shocked and they fell over the edge together.

Afterward, Adam rolled off onto the floor and settled Noel on top of him. The hardwood wasn't exactly comfortable, but they were both dripping sweat, and he didn't intend to shut Noel up permanently by smothering him.

"What the hell you got against AC?"

Noel mumbled something sleepily about magnolias. Hell, if that was all he wanted, Adam would pick some damn blooms and bring them inside. He let himself drift for a little while, enjoying Noel's weight against him despite the heat.

He was about to suggest they move the party upstairs, maybe to the shower, when he felt Noel's foot start a slow jiggle. His next words weren't so sleepy. "So, what's the story up in Natchitoches?"

Chapter Two

Bergeron leaned against the partition that separated Noel's cubicle from the others in the office. He was tall anyway, but with Noel seated, the height differential was enough to irritate.

"What?" Noel stood to prevent a kink in his neck from craning.

"The memo said casual Friday, not dress like your favorite gay anime."

Flipping the brim of his ball cap to stand it up straighter, Noel grinned. "And I guess your memo said *dress like you plan to spend the afternoon in the weight room*?" Bergeron always used casual Friday as an excuse to wear what the marketers called activewear. "I know Charisse down in accounting has got all your numbers." He emphasized his statement by giving Bergeron a wicked once-over.

"So now you're an expert on the ladies." Bergeron rolled his eyes.

Noel feigned indignation. "I may be gay, but I do pay attention to these things."

"Uh-huh."

"Look, did you just come in here to give me grief, or is there a purpose to this visit?" Noel adjusted his vintage-style horn-rims with the amber lenses. "Because I'm on my way out, so…"

Bergeron shook his head. "Skipping school? All right. I see how you are."

"Shut it. I closed the Hutcherson account, and the Tanakas'. The rest'll keep till Monday."

"Damn. You're too good for this grind, pretty boy."

"I am pretty." Noel gave him a head toss and a grin, and Bergeron rolled his eyes.

"So where you headed?"

"Adam wants to take me to Natchitoches for the weekend."

At that, Bergeron burst out laughing. "I wouldn't have figured Natchitoches as a mecca for the gays. Y'all gonna have a few meat pies?"

Stuffing his Mac in its case—the leather Bottega Veneta case his sister sent him because she felt guilty about some bullshit he'd tried to ignore—Noel shook his head. "I don't know what you're talking about, and I don't want to know."

"Nah, man. You gotta have a meat pie while you're there. They're the best." Bergeron pursed his lips like he was trying to keep from saying something else. Then his grin broke free. "Because I know you're all about the meat."

Noel tipped his head back, stifling a laugh. He hadn't come out to Bergeron until they'd known each other a few months, and now he couldn't remember what had held him back. The guy was more than cool with it; in fact, sometimes Noel wondered if his workmate didn't have a touch of the gay himself.

"I will take that under consideration." He slung his case over his shoulder and slid past the taller man. "You have a good weekend, and if Bonny asks, tell her I sent her an email with updates on all my cases."

"Too good for us, and too pretty to boot. I'm just sayin'..."

With a wave, Noel left the office. He'd taken the position at Hughes Wallace Insurance when he'd left the LAPD because the skills required were similar and people were a lot less likely to end up dead. This job didn't piss his mother off nearly as much as policing had, which was both good and bad. He also didn't have to wade through a daily upchuck of humanity's worst, which was an unanticipated bonus. People who tried to skate on their insurance policies were losers, but mostly he interacted with honest individuals making the best of shitty circumstances.

He could deal with that.

Flipping Bergeron shit had given him about ten minutes when he didn't have to navel gaze. He'd agreed to a weekend in Natchitoches more or less under protest. Like, Adam was a good guy, and Noel liked having him around.

Needle scratch.

Noel more than liked having Adam around. He'd begun to rely on him, unlike any other man he'd been with. Guys from his past, whether Stephen the hissing sissy or Alex the great unwashed or that dude from the gym who liked a good blow job? Compared with Adam, they were distractions. Toys. Adam was real, and smart, and strong. That was the reason—the *only* reason—Noel had agreed to go along.

Of course, there were times when that reliance felt a little too much like need, and Noel had to talk himself down from running the other way. Noel made a face at himself in the Lexus's rearview. More than one guy had told him he had intimacy issues.

So what?

He pushed on the accelerator as if he could speed

away from his own baggage. New town, new job, new life, right? Somehow, he had to drive across the state to walk into a place where something unexplainable had happened without tanking the little thing he had going on with Adam.

Shit. He couldn't even call it a relationship in the privacy of his own head.

Getting across town took way too long, though when he pulled up in front of Adam's house, it didn't seem long enough at all. Adam had a garage apartment behind a house in the Garden District, far enough back from the street that Noel couldn't be sure he'd hear the Lexus's horn. He could go knock on Adam's door, or...

He picked up his phone and sent a quick text.

```
Noel: I'm out front.

Adam: One second.

Noel: Don't keep me

     waiting, baby.

Adam: ffs...
```

Noel grinned and set the phone back in its holder. He spent the next few minutes considering all the reasons he didn't want to walk into someone's haunted old plantation, till a sharp knock on the back of the Lexus brought him around. He hit the Unlock button, and Adam opened the hatch, dumping a small black bag next to Noel's own luggage.

"You sure you brought a change of clothes?"

Adam responded by slamming the hatch shut, then came around and climbed into the passenger seat. "What in the..." He gave Noel an obvious once-over.

"You look like one of the Little Rascals, but gayer."

Noel slammed the car into gear. "Did Bergeron text you? I'm in shorts and a tee, for fuck's sake."

"No texts from Porter." Adam smirked at the street. "I came up with that observation all on my own."

They were both quiet till Noel had them heading down St. Charles Avenue toward the freeway. "It's the cap," Adam said, laughter in his voice. "And maybe the glasses." He poked Noel's bare thigh. "And how short are those shorts?"

"Long enough." Noel gritted his teeth. Clothing was a tool, and he'd dressed in something deliberately upbeat to chase off the ghosties. *Strategy fail.*

Another stretch of silence, broken up by Adam fiddling with his cell phone. "I've got the address in Google maps."

For a minute, Noel didn't answer. But if he didn't answer at all, Adam could call him a pouting princess, and if he was acting the princess before they were twenty minutes into the trip, this was never going to work. "So, tell me again why we're doing this." Because he didn't really give a fuck about Google fucking maps.

"Um..." Adam set his phone in one of the cup holders. "Doing what?"

"Making this damned trip."

Adam nodded like he was calculating his best approach.

Or maybe he was just trying to decide between giving a history lecture and answering the damned question.

"So...Magnolia Plantation's part of the Cane River complex. The main house is still a private home, and there's research happening in the National Park section, but mostly it's a tourist destination." Adam shifted in his seat. "We're just beating the crowds who'll show up for Mayhaw Days."

"Mayhaw Days? What the hell is a mayhaw?" Noel grabbed on to the topic to derail the budding lecture.

"No clue. I think it's a fruit of some kind."

"And what happens during Mayhaw Days?"

"Festival stuff. You know, food and music and craft displays." He slid his gaze in Noel's direction. "I hear they try hard not to sugarcoat history." He shrugged. "One of the high points is a reenactment of the story of Marie and Valsin, which is a local legend about an enslaved woman who escaped to freedom with her lover."

"Huh." Noel hit the blinker, cursing under his breath when a shitty little Prius cut him off. "Sounds like we'll miss all the fun."

"I don't know about fun—"

"So why now? What do you really want from me?"

Yes, it was the one thing Noel really wanted to know, but he hadn't meant to phrase it so baldly. Adam's slow blink made him want to grab the words back. They drove in silence for a while and Noel tried to keep his eyes on the road. Even so, the way Adam twitched and shifted in his seat made it plain he was reluctant to wade into these murky waters.

"Highway Ten, next left."

Siri's disembodied voice gave Noel something else to think about. Adam didn't break the silence until they were sitting in traffic on the highway.

"Look, I know we've never really talked about what happened last spring, but maybe we should."

And maybe we should run this thing right off the road. Noel inhaled, fighting the urge to open the door and jump. Half the reason he stayed was that he liked the Lexus too much to wreck it. "Which part in particular? The time when I busted you for stealing evidence from a crime scene?"

"Don't be a bitch," Adam huffed. "You know what I mean."

"Do I?"

"I'm talking about when we went to the Lafayette Cemetery and you had some seizure thing and collapsed and woke up yelling for help because of something that wasn't there."

Noel didn't answer. In fact, he debated never answering, because he remembered all that with painful clarity, and because he'd then told Adam about the thing that had chased him out of LA.

He'd managed to go two months without having anything weird happen. *Why now?*

"Hey, I'm sorry. I don't want to piss you off, but something happened to you in the cemetery, and...maybe before that."

Noel nodded, his brain scrambling to come up with something to say. The tension between them was thicker than the humid air.

"Shit." Adam shifted further away from Noel. "We don't have to talk about it if you don't want to. We can just...drive out to the country and get drunk tonight and see what happens."

Noel eased off the accelerator before he crawled up the tailpipe of the hulking SUV in front of him. "Meat pies."

"What?"

"Bergeron says we should have meat pies."

Adam nodded, lower lip caught in his teeth.

"But first I have to change."

Noel caught Adam's smirk out of the corner of his eye. That one gesture eased something in Noel's chest. He'd do...whatever it was...but not tonight.

"Catfish."

Noel raised an eyebrow. "What?"

"And beer. That's what I heard we should eat."

"Noted."

They rode in silence for a while, the Lexus smoothly chewing up the miles. Out of the blue, Adam dropped a small bombshell. "They practiced voodoo."

Noel shook his head. Adam must have spent the last thirty miles figuring out which little factoid Noel absolutely had to know.

"The enslaved people who lived at Magnolia plantation. That's one of the reasons it's supposed to be haunted."

Stuffing his hand in the pocket of his shorts, Noel wrapped his fingers around the old gris gris from the burned-out house in Adam's neighborhood. Silly, but it was a token of when he and Adam first met, stalking each other through the house neither of them should have been in. *Got a feeling I'm going to need whatever juju it can come up with.*

When the show traveled, Adam and the other on-air talent sometimes got lucky enough to stay on the featured property. If not, accommodations were usually basic. *Haunts and Hoaxes* had a cult following and a decent budget for cable, but the expense accounts didn't stretch to luxury rooms. The crew stayed at a chain hotel off the highway while they filmed in and around Natchitoches.

Adam had been halfway through entering his credit card information into the booking system for the same place when he got a mental image of Noel faced with polyester bedspreads and the "continental" breakfast laid out in the lobby.

He'd backed out fast and booked them into the Judge Porter House instead, arguably one of the poshest accommodations in town.

Noel, of course, had taken the upgraded rooms as his rightful due and made himself at home. He'd charmed the innkeeper with a few words about the antique chandeliers, located the wet bar in the downstairs parlor in under thirty seconds after entering the building, and magically produced an expensive-looking bottle of gin from somewhere up his nonexistent sleeves.

Adam dealt with check-in and their luggage. Had Noel given him shit about his duffel and laptop case this morning? Because it wasn't Adam who required a suitcase, garment bag, and tiny third bag he bet Noel called a shaving kit and probably contained half the Nordstrom men's care counter. He dumped the suitcases and garment bag in the closet, put the shaving kit in the bathroom, and sat his laptop on the dresser next to their welcome gift from the inn. The wicker basket included a bottle of wine, a box of pecan pralines, two jars of local mayhaw jelly, and coupons for local restaurants and tours.

Adam flipped through the coupons and a brochure for Mayhaw Days before heading out to the second-story gallery. Noel had two G&Ts sweating in tumblers on the balcony rail while he took in the view of small-town charm.

Adam approached cautiously, wondering if the second drink was supposed to be for him or just *look* like it was for him. He wasn't very fond of gin. On the other hand, Noel wasn't generally coy about his drinking when he decided to lay one on. Maybe he'd just taken Adam's suggestion in the car seriously.

"You okay?"

Noel had ditched the lenses, and the gold flecks in his normally sleepy eyes glinted when he turned his regard to Adam. "No one's ever rented an antique bed to boink me on before. You're definitely getting lucky tonight."

Adam wouldn't bet on it. Since their little chat in the car, Noel had alternated between silence and bursts of frantic conversation. Not the good kind of quiet either. And not the conversations they ought to be having.

A knot of tension settled in Adam's stomach. He shouldn't be pushing this. He was going to lose Noel over it, and he'd be lucky if that was all that happened. For all he knew, exposing Noel to whatever was out at Magnolia could be dangerous.

Who was he kidding? It *was* dangerous. The only question was if the danger would be physical or purely psychological. Either way, he would be subjecting Noel to an uncontrolled experiment with the possibility of lasting damage.

Real romantic. He was getting lucky tonight for sure.

Or they could go home without learning anything and wait for some random psychic energy to hijack his boyfriend again.

Noel sucked down the last of the liquid in his glass and set it next to its twin on the balcony railing. He moved closer until they were chest to chest, then tilted his head into Adam's neck and inhaled. "You smell like my Lexus and guilt. I can work with that."

He grazed his teeth over Adam's earlobe. "We're here. Stop thinking and have a drink."

Adam's body tightened, and he clenched his hands to keep himself from yanking Noel closer and taking him up on the offer. "You know I hate gin."

Against his better judgment, he cupped his hand around Noel's neck and pulled him closer until the ridiculous flowered shirt was pressed against his own blue polo. Noel smelled like Le Labo and liquor. Adam inhaled all the bullshit, searching underneath for something real. Before he could sort through all the chemicals, Noel bit his neck. "So skip the drink, Professor. We can go right to the boinking."

Adam sighed. Someone had to be the adult in the room. "We've got dinner reservations, remember?"

"Suit yourself." Noel stepped away way too easily, proving he hadn't really been into the seduction. He picked up the second glass and took a healthy swallow. "Let me get changed and we can head out, maybe hit the bar before we eat."

Adam directed a meaningful look at the second G&T. "Don't forget the anthropologist from the park is joining us."

Noel's smile was all white, perfect teeth and perky enthusiasm. He drained the glass in one long swallow. "Can't wait, baby."

Chapter Three

Adam changed his shirt, because a day on the road was a day on the road, even in a Lexus.

Noel ditched the cap, kept the shirt, and swapped the shorts for a pair of jeans with a fit that had to be illegal in half a dozen states. Adam tried not to stare at his ass while Noel stood in front of the mirror and scrunched his hands through his hair. In the last couple of months, he had abandoned the designer bed head. The new cut was shorter and neater, but still managed to look like Noel had just rolled out of bed. The scruff along his jaw had gotten neater with the hair. The green-and-gold bedroom eyes hadn't changed a bit, and they still drove Adam crazy.

"Who's this guy again?"

The question sounded offhand, but Adam wasn't fooled. Noel had been a cop. A few drinks didn't change that.

"Jason Pham. He was the show's liaison while we were filming, and we go way back. Be nice to him. He's the guy who's going to get us in after the park closes, even though we aren't good for any more free PR."

"Be nice to the park ranger, got it." Noel smirked at him in the mirror. "He cute? How nice you want me to be?"

Adam tamped down on the unexpected anger that tightened his gut. Noel was just being Noel. He was freaked by this whole trip, and all his defense mechanisms were out. There was no reason for Adam to get all bent out of shape, so he kept his voice calm when he replied. "Dr. Pham, actually. He's teaching some classes at NSU, but his main funding is a grant from the Park Service. His area of expertise is African-American folklore, so we have a good bit of overlap in our interests."

For a second, Noel went completely still at the mirror. Then he turned, cocked a hip, and gave Adam his most devastating smile. "Ooohhh. Mama would approve of a doctor! Let's go meet Dr. Pham."

No reason to get bent out of shape, Adam reminded himself. None at all.

His gut didn't agree. Noel might or might not be joking about flirting with Jason. Noel flirted with the same consistency he breathed, and Adam had learned to live with that fact early on. But Mr. G&T wasn't the only one anxious about this trip.

The whole situation brought home just how tenuous their association was. The psychic stuff wasn't the only thing they never discussed. Their *relationship* didn't even have a name. Friends with benefits? Fuckbuddies? Adam would like to think it was more, but Noel had never given him any indication he was ready to take things to the next level.

Adam thought he'd come to terms with the idea they were killing time until Noel went back to California, his high-profile job, and his rich family. Or Noel was killing time. Adam spent too much of his own time wondering what the extensive Morales family would think of his prickly California cop.

"So, we doing this?" Noel's smirk slipped into a scowl.

"If you're done primping." Adam tried for light and was pretty sure he fell short. Noel scowled again but didn't say anything as he headed for the door.

The restaurant was within walking distance, and Adam figured they could do with stretching their legs after the long car ride. Natchitoches sat between the Cane River and Sibley Lake, a classic slice of northern Louisiana. The town was older than the plantation they had come to see, and its residents had made an effort to revive the historic district. Many of the stately old homes had been preserved, although some—like the Judge Porter House—had been converted into inns and B and Bs.

The heat of the summer hadn't hit yet, so they weren't the only people out enjoying the temperate weather with a stroll along the picturesque streets. The well-tended lawns featured bursts of colorful azaleas and hydrangeas as well as the fragrant magnolias Noel was so fond of.

Adam pushed aside his misgivings and let himself pretend they were any other couple on a weekend getaway. Noel seemed to settle back into his skin too. He was in one of his quiet moods, and Adam filled the silence with trivia about the town like the nerdy history professor he really was.

He kept it light, regaling Noel with a version of the Marie and Valsin legend that had the local grocer smuggling Marie off Magnolia in an empty rice sack. He was rewarded with an incredulous laugh at the end. "Are you kidding me?"

"That's just one version."

"No, really, though. How did she get out?"

"The truth is lost to the ages." Adam put on his best

TV Professor voice, then suppressed a smile as Noel threw him a dirty look. Love story of the century? Not interested. Unexplained getaway? He could see the wheels turning in Noel's head as he pondered the problem.

He changed topics to point out some interesting history about a few of the houses they were passing. By that point, he didn't expect Noel to be paying any attention, so it was a surprise when he stopped short and pivoted, arms wrapped around his waist as if he'd caught a sudden chill.

"Noel?" Adam turned with him, prepared to see something more dramatic than the old Southern houses, live oaks, and a few random tourists.

"What about that one?" Noel jutted his chin in the direction of large brick home set back from the street. "That one looks old. Don't you have anything to say about it?"

Adam glanced at the house. "That's where they filmed *Steel Magnolias.*"

Noel cocked his head as though confused, so Adam clarified. "Movie? Shirley MacLaine, Dolly Parton? Julia Roberts?"

Noel stared at the house a little longer, then shook his head and resumed walking. "Never saw it."

He took a few more steps, then stopped again. Adam could see the tension in his body, as though he were holding himself still with an effort. "Just the movie? No...history?"

Adam glanced back across the street. "What is it? Do you...?"

"No." Noel spat out. "Come on, I'm hungry."

He didn't remark on the fact that Adam hadn't actually answered his question. The Steel Magnolia house mostly drew movie buffs as tourists, but it was old. Of course it had history. Adam had booked the Judge Porter House instead of Steel Magnolias for that very reason.

He spent the rest of the walk wondering if he should mention the history and get Noel to talk about whatever had drawn his attention to that particular house. In the end, he held his tongue. Noel was under enough stress this weekend. Their agenda was Magnolia Plantation. They didn't need a side tour.

Despite the rough start to the evening, Adam got a little thrill as he spotted Jason across the restaurant. Adam had met Porter Bergeron and a couple of other people at the insurance agency where Noel worked, mostly by showing up and forcing the issue. This was Adam's first chance to introduce Noel to one of his own colleagues. He was ridiculously excited at the chance to show him off.

He waved at Jason, who was already seated at a table out on the deck overlooking the river.

"*That's* Dr. Pham?" Noel muttered under his breath.

Adam slid him a look but couldn't tell what he meant by the remark. Maybe he'd expected someone older. Or in a tweed jacket. Noel had weird expectations for academics sometimes. Adam had to admit he played to stereotypes, both for the show and Noel. Jason, however, preferred a more laid-back look. Tonight, wearing a Vic the Demon tee and board shorts, he could easily pass for an NSU undergrad rather than a PhD in mythological studies.

"Adam." Jason rose to greet them as they approached, smiling and obviously excited.

Adam did the introductions. For once, Noel *didn't* flirt. Instead, he wore an expression that looked like what Adam thought of as his cop face, serious and sharp-eyed, with no hint of what he was actually thinking. From the way Jason's eyes narrowed at their handshake, he also did the macho-man squeeze, which was so out of character, Adam couldn't even begin to guess what was going on in his head. Still rattled by the trip, maybe.

"Adam," Jason said as soon as they were all seated. "I'm glad you decided to come back up this weekend. We didn't get a chance to catch up while you were filming."

Adam nodded. "Definitely worth a second trip. I don't know why it took the show so long to take you up on your offer of access. You couldn't have kept me away if I'd realized the scope of what you were doing."

He turned to Noel. "Jason is researching how enslaved African Americans on the plantations blended elements from their disparate backgrounds to form a common culture. He's put together a really impressive collection of lore from various sources."

Jason waved a hand dismissively. "Please. I hope I can contribute something, but of course it's all derivative of Stuckey's work on the African diaspora. When it comes down to it, I'm just like Adam. The thrill is in finding a new story.

"Speaking of which" —he turned to Noel—"I bet you've got a few you could tell."

"Me?" Noel looked blank.

Jason went on blithely. "Adam couldn't shut up about you last week. I'd love your perspective on a few mysteries I've stumbled on in the historical record."

An obvious silence hung in the in the air while Noel digested this remark. Then he smiled lazily. "What, and miss out on you two professors comparing notes? Let's order, and you can have at it."

Jason picked up his menu with a laugh. "That works."

Adam started to relax. Noel had been kidding back in the room. Of course he wouldn't flirt with Jason. As long as Adam could steer the conversation away from what they actually hoped to accomplish at Magnolia, everything would be fine.

dam couldn't shut up about you last week. And what could Adam possibly have said to make Dr. Pham think Noel could help with historical mysteries?

His special talent. Had to be. Noel wasn't drunk. *Yet.* He tipped his head at the waitress, who ambled over. "I'll take a double gin and tonic."

The waitress was short and stacked, her too-tight, too-long dress emphasizing both those attributes. "Tall glass?"

Noel sat back in his seat, moving out of range in case her straining top button broke free. "Any glass is fine." He just wanted the gin because Adam had a big fucking mouth, and Noel was close to saying something they'd both regret. The whole day—the "we need to talk" bullshit on the ride over, the surprise work buddy who knew Noel's secrets, the weird-ass cold spot he'd stumbled over on the way to the restaurant—combined to make Noel thirsty. Real, real thirsty.

Adam ordered a glass of white wine and Jason ordered a Coors Lite. *Really? Coors Lite?* Noel stifled a snort.

The waitress drifted in the general direction of the bar, her slow pace necessary to keep her from busting a seam. That, or to make sure every man in the place got an eyeful. Every man except him and Adam.

And possibly Jason, who watched Adam as if memorizing every inhale, every pause, every thoughtful smile.

Noel had pretty strong observational skills too, and this hot Asian dude—with his gelled hair and bad-ass goatee—was paying way too much attention to Noel's...whatever Adam was to him. Jason had an accent too, but not from the South. Something familiar. *Where have I heard...* "Are you from Hawaii?"

Adam stopped talking about folktales and Jason stopped staring at Adam while he talked about folktales.

"Yeah, I grew up on Kauai and did undergrad at UH," Jason said. "Haven't lived there in a while, though."

The waitress strolled over with their cocktails, and Noel took a healthy swallow of his gin and tonic. He grimaced at the chemical juniper taste but a couple more swallows washed it away.

"I'll be back in just a sec to take your food order." She gave them an inviting little smile, probably figuring it'd help her tips.

Noel downed more gin to disguise his eye roll. "Wanna bring me another one of these when you come back?"

She blinked, and her smile broadened. "Sure thing, hon. Just a sec."

Adam was giving him side-eye, and Jason's expression had that careful blankness of someone who disapproved but didn't want to actually say anything. "What?" Noel mostly addressed Adam, but if Jason wanted to respond, he could have at it.

"Nothing."

Adam's mouth said one word, but his eyes shouted paragraphs of displeasure. He'd never seen Noel really drunk.

First time for everything, my dude. "So, come on"—he echoed the words with a wave of his hand—"tell us how a boy from Kauai ended up poking around plantations on the bayou."

"Kidnapping." Jason maintained his impassive expression, but Adam snorted into his wineglass.

"That line might have worked with me, Jay, but Noel's not nearly as gullible."

Jason cracked a smile, his gaze on Adam, and for one sharp moment, Noel wanted to reach across the table and smack him. Nobody got to look at Adam that way, and Adam didn't get to make up cute little nicknames for dudes.

Not while Noel was sitting right there, anyway.

Noel swallowed the remainder of his drink, impatient for the waitress's return. "So if it wasn't kidnapping, what? There weren't enough weird folktales to keep you busy back home?"

Between his mother's house on Diamond Head, with a view of Waikiki in one direction and the entire Pacific Ocean in the other, and her Maui condo where she went to watch the whales, Noel had spent a fair amount of time in Hawaii. He knew a few of the local legends—the night walkers, Madame Pele, the *menehunes*—and from what Noel could tell, a guy who was into that sort of thing wouldn't need to come all the way to Backwater, Louisiana.

"Eh, long story, brah." He'd thickened his accent. "My dad was in the Army, but he grew up in Shreveport. I got family..." His voice faded, and they all watched the waitress put a fresh drink in front of Noel.

"Are y'all ready to order food?" Her words had the same leisurely pace as her walk.

Noel had pretty much lost his appetite, but he scanned the menu, because no way was he leaving Adam alone with Hawaii Boy. No *fucking* way. Fortunately, the combined effects of many gin and tonics dampened the grinding whine of anxiety that had tightened his jaw till Noel could barely open his mouth. He pointed at something random. "I'll have that."

"Sure thing. How would you like your burger?"

Damn. Noel squinted at the menu, willing his eyes to focus. Had he just ordered a hamburger? "Medium rare." He hated—

"I thought you hated hamburgers." Adam's voice was low and possibly soothing, except for the way it took the anxiety whine to eleven.

"Forget that." Noel shut one eye, since apparently the two of them were confusing each other. *Drunken fuck.* There. Salad. He liked salad. "Can I have the Caesar salad with chicken instead?"

The waitress made a note on her pad and turned to Adam. He ordered something, and then Hawaii Boy asked for a burger. *Make your breath stink like old beef, brah.* Wouldn't matter. Not like Hawaii Boy would be kissing anybody.

Wait.

Who would he be kissing? The room shifted, and everything more than two feet away started to blur.

Not Adam. Noel would kill him.

Yes. Kill him. Kill Hawaii Boy. That was the answer. With that issue settled, Noel took another long pull of his drink. Adam and Jason slid off into some side conversation about how hard it was to document anything about the early African Americans because nobody kept any records. "But what do you do, then?" Noel surprised himself by asking a question. "Make shit up?"

Jason chuckled, but Adam's expression was the exact opposite of amused. "I think you've had about enough." He reached for Noel's glass.

Noel grabbed his wrist, hard. "I'm fine."

"All right, then." Speaking carefully, Adam gave a little jerk and pulled his hand away. He didn't look angry. Maybe disappointed? Disappointed that Noel was acting the fool in front of his work friend. His work friend who knew all about Noel's special talent. *That's right!* Move that to the top of the list of shitty things that had happened today.

Anger pulled all of Noel's feelings into focus. "It's your own damned fault. You had to go tell him."

"I...what? Tell him what?"

"About me."

"What are you talking about?"

Adam's blank expression just made Noel angrier. "My *thing*."

"It's cool, man." Jason stood, his hands out like he wanted to smooth over the turbulence at the table. "I'll just... See y'all another time."

Adam half rose from his seat too. "No, I'm sorry, just—"

Noel shoved his chair back from the table. "I guess I really am the problem. You two have a good dinner." He grabbed his glass and downed the rest of his drink. "I'll see you...later."

He managed to make it out to the street without walking into anything, which he counted as a win. The scene was blurry, ordinary traffic sounds muffled, the anxiety whine rising. Which way was the hotel? He couldn't remember. Picking a direction at random, he started walking. He just needed to find a bar anyway.

So much for staking his claim on Adam. He and Hawaii Boy could have a heart-to-heart conversation on the importance of preserving the knowledge of dead people since living people were clueless. He walked farther, finally smacking his knee on a fire hydrant that jumped into the middle of the sidewalk.

Farther still, and he hit it again. Not the fire hydrant, the cold spot. It brought him up short. His blurred vision found the gold plaque on the building across the street. Steel Magnolias. Whatever. He'd been raised by the titanium poppy. *But what the hell?* It was so cold, right in this spot. So cold, and so saturated with fear.

His knees gave way, and he might have started screaming.

Chapter Four

hat?" Noel sat up fast, clutching the sheet. Screams echoed and the pounding in his head rolled his stomach. He eased back, heartbeat thudding in his ears, mouth so dry he could barely unstick his tongue.

"Where the hell...?" He pried open his eyes, or his right eye, anyway. The room was dark except for a thin gray light from the window. Streetlight, or maybe dawn. He was in that shabby chic nightmare of a room Adam had booked.

Adam. Was he...?

A snorting snore answered his question. Adam was beside him in the bed, a big, warm, security blanket. Noel tipped his head up against the pillow. His mouth tasted like he'd been eating tree bark, but bitter and ugly. What the hell had he done? He drew circles on the sheet, trying to retrace his route to this moment in this bed.

He'd started drinking early, spiking his water bottle with gin before he'd picked Adam up. Then...more drinks at the hotel, plus a Xanax because this whole little adventure had him strung out in the extreme.

Then...fuck... Had he ordered a double at the

restaurant? He'd needed it. Adam's friend... What was his name? Noel couldn't remember much, except the guy had been dangerously sexy, and he and Adam had a lot to talk about.

The second double had been the bridge too far. After that, everything went a little nuts. The memory had him breathing faster, except that made his head hurt and he forced himself to slow down. Water. He needed water. Slowly, mindful of the heavy thudding in his head, he turned toward the nightstand. A bottle of water sat there, with two white tablets beside it.

Tylenol. *Sweet.* Raising himself onto his elbows, he picked up the pills one at a time. Something—either the pain in his head or the thoughtfulness behind the gift on the nightstand—had his eyes burning with moisture. He tossed back the pills, downed about half the bottle of water, and eased himself onto the mattress.

He'd appreciate the relief as soon as he was sure his head was going to stay attached.

"You alive?"

Adam's gruff voice set off pain of a different kind. Noel couldn't have made a bigger ass of himself if he'd set out with a checklist. Why was Adam even here? "Yeah." His voice cracked and sagged. "Just don't ask me to move, because it might kill me."

As if called to attention by his words, pressure built in his bladder. *Fantastic.* They lay together, the room's hushed quiet enveloping them. For his part, Noel didn't have a fucking clue what to say. Dinner had been such an epic debacle, Noel couldn't even remember the other guy's name. And then...and then...

Cold. The kind of cold that made him forget he'd ever seen the sun. A cold fueled by rage and by despair, defiance, and hopelessness.

And he could never give in. *Never.*

"I'm pretty sure we've got stuff to talk about, but—"

"Dude." Noel's groan reverberated in his head, and he hissed against the pain.

"Later." Adam rolled up on his side, edging closer to Noel.

Noel slid a hand in Adam's direction. Adam's hand found his, their fingers interlacing. "Later," Noel whispered. He drifted off, dozing until the Tylenol kicked in, and then he slept.

Chapter Five

Aside from waking up to take the Tylenol and later a trip to the bathroom, Noel slept until after noon. Adam briefly considered dragging him down for their included breakfast as a form of revenge, then immediately felt like shit.

Last night—whatever last night was—he had massively failed.

He had lost sight of his responsibilities at some point in the evening. His vision cleared up fast when he found Noel curled on the porch of the B and B, shivering as though it were the dead of winter instead of almost eighty degrees.

So he had no reason to hang on to this residual anger. He knew Noel tended to self-medicate, he just hadn't expected him to try to completely anesthetize himself. He'd been too busy wallowing in his fantasy relationship to notice how bad things were.

A creak of the bedsprings brought his gaze up from his tablet, where he had been responding to a spate of postproduction emails from the show.

Noel's eyes were open.

For maybe the first time ever, he didn't immediately make an off-color comment or crack a joke. He just lay there, looking small and pale and sick and so un-Noel-like that Adam felt his own bile rise.

"Hey." He wasn't sure what else to say.

"Hey."

Adam waited, then finally prompted, "You okay?"

Noel winced as he struggled to sit up. His voice sounded raspy and subdued when he replied
"Yeah. I'm good."

Good? So they were going to start the day with lies. Noel's state was anything but *good* at the moment. The flutter of fear in Adam's stomach made him speak more sharply than he intended. "You look like shit. It's a wonder you didn't choke on your own vomit last night before I found you."

Noel's lips thinned. "Okay. Thanks for tucking me in, St. Adam, but I didn't need your help."

Adam squeezed his eyes shut, counted to ten, and tried again. "I'm sorry. I didn't mean that. I was just... You worried me, okay?"

Noel didn't reply, so Adam prompted, "Did something happen on the way home?"

Noel scowled at him. "Yeah, I tripped over two fire hydrants, then blacked out. I guess I didn't walk in front of any cars, because here I am."

"Nothing else?"

"What else would there—" Noel stopped abruptly. If possible, his face paled further. "No. Nothing else. I was drunk. I do that sometimes. Sorry."

They stared at each other for another minute. Then Noel rasped out, "Why?"

He didn't sound like he wanted to know. Looking at his ashen skin, Adam seriously debated whether to tell him. "I found you out on the porch. You were shivering and ice cold, like you were going into shock. You looked pretty much the same way you did that day in Lafayette

Cemetery." The last time he had been hijacked by some kind of external energy, unless they were both crazy.

Noel's fingers clenched in the sheet. "So I'm an ugly drunk. Again, sorry."

"Noel, are you sure..." Adam paused. He'd thought he was prepared for this weekend, that the test of Noel's abilities would happen in as controlled an environment as he could make it. But nothing about this trip was going as planned.

The direction of the conversation helped Adam come to a decision he'd been circling all morning. "How soon do you want to leave?"

Noel scrubbed his fingers through his hair and squinted at the window. "Uh. What time is it? Are we late for something?"

"A little after one. And no, no particular schedule. The room's paid for for the weekend. If you don't feel up to the drive today, we can stay over until tomorrow."

Noel turned the squint on Adam. "What are you talking about?"

"This was a mistake. Obviously. I'm taking you home."

"The fuck you are." The squint turned into a glare. "You wanted to come, we're here."

Adam shook his head. "Noel, you aren't in any state to..."

Noel rolled out of bed with more grace than Adam would have thought possible, dragging the sheet with him. He swayed a little as he landed on his feet, but his jaw came up, daring Adam to call him on it. "I just need a shower. And some kombucha. Maybe another Tylenol or two."

"I really don't think..."

"No. Don't think. You wanted to do this, we're doing it." He shuffled toward the bathroom, then hesitated.

He looked almost uncertain for a second, then threw out, "Sorry I fucked up dinner with your asshole friend."

He didn't sound sorry. He sounded angry. What the hell did Noel have against Jay? He hadn't even given him a chance last night. "Jason's not an asshole. He's actually a very nice guy."

Noel snorted. "Yeah, I'm sure you think so."

"He was looking forward to meeting you."

Noel's face darkened. "Yeah, because you told him *all about me*. Thanks."

What the hell? Because it was a crime to talk about his boyfriend?

And all the air went out of Adam's lungs in a rush because...because he thought of Noel as his boyfriend. He *wanted* Noel to be his boyfriend. Or whatever relationship term Noel wanted to use that meant they were more than friends who fucked. He thought he might want to be a lot more than friends. And...Noel obviously didn't want that.

"I..." He couldn't talk to Noel about this right now. He scrambled for the threads of the conversation they'd been having. "He's from Hawaii. He surfs. He used to do the Haleiwa Open every year. I thought you two would have a lot in common."

Noel's lip curled. "Amateur." Then, "It's not me he's wants to impress."

"He doesn't need to impress anyone. His work speaks for itself."

Noel glared. "I get it, Professor. You were obviously into his *work* last night. Almost as much as he was into you."

"Well, you weren't into anything but the gin," Adam shot back before he could censor himself.

"Just admit you got off on talking about census lists

and diaspora and circle rituals with someone who could follow all that shit." Noel blinked as though he'd surprised himself.

"You're not stupid. You could have joined the conversation any time."

"Not. My. Field," Noel bit out. "Whatever. You both like history. I get it. Glad you found someone who appreciates you. He's still an asshole."

The unfairness of the accusation hit Adam's last nerve. "*Yes.* Okay? It was nice to talk to a colleague. It was nice to talk to another academic who still treats me with respect. You know what it's been like since I started doing the show?

"I'm *the ghost guy.* If I go to a conference, everyone assumes my degree is in parapsychology—that's if they think I have any kind of degree at all. Most just assume I'm an actor. The only questions I get asked are about EMF meters and if the minions are as hot in person as on TV.

"Submit a paper? Want to sit on a panel? Forget it. I love my job, but *I miss being taken seriously by other historians.* So fuck you. Yes, I enjoyed talking to Jay last night. It was nice talking to someone who knows my master's thesis wasn't on spirit globules, much less someone who's actually read it."

He was breathing hard. He'd somehow moved across the room until he was only a foot away from Noel, who was watching him warily, as though he might suddenly sprout fangs or burst into flames.

And fuck everything. Noel still looked like death warmed over. His skin had the healthy glow of a dead fish. His eyes were bloodshot. His hair stuck up at every angle. Sour gin was literally seeping out of his pores. And he still looked...delicious. Fuckable. Unattainable.

"Take your damn shower," Adam growled. "Pack

your bags. God knows where I'm going to find your godawful kombucha in this town, but as soon as I do, we're going home."

None of it was what he'd meant to say. All he knew was his instincts yesterday had been right. This trip had cost him Noel.

Noel's bloodshot gaze gave no quarter. "I said no. We're going out to that damn plantation and doing what we came here for."

Pain spiked behind his eyelids from the pressure of his clenched his jaw. They could not possibly be fighting about this. Except they were. "It's not safe."

"What, I'm going to fall over again? We brought a helmet."

He'd practically had to drag Noel up here, and now he wouldn't leave. It didn't make sense. Why did Noel have to be so difficult? Why couldn't Adam have fallen for someone like Jay, who was easy-going and didn't take unreasonable offense to meeting someone new? Adam smiled. Bingo. "Going out to the plantation means seeing Jason again."

Noel flinched. "Fine. Call him and set it up. That's what we came here for, right? So you could impress him?"

"What?"

"Yeah. He said you wouldn't shut up about me. And what is it about me that's so darn interesting, Mr. History Professor? Gee, I can't put my finger on it. Now call him and set it up. Let's go get this over with."

Noel stood under the spray of hot water, hoping the shower would wash away the last ten minutes. Or that the second dose of Tylenol would kick in. Or something. Anything.

What was he sure of? Adam had a thing for Noel's superpower, had wanted to test it since that day in Lafayette Cemetery. Noel had put him off, making excuses for why they couldn't go exploring every damned pseudo-haunted house Adam tripped over. Adam didn't talk much about it, but something had happened to an old girlfriend, and Noel hadn't wanted to deal with anything that messy.

Noel squeezed his eyes shut and turned his face to the full blast of the water. *I'm not your answer, dude.* If he'd been reluctant to help Adam work things out with an old girlfriend, coming here made even less sense. Here: this stupid B and B, the Magnolia Plantation, Natchitoches, this place where *Jay*—why did the name have multiple syllables when he heard it in his head?—was eager to be helpful.

And as Noel's reward for vacillating, Adam had apparently told *Jai-ai-ay* all about his superpower. *Fucking awesome.*

At least the shower's water pressure was good. Noel pivoted, head tipped back, though a wave of dizziness almost knocked him over. *Damn it.* He shut the water off and stood there dripping. Adam had even given him a free pass.

This was a mistake. Obviously. I'm taking you home.

Fuck that and fuck that and fuck that again. Whatever this *thing* was, this whole cold-fear-weird-spirit thing that highjacked his mind, Noel needed to figure out a way to stop it from happening. If Adam's haunted plantation test didn't work, maybe antipsychotics were the answer.

But he wasn't crazy, or at least he didn't think the ghosts were a sign of insanity. He could count two episodes, well, three if he included whatever had happened last night. Okay, four if he counted the voice in the house in New Orleans. There had to be a way to link them together.

Both the incident in LA and the one in Lafayette Cemetery had occurred when his mind was focused on a task. He'd been occupied, searching for something. Cemetery aside, there'd been nothing woo-woo about either scene. While his knowledge of medicine was limited, the lightning-bolt nature of these attacks made them seem more like seizures than anything else. Episodic psychosis wasn't a thing, was it?

Although, his doctors had cleared him of seizures, so…

So he was either crazy, or he did have some kind of superpower. The thought caught him somewhere between disbelief and fear. He didn't feel like dealing with either.

He could take Adam up on his offer; drive them both home, spend the rest of the weekend drowning in a bottle of gin, and maybe make a doctor's appointment Monday morning. Because yeah, telling Karen the Receptionist that he needed an appointment because the haunts kept hijacking his mind was gonna go over real well.

Or he could ball up, check out the plantation house

and any other place Adam wanted to go, and hopefully put all this behind him. His stomach gurgled loud enough to make him chuckle. "Kombucha and an Egg McMuffin dude. I hear you."

He could help Adam out. He was a cop, or he had been. Clutching his metaphysical 'nads, he got dressed, determined to see this whole charade through.

He came out of the bathroom to find Adam had magicked a kombucha from somewhere. The honey-and-vinegar taste bolstered him, and after another round of are-you-sure-you-want-to-yes-I'm-sure, they managed to make it to the Lexus without a real argument.

A few blocks from the B and B, a set of golden arches caught Noel's eye. He flipped the turn signal on, easing into the center turn lane.

"Where are you going?" Adam's retro Ray-Bans were perfect for his hipster-professor vibe, though Noel figured he'd chosen them at random.

Noel made the turn and pulled up in front of the drive-through speaker. "Breakfast."

The tinny speaker sprang to life. "Welcome to McDonald's."

"I'll take an Egg McMuffin and a large fries." He tossed a glance at Adam. "To share."

Adam snorted. He leaned against the passenger door, elbow on the armrest, knuckles covering his mouth.

At the clerk's invitation, Noel rolled up to the next window and paid for his breakfast. The salty grease smell from the bag made his stomach gurgle. He grabbed his McMuffin and set the open bag on the console between the seats. "Help yourself."

Adam scowled. "You're a dick, you know that?"

Noel grinned around a mouthful of food. "What?

You like fries, and I like you." Besides, Adam's body was perfect. *Perfect*. "And I want you to be happy."

Still glaring at the bag, Adam slipped in a hand and pulled out a single fry.

"Dude...no one can eat just one."

"Fuck you, Noel." Adam grabbed a handful of fries, and Noel grinned again, glad they were back on more solid ground.

The map app on his phone blurted out instructions, and with one hand on the wheel, Noel pulled back out into traffic. "So on the way down here, you said something about voodoo."

"Hmph." Adam raised a finger, swallowing fries. "Yeah, that's the angle we played on the show."

"Angle you played? You mean it might not be true?"

Adam's brow creased, a sign he was putting his teacher face on. "No, I think the enslaved people—the early African Americans—did practice voodoo. It was a mélange of their traditional religious beliefs and the Christianity they were forced to adopt."

He reached for another fry, and Noel didn't interrupt him.

"Like, on the show, we emphasized stories that claimed the enslaved laborers used voodoo to put curses on their oppressors, but I don't know. The winner gets to write history, you know? And I think it was in the white people's self-interest to cast everything about the enslaved Black people in as negative light as possible."

"So no voodoo curses?"

The map app reminded them they'd need to turn left in 400 feet.

"I can't say it never happened, but..." Adam paused. "Let's just say voodoo curses get better ratings than whatever the truth might have been."

Noel wadded up the McMuffin wrapper. "I can see that."

"It's frustrating because it's so easy to reduce history to cartoon stereotypes. Instead of doing a show about the real experiences of enslaved people, our focus was on ghosts and voodoo curses." Adam snorted. "I mean, even if you want to stick with ghosts, there's plenty of material. This area has seen explorers, treasure hunters, outlaws. There are plenty of stories. Even that Steel Magnolia house we passed last night. Some people say that house was a hospital during the Civil War, but now when they see it, all people think about is Shirley MacLaine and Julia Roberts."

Noel fought back a chill at the mention of the house on the street where he'd...well, something had happened, something weird if not truly supernatural. If he hadn't been dead drunk, he might remember more of the details.

"It's important to preserve as much real history as possible, before it's lost completely. That's what Jason's trying to do." Adam shot Noel an unreadable glance. "By the way, he's going to meet us there and let us into the non-public areas."

"Oh yeah, your buddy Jay." Noel gave the name two syllables, or maybe three. "Good thing you told him *all* about me. I'd hate to surprise him when—"

"Yeah, about that. I owe you an apology. I should never have implied that we were anything more than friends."

"—I acted like a complete...what?"

Damned if Adam's cheeks didn't turn pink. Noel blinked, confused, and forced himself to keep his eyes on the road.

"I might have said..." Adam stopped to clear his throat. "Might have said you were my boyfriend, and that—"

"Wait. No. That's what you told him? That we were a couple or something?"

"Like I said, I'm sorry, man."

Noel raised a hand, shushing Adam. "Let me spell this out. I thought you told him about my superpower."

Adam stilled. After a long moment, he swallowed. "No, I would never have told him that."

"Oh."

The map app informed them their destination would be on the left in three-quarters of a mile.

"So if he doesn't know about my superpower, and he's going to be there to escort us to off-limits areas, what are you going to tell him if I curl into a quivering ball?"

"You mean like you did last night?"

Noel locked his jaw against the first fifteen things that wanted to spout out of his mouth. Instead, he reached up to massage the back of his neck, where a tension headache had begun to spiral up. "Guess we'll see what we'll see."

Adam crossed his arm, his tone all pissy. "I guess we will."

Chapter Six

They should get out of the car. Neither of them moved. Adam was angry and not sure why.

No, he did know why. Because Noel thought he had betrayed his trust. Because he'd jumped straight to that and not said a word, *a word*, about what Adam had actually done. No *Hey, no worries, we* are *a couple*. No *please don't do that again*. Yes, the second would have sucked, but Adam would know where he stood. Then, to add insult to injury, he had jumped straight to *I assumed you told somebody something you swore was between us*. No apology for it either.

Adam had done all the apologizing, something he was starting to regret since the thing he had apologized for apparently meant so little to Noel, he hadn't said a word about it.

Noel *had* acted like a dick last night. At least he had admitted that. No apology, though. Or not a real one, anyway. Adam had every right to be angry. He had every right to demand an apology on all counts.

He looked at Noel's grumpy, still-pale face.

"We can call things off and head home. You don't have to do this," he offered for the millionth time that morning. Shit.

Noel opened his mouth to respond, then his attention focused on something over Adam's shoulder, and he abruptly swung his door open. "Nah. Let's move before I change my mind."

Adam reluctantly unfastened his own seat belt, not sure whether he was more annoyed or impressed. Whatever Noel's faults, backing down from a challenge wasn't one of them. As he climbed out of the car and walked across the parking lot to greet Jason, it wasn't Noel's non-apology that occupied Adam's thoughts. *I like you. And I want you to be happy.*

He had a damn funny way of showing it. Except...except Noel was striding determinedly across the parking lot toward an experience he had literally fled halfway across the country to avoid. And Adam was letting him. He picked up the pace, almost running to catch up.

He joined the party just in time to watch Noel drop into his usual sleepy-looking posture, somehow making the tell-tale signs of hangover into a fashion statement. He tilted his chin at Jason in greeting. "Sorry about last night, brah."

Jason gave a casual roll of his shoulders. "No worries, brah."

Adam mentally rolled his eyes. *Et tu, Jay?* The nonchalance had an aggressive edge, like some sort of surfer-dude chill-off.

Jason flicked a sympathetic glance at Adam, and then flashed a more genuine smile. "Seriously, don't worry about it. Adam explained about the PTSD. That's harsh, my man."

Noel sputtered. "I'm not..." He turned a furious look on Adam. "Why would you say... I'm not some damn wounded warrior, okay? Save your sympathy for the real heroes."

Jason flicked another look between them and appeared to decide a subject change was in order. "So, exactly what did you have in mind? I thought you got everything you needed for the show last week."

Adam nodded. "We did, but there was an anomaly with the equipment the last day."

Jason perked up, obviously excited to get some insider show intel. "For reals? Something freaky?"

That brought Adam up short. He knew Jason watched the show, but he'd never seemed like the type who took any of the paranormal stuff seriously. Adam figured him for an entertainment-only type viewer who mostly watched so he could rib Adam about it. Last week, most of their conversations had either centered on the actual history or the publicity *Haunts and Hoaxes* could bring the site and Jason's research.

Now how do I spin this?

"Yeah, umm, freaky." He glanced at Noel. He had his cop face on again, his hooded gaze steady on Jason. No help there.

"We didn't have a good historical event to pair with that spot. If I can find a better story, we can edit it in, so I figured we could poke around some before the Mayhaw Days crowd starts rolling in." He smiled and played his trump card. "Depending on what pops, maybe we can even get the show to do a follow-up episode."

"Tourists out the wazoo," Jason complained, but his gaze was calculating. More tourists equaled more funding. "The Historical Society will love you. Was there a reason you needed to be here after the park closes?"

"I'm a spoiled celebrity?"

It was an ongoing joke, and Jason responded with the expected "Diva."

Noel let out an annoyed huff, but declined any other contribution to the conversation.

"You don't mind if I show Noel where we were filming, do you? Maybe soak up a little atmosphere, let some ideas percolate?"

Fortunately, Jason had run out of questions. "Cabin 1 is still closed off for excavations, but I know I can trust you not to disturb anything. I'll meet you up at the store when you're ready to leave."

Adam thanked him again. Without knowing the real reason they wanted the park to themselves, he must seem like the diva Jason teased him about being.

Jason waved him off. "Hey, if you want to pay me back, you and Noel can help me play detective later. I got something I think will interest you."

Another huff from Noel. Adam ignored him. "What's up?"

"You got into the Marie and Valsin story, right?"

"Where'd I hear those names before?" Noel glanced from Jay to Adam.

"We talked about them on the way here. The local legend," Adam said.

Noel nodded. "Oh yeah. The runaway slaves."

"Valsin was born free." Adam tried to tone down his lecturing voice. "Since Marie was still enslaved, when he left with her, he became a criminal and a fugitive. He wasn't a runaway."

"But, yes, the freedom seekers were Valsin and Marie," Jason confirmed. "Anyway, I got an email a few days ago from a Ms. Angela Davenport. She's researching her family history, and you'll never guess who she is."

"Not one of their descendants?" Adam couldn't help himself; he felt a grin spreading over his face. "You're shitting me. Tell me you're not shitting me? We *never* get this kind of lucky." He grabbed his phone, ready to call his producer for permission to schedule an interview.

"Not sure I'd call it luck." Jason sounded bemused. "I mean, the story's great. Two people risking everything for freedom and true love."

Noel made a gagging sound under his breath.

"And they make it," Adam said, not willing to let Noel spoil his excitement. "Against almost impossible odds, they ride off into the sunset."

Jason's phone rang. He glanced at it distractedly before replying. "Yeah, about that..."

"I can't wait to hear the legend from the other side." Adam was practically bouncing. "Tell me she has the rest of the story for us. It's so rare when these old stories actually pan out the way they're told. The fans are going to eat this up."

"Hold that thought." The smile dropped off Jason's face as his phone rang again. He made a shooing motion with his hand. "Go enjoy the grounds. We'll talk later."

"Absolutely. I want to hear the rest of this story."

Noel shifted a little closer to Adam as Jason walked away. "Man knows how to set a hook."

"What now?" Adam murmured absently, his mind still stuck on the legend and the way Jason had stopped smiling. Aside from the voodoo bit, they'd done a segment featuring Marie and Valsin and a shorter one on Murrell's Cave, based on the tale of a deadly feud between outlaws. Marie and Valsin didn't feature any ghosts, but the legend was popular enough the show's PR department wanted the name drop for extra publicity. The episode was scheduled to air right before the Mayhaw Days festival.

"What nothing." Noel sounded put out. "Asshole

started with a descendant, ergo the story is true. He wants your attention. Don't be gullible."

Adam tried to shrug off the insult as they turned and made their way toward the cabins that had once housed the plantation's workers—first enslaved people and then tenant farmers. "I'm a researcher. I deal in historical fact. I'm not gullible."

"So you say."

Noel probably had him there. Historical fact and established scientific thought didn't exactly cover the reason they were here. *Open mind*, he reminded himself. He was here to apply as much reason to...whatever...was going on with Noel as possible. "Look, let's set all that aside and check out the cabins."

"Sure." Noel barely glanced at the tape and barriers marking Cabin 1 off-limits as they passed. His gaze scanned the fields and tree line instead. "Gotta admit they had some 'nads, though. I mean, even in a car, you're talking serious travel time to get from here to anywhere safe. And they were, what? On foot?"

"Horseback." They were approaching Cabin 2. Adam relegated Valsin and Marie to a back burner. "Noel?"

"Yeah?" He sounded distracted.

"Umm..." Neither of them knew what prompted Noel's episodes. Adam was struck with the sudden realization of just how much they didn't know.

He should give Noel another opportunity to leave. Except what if it was real? What if Noel really could connect with the past? Excitement warred with apprehension. To quell both, he picked an easy option. "You want to see number two? It's normally open to the public." And hadn't elicited a single blip from any of the minions' equipment.

"Is that where...?"

"No. I just thought we might get a sort of...um....baseline reaction."

"Baseline reaction?" Noel sounded disbelieving. "You mean where I walk around and don't froth at the mouth? Like I'm doing *right now*?"

Put like that, it sounded stupid.

Noel shrugged. "Yeah, sure. Might as well take advantage of my VIP tour, right?"

"The bricks used in construction were made on-site." Adam dropped into lecture mode, his usual coping strategy. "These cabins were actually in use by tenant farmers up until the 1970s. But by the time the NPS took over thirty years later, they were in pretty bad shape. This one's been fully restored."

They were at the door. Noel didn't hesitate, but Adam heard him suck in a breath, as if he were preparing for a dive, just before he stepped over the threshold. He paused inside and let it out slowly as he looked around. His voice didn't betray any nerves at all when he spoke. "Kept the original track lighting and all, huh?"

Adam stepped next to him and reached out to twine their fingers together. "Tourist model."

He waited while Noel took in the small room. Eventually, Noel pulled away and wandered over to look at the vintage pictures displayed on a small folding table in the corner. He ran his fingers over the brick walls and touched the wooden slats at the windows.

Adam trailed behind him, trying not to fall back into lecture mode and unsure what to do with himself otherwise. "Okay?"

"Yeah." Noel sounded subdued. "It wasn't here, was it? Whatever happened to your crew?"

"No." Adam swallowed. "Cabin 3."

Noel simply turned, walked to the door, and waited

for Adam to lead the way.

They stepped out of the cool interior of Cabin 2 into bright sun, muggy heat, and the smell of recently mowed grass. Normal. Cabin 3 was directly across from 2.

Adam's heart began to pound. As they walked the few yards to their destination, time and distance expanded, the way it sometimes did in dreams. Adam's feet moved, but he didn't cover any ground. He walked and walked, and all he could see was Noel in Lafayette Cemetery, eyes wide and harrowed, mouth moving but no sound coming out. Adam had touched him...

...how had he forgotten the next part...

Hot wind, a woman screaming and... Something. Something so terrifying, his mind shied away from it. The whole episode took no time at all. The entire thing happened between one breath and the next. One breath when he'd felt like he might never take another. And when it was over... Noel lay on the ground, pale and bleeding.

He forced his feet to keep moving.

Step. Step.

No closer.

Suddenly, they were there. Like before, no time at all had passed.

From the outside, the cabin looked almost identical to the one they had just left. Except outside Cabin 3, Adam couldn't force his feet to move. Couldn't take the few final steps to...

Noel surged ahead and disappeared into the cabin.

Adam unstuck his feet and followed.

He barreled into something just inside the door. For a single moment of fear, he was back in Lafayette Cemetery, the landscape reduced to gray and shifting shadows.

"Watch it, professor!" Noel's annoyed voice cut through the panic. The shadows resolved into an empty room with no light except the rectangle of sun from the still-open door.

"Sorry." Adam sucked in a breath. "Sorry."

"Hey, no track lighting in here, huh?" Noel sounded completely normal, not even breathing hard from their collision. "You okay?"

"Fine," Adam wheezed. "Shouldn't I be asking you that?"

"Good so far." Noel sounded far too cheerful for the occasion. Unreasonably, this annoyed Adam.

He spent the next few minutes watching Noel wander around the space the same way he'd wandered around Cabin 2. He ran careful fingers along the crumbling mantel, ducked into the nearly pitch-black adjoining room, and finally came back to stand next to Adam and simply look around.

"Well?" Adam tried to keep the impatience out of his voice.

"Well, what?"

"Are you even trying?"

"Are you kidding? What am I supposed to do?" He raised his voice, "Here, ghostie, ghostie. Come and get me."

"Cut it out. You aren't taking this seriously."

"Taking *what* seriously? I'm here. I've never had to do anything to get hijacked before. I just show up. Maybe your stupid equipment is bunk."

A month ago, Adam would have mostly agreed with this statement. But he'd spent the last week positive he'd found a way to test Noel's abilities. How were they ever supposed to know if Noel's episodes were anything other than some weird brain chemistry if there was no correlating external data?

"Hey." Noel interrupted his thoughts. "Which cabin did Marie live in? Let's go look at that one."

"Forget about Marie. She left. Obviously, she's not haunting the plantation."

Noel narrowed his eyes. "Well, maybe *nothing* is haunting the plantation. You've been talking about her the whole trip. Now why can't we see her cabin?"

Adam ran a frustrated hand through his hair. "Look, there's no way to know, okay? It could have been this one. It could have been one or two. Honestly, it likely wasn't any of the few still standing."

"There were more?" Noel went to the door and looked out speculatively.

"Yeah, there were around seventy at one point. But a lot of them were wooden structures that haven't survived." He walked over to stand next to Noel and tried to shake off his disappointment. His emotions had been all over the place the past twenty-four hours. How did Noel stand living with this day after day, never knowing when *something* might happen?

He bumped Noel's shoulder. "Nothing, huh?"

"Yeah, it's a bust. Sorry, baby." Noel's foot tapped idly as he stared across the yard at Cabin 2. "Hey, look on the bright side. Maybe ghosts don't exist. Maybe I'm just crazy."

"You're not crazy. Maybe the equipment was faulty." Adam was aware he didn't sound massively convinced, but he'd just freaked the fuck out walking across a few yards of grass. Maybe they were both crazy. Maybe he was enabling Noel's psychosomatic seizures. Maybe they both needed therapy.

"One experiment doesn't mean anything." He turned to pull Noel into his arms and resisted saying something non-helpful like *it won't change how I feel about you either way.* Noel didn't need *either way* right now.

"You want to walk around some more or something?"

Adam didn't see any point in it. The creepy-ass noise had happened here. "We can do whatever you want."

"Meat pies?"

Trust Noel to lead with his stomach. Adam was going to have to either take up jogging or buy new clothes. "Sure. Why not? All the meat pies."

Surprisingly, it seemed Noel wasn't eager to leave. He asked a few leading questions until Adam went back to lecture mode, then seemed content to stroll at his side and listen as they walked the grounds. They were finally headed back to the car when he suddenly stopped and stared hard at a grove of pecan trees behind the pigeoneer. "Hey, we're the only ones supposed to be in here, right?"

Adam followed his gaze but didn't see anything. "Maybe? I'm not sure. Jason's up at the plantation store. There might be a few rangers left around. Why?"

Noel shook his head. "Never mind. I thought there was a woman over by those trees, but I don't see her now. Probably just a shadow or something."

Chapter Seven

A shadow. Right. Just a shadow, because a shadow often dresses like she's part of a historical reenactment, in faded gingham with a tattered wrap on her head. *Pull it together, Chandler...*

It wasn't the clothing that bothered Noel as much as the detail: the frayed edges of the cloth, the careful way she held her hands over her belly. She'd been visible for less than the time from one heartbeat to another, but she'd etched herself in his memory.

Why get all twisted up by the sight of a woman who was likely just a remnant of his hangover? Noel shook off the chill running down the back of his neck. No reason. No reason at all. "You promised me meat pies."

Adam made a poor attempt to stifle a snicker. "We just went to McDonald's."

"Hmm." He wasn't sure what you called the next meal when breakfast was an Egg McMuffin at three p.m. "I'm sure it's time for something."

"We'll check out with Jason and ask him if he knows a place that has a senior citizen deal starting at four thirty."

Noel bit back a hunk of sarcasm regarding how unlikely he'd be to go to anyplace Jason suggested. He strode along beside Adam, fishing for something less inflammatory to say. He had no real reason to dislike Jason, well, beyond the way he looked at Adam.

It wasn't as if he and Adam had made any kind of commitment to each other. Hell, Noel had to admit he'd been pretty much out of line from the start. Getting fucked up had been an asshole thing to do, but dammit, Jason looked at Adam like he was the highlight on a buffet table.

And Adam had no fucking clue.

Think about something else.

"This place is wild."

"Why?" Adam's one word managed to edge into eagerness territory, as if Noel was going to spout some semi-magical bullshit that would make this whole trip something besides a tremendous waste of time.

"I just meant that, well, when we talked about visiting a plantation, I pictured Scarlett O'Hara or something, running up the steps of a big-ass mansion with Grecian columns. That place—" Noel nodded in the direction of the main house, the entrance nearly obscured by an abundance of shrubbery—"looks like it's seen better days." And those slave cabins. *Damn.* "You think they'd at least do some pruning or something."

Adam didn't answer for a long moment. *Probably adding to the list of ways I've disappointed him.*

"The owners kept the fields and the main house," he said at last. "So maintaining the place is up to them. As for the rest, that's why Jason let us do the show here. He relies on grant funding for his own work, but the more visitors, the easier it'll be to keep the park open."

This time, it was Noel who clamped his jaw shut to keep from saying something stupid. He'd fucked up last night, both for getting blind drunk and for jumping to the wrong conclusion about what Adam meant. *Love means you'll never have to say you're sorry, right?* He bit back a chuckle. The best he could come up with was a bad cliché from some from old movie his mother liked.

Noel scanned the scene as if he was still a cop, ready to find something threatening. There was the Lexus and half a dozen other vehicles in the parking lot, a faded wooden sign announcing they were in a National Park, home of the Magnolia Plantation, that woman in the head wrap standing— "Dammit."

"What?"

Noel massaged his bicep, fighting against the lightness in his head. *I'm not going down this time. I'm not.* He should say something, tell Adam what he'd seen. He should tell him what really happened last night. If he wanted to talk about commitment, he couldn't keep big-ass secrets.

He cleared his throat and nodded at the old plantation store up ahead. "We should go find Jason."

Because why not? He didn't tell Adam his secrets because he didn't want anyone to know how fucked up he was. He didn't tell Adam they needed to come to an understanding because he didn't deserve a guy like that, someone smart, and solid, and handsome as fuck.

He didn't want to hold Adam back, to keep him from finding someone better.

Still rubbing his bicep with cold fingers, Noel managed to walk along beside Adam without falling on his ass. *Improvement.* "It's nothing. I either need more food or more Tylenol or both."

Adam's quiet spoke more of disbelief than anything else, but Noel didn't have a better answer for him. The store was on the far end of the property, and Noel fought to regulate his breathing, each inhale dragging more oxygen into his lungs to fight the disconnect in his mind.

Each exhale carrying tension out into the atmosphere.

"You guys done?" Jason called out from the small room at the back of the store. The place had been converted from its older purpose. Now it was lined with racks of tourist flyers, a solid antique desk in one corner, INFORMATION stamped on a brushed gold nameplate.

"Yup." Adam's brusque response startled Noel. *Okay, enough.* He would get through this conversation without being an asshole if it killed him.

Jason had been talking on the phone. He murmured something, then covered the phone with his palm. "I gotta deal with this, but I still want to tell you about the Valsin and Marie story. Can we meet later?"

"Sure," Adam said.

"Tell us when and where." Noel managed to get the words out with reasonable sincerity.

"Cool. Let's say Brady's Diner, over on Bossier Street. At about"—he glanced at his phone—"six o'clock?"

"We'll see you there." Adam had brightened some.

Noel smiled with more enthusiasm than he felt. "That'd be great. Something about the story grabs me, you know?"

Adam gave him a slow blink, which turned Noel's smile into a sincere grin.

"Awesome." If he was surprised by Noel's change in tone, Jason managed not to show it. "See you boys later."

They were halfway to the parking before Noel broke the silence. "Boys." He laughed. "If that man doesn't play for our team, I'll kiss my own ass."

"What?" Adam gave him an annoyed look. "Far as I know, he's straight."

Noel wrapped an arm around Adam's waist. "He may not fly his freak flag very high, babe, but he is as queer as you and me."

"Why would you think that?"

Noel stopped short, his face tipped up to the sky. It might have looked dramatic, but he had to blink hard against the brightness of the late-afternoon sun. Adam took another couple of steps before turning back to Noel. "Why?"

Noel met his question with a wry grin. "Because, my dude, he looks at you like he wants you laid out naked and covered in oil."

Adam laughed and shook his head. "Nah, that's not—"

"It sure enough is how it is. Look..." Noel paused, surprised at himself. He'd been about to explain why he'd been such an asshole when they first met Jason, except...except...he really didn't have a claim on Adam. "Sure. Whatever you say." If he and Adam were only temporary, he might as well take what he could get. "We've got a little over an hour before we meet him." He walked as he spoke, ending up very nearly nose to nose with Adam.

"Yeah." Adam's voice was husky all of a sudden.

"Tick tock, Morales..." Noel rubbed his knuckles up and down Adam's fly. "Let's head back to the hotel."

Adam wrapped his hand around Noel's wrist. "I'll race you to the Lexus." He took off running, and, after wasting a good thirty seconds laughing, Noel followed.

They were equally efficient at getting to the room at the B and B. Once the door was closed, Adam reached for Noel, but after a short kiss, Noel took a step back.

"What?" The rough edge to Adam's voice jacked up

Noel's heartbeat, and he knelt with as much grace as he could muster.

"This."

Noel reached for Adam's fly and made short work of zipper and buttons and shirttail and briefs. Adam's cock was thick, a shade darker than the skin of his belly. *Goddam gorgeous.* For a moment, Noel simply inhaled, savoring his musky scent.

"You don't have to, I mean, after last night—"

Noel silenced him by swallowing as much as he could in one motion. He waited another moment, using the light brush of curls on his nose to distract his gag reflex with something more pleasant. When he'd gathered himself, he set a leisurely pace, tailoring his action to the swell of Adam's cock. He wrapped one hand around the base and cupped his balls with the other, tugging and teasing just this side of rough. *This, man. Nothing better.*

He drew back, nibbling the very tip and stroking with his hand. Adam gasped, half bent from the waist, his fingers gripping Noel's head. "You're killing me."

Noel grinned around his cock. He could have come up with some snark, but was too happy to have his mouth full. A few more deep swallows, and Noel was ready to burst. He left off massaging Adam's balls and unzipped his jeans, dragging out his throbbing cock.

"Commando? Fuck."

Adam's obvious enthusiasm made it hard for Noel to sustain such a slow pace, but he'd be damned if he'd rush. For however much time they had left, he was going to milk every drop.

Finally, Adam took control, fingers digging into Noel's scalp, the force of his thrusts impossible to ignore. He set a much faster pace, and Noel relaxed into the peaceful space brought on by having his mouth thoroughly fucked.

No man had ever given Noel the space to let go. *No man but Adam.*

Too soon—really, much too soon—Adam's hips lost their rhythm. His breath grew harsh, and the taste of cum spread through Noel's mouth. One thrust, then another, and Adam let loose, his cry a mix of agony and joy.

With a practice stroke, Noel brought himself off, the familiar spasm of pleasure almost an afterthought compared with the vibe he felt from Adam. Noel slid down till he was sitting on the floor, and Adam joined him, pulling him into a soft embrace.

"Thank you." Adam leaned in for a kiss.

"My pleasure."

"Mm." Adam nuzzled his ear, making him shiver. "We have time to do that again."

Noel teased the dark hair running south from Adam's navel. "Or we could, you know, climb into bed and..." Noel stopped himself, appalled that he'd been about to suggest they cuddle. "Nap?"

"Sure." Adam straightened just enough for Noel to feel cooler air slide between them. Though he couldn't tell if Adam was disappointed or not, they did make a slow move toward the bed.

"I'm going to set my phone for thirty minutes," Adam said, his voice soft and slow.

Noel curled up against him, lethargy swamping his muscles. "Cool." He didn't hear anything else Adam had to say, because he drifted into a doze.

Seemed like ninety seconds later when Adam shook his shoulder. "Shit." Noel rubbed his eyes, wondering if he could persuade Adam to cancel with Jason. But...no. Adam would probably suggest he go alone, and...no. Hell no. Adam's gaydar had a glitch, and Noel was so not going to let him go off unsupervised. They might not be a permanent thing, but for now, Noel was the one sharing Adam's bed.

After deciding a shared shower would definitely make them late, they took turns putting themselves together. On the way to the B and B's main floor, Noel asked how far they were from Brady's Diner.

"Should be about a ten-minute walk," Adam said, his attention on his cell phone.

They crossed the street and headed down the block. "I want you to know something." Noel put on his shades, the setting sun still too bright. "I'm only drinking soda. I want...I want to hear what you all have to say."

Adam shot him a glance, one Noel pretended to ignore. In another couple of blocks, he realized they were coming close to the cold spot he'd hit the night before.

"We gotta cross the street."

"We do?"

"Yeah, just, let's walk on that side." The plaque on the Steel Magnolia house caught the dying sun's rays.

Adam stopped, hand raised and finger pointed like he was going to start a lecture. "All right, then. We'll cross the street, but..."

"But what?" Noel stepped out into the street, ignoring Adam's tense silence. At a break in traffic, they jogged across. Adam still hadn't answered Noel's question, and heading down the block, Noel felt like they were walking in different zip codes. *Fuck.* He kept up with Adam's angry pace, passing the house without tripping over any weird-ass cold spots. *I'm really going to blow this.* The thought left him with enough sadness that he had serious doubts he could keep his nonalcoholic promise.

Meat pies, as it turned out, were nothing like the Thanksgiving-leftover type pot pie Adam had vaguely pictured. After catching *fried* in the description, he had conscientiously ordered a grilled chicken salad despite the fact that the scuffed counter, dingy linoleum, and heavy smell of grease screamed they were not in a salad kind of establishment. Noel smirked at the salad order, then changed his own order from the same meat pie dinner Jay had ordered (one pie with sides of fried vegetables), to half a dozen pies split between meat and crawfish.

"What?" He blinked innocently at Adam. "We can share. I'll eat some of your salad, even if it turns out to be a bunch of shredded iceberg."

Adam had been in enough small-town eateries to know the iceberg might be a real possibility. He didn't exactly give in, but he didn't protest much more beyond, "You're going to have a massive coronary one day."

"Nope. Good genes. Got great-uncles over a hundred. Both swear by bacon and eggs every morning. Cigars and scotch every night. Anyway, lighten up. We're on vacation. We can eat healthy at home."

For once, he and Jason seemed to find common ground. "Noel's right. You can't possibly need to count carbs, and it's a local specialty. When I was a kid, my grandparents used to bring me down here to see the lights every Christmas. I looked forward to the pies more than the lights."

Adam spent the next ten minutes watching Jason and Noel make careful conversation about beaches where they'd surfed. He supposed he should be happy he had two people willing to make the effort for him, but somehow, having his two buds get along didn't improve his mood. He sat out the conversation. He'd never been to Hawaii, didn't surf, and didn't feel up to faking an interest.

Instead, he spent the time obsessing over a stray lock of hair curling above Noel's ear and wondering if it was the same one that had tickled his nose as they lay tucked together in bed earlier. He wondered if it was all sex for Noel or if it meant something that he was having sex with Adam specifically. He wondered if he was crazy to think any part of his relationship with Noel was a good idea. Mostly, he wondered what secrets his cop was keeping.

They were finally rescued by having their number called. Jay snagged his plate and headed to the condiment station. Adam picked up his salad—iceberg, but thankfully not shredded—while Noel collected two plates piled with something that looked like deep-fried empanadas.

"That's an insane amount of food." Adam put his salad on the table. Next to him, Noel chose a pie at random and cracked it open.

"Meat," he pronounced with glee before taking a healthy bite.

A spicy aroma filled the air.

Noel put half the pie on a napkin and used one finger to push it slowly across the table until it rested next to Adam's untouched salad.

Adam's mouth watered. "Why are you such a dick?"

"Half a pie." Noel wheedled. "You'll like it."

The second sentence was, in Noel terms, almost timid. Maybe because Adam had totally overreacted to an offer to share food. *I want you to be happy.* Apparently, Noel thought fried foods were how Adam experienced happiness. Or maybe he was trying to make up for being a secretive, mistrustful bastard.

The pie, a slurry of ground pork, beef, onions, and Cajun spice in a flaky crust, was amazing. Adam choked back a sound suspiciously like one he'd made earlier in the evening when Noel was on his knees.

Jay, who was just sitting down, grinned at him. "Told you they were good."

Noel didn't make any comment, just pushed another pie within easy reaching distance.

Adam spared a final glance at the rubbery-looking chicken bits sprinkled on a mound of iceberg lettuce and admitted defeat. Hey, they were on vacation.

Maybe Noel knew him better than he thought, because his mood did improve after the second meat pie. By that point, he also remembered why they were here. "So"—he gave Jay what he hoped was a piercing stare—"Marie and Valsin."

But instead of launching into details, Jason hesitated. "I don't know, Adam. I was kidding earlier. You don't owe me anything, if you don't want to help with this..."

Adam frowned at him. "Come on, man. Quit holding out on us. What'd she say?"

"Well..." Jason hesitated again. "Some significant details of Angela's family story don't match up."

Adam laughed. "Is that all? Buddy, you and I know the details *never* match up. That's what makes it so exciting to try to piece together what really happened.

C'mon, don't hog this. I promise we won't use it on the show without giving you credit or letting you approve it or whatever you're angling for here."

"It's not that," Jason protested.

"Maybe you got your ancestors swapped," Noel drawled. "Maybe Ms. Davenport doesn't have anything to do with Valsin and Marie. Maybe she just liked the story same as everyone else. Maybe *she* wants on Adam's show."

"Give me *some* credit," Jason snapped. "She sent me a scan of her family Bible, and I was able to use birth records to confirm their claim back to the woman we think was Marie. I'm almost positive she's Marie's four-times great-granddaughter. That isn't the problem." He turned his gaze back to Adam. "Are you sure you want to do this? You won't like it."

Adam stared at him. "Are you kidding? You can't hold out on us now."

Noel let out a slow breath that sounded a little like *asshole*. Adam shot him a warning look, but Noel just slouched back in his chair looking bored and sleepy as he studied Jason across the table. "Stop jerking Adam around. How bad can it be? We know they made it out, or Ms. ...Davenport, right?" Jason nodded. "Ms. Davenport wouldn't exist."

"Oh, she exists, and her family story is close enough to the legend, I'm pretty sure we're all talking about the same people."

"So let's hear it," Noel said. "Stop stringing us along and spit it out."

"Don't say I didn't warn you." Jason took a deep breath. "Okay, so according to the stories handed down by her family, Ms. Davenport's great-great-great-great-grandmother was a forced laborer on Magnolia Plantation named Marie, who escaped just before the

Civil War and eventually wound up in Pennsylvania.

"Forced laborer?" Noel interrupted.

"What did you think slavery was?" Jason asked.

Adam waited for some pushback over the accurate but stark academic terminology.

Noel shrugged. "Fair."

"And actually," Jason continued, "Ms. Davenport can place the date when her ancestress escaped pretty close. According to the story passed down in her family, Marie hadn't originally intended to run away."

Noel grunted. "Well that's different enough. You saying she was happy where she was?" He sounded personally affronted at the thought. Adam smothered a grin. Noel might put on a good front, but his not-boyfriend had never met a mystery he didn't want to solve.

"Don't hold it against her," he soothed. "Escapes almost never worked. We know from plantation records that Marie was a skilled seamstress and a valued worker. From her viewpoint, the risk of getting caught and jeopardizing her standing might not have seemed worth it."

"And according to Ms. Davenport, she might have had even more reason to stay." Jason said. "She believed her situation would eventually improve."

Noel frowned, obviously not liking this twist on the legend. "How so?"

"Valsin," Adam said. "He intended to buy her. One of the older versions of the legend says he tried to buy her, and when he couldn't, he helped her escape and they went north. Most contemporary versions don't include that part. They skip from them falling in love to running away together. Valsin would have wanted to buy her if he could, then manumit her. It would have been expensive, but legal and much safer than attempting an escape." He looked to Jay for confirmation. "Am I right? I don't know the specifics of Louisiana law in that period."

"Yes," Jay approved. "Exactly right. In fact, Louisiana law is the reason we're almost certain that her Marie is *the* Marie. In 1857, Louisiana passed a law prohibiting manumission.. The story, according to Ms. Davenport, is that Marie had a lover who she expected to buy and then free her, but the law passed before he was able to do so. Then the situation got worse. She found out she was pregnant. Faced with bearing a child who would never have a chance at freedom if she stayed, she began pressuring her lover to help her escape before their child was born."

"Stop," Noel cut in. "Her lover? You mean Valsin, right?"

Adam played back what Jason had said. "Jay?"

"And now we get to the interesting part." Jason leaned forward. "Yes, I think Ms. Davenport is talking about Valsin, but she never used his name. That's the reason she contacted me. She's trying to track down who her great-great-great-great-grandfather was."

Adam's mind went blank for a minute, trying to adapt the legend to the new facts. "She...what?"

"She doesn't know anything about the legend. All she has is a family tree starting with a Marie Tisdale and a story handed down from mother to daughter. According to the family history, Marie escaped with the help of her lover. He made arrangements with an abolitionist who would shelter them the first night and even provided the horse Marie used on that first leg of her journey. At some point, they were separated. No one in the family knows exactly how. Maybe splitting up was part of the plan. To the day she died, Marie protected the names of people who had helped her. At any rate, Grandpa never showed. Marie waited as long as she dared before continuing on to Pennsylvania, where she would be safe."

"But...Valsin." Adam knew he sounded bewildered. "You've done more digging into the actual historical aspects of the legend. Do we know Valsin actually existed?"

"Before last week, if I had to pick one of them to be pure fiction, it would have been Marie. Valsin was a local businessman, a homeowner, cousin to one of the wealthier families in the area. There are a lot of documents with his name on them. Yes, we know Valsin Ferrier existed." Jay paused to take a sip of his iced tea while he thought. "I guess it's possible he wasn't Marie's lover, but I don't know how his name would have gotten tangled up in the legend if he wasn't. Either way, it doesn't solve anything. Whoever helped her escape disappeared."

A quiet huff of disbelief drew Adam's gaze back to Noel. His bored slouch hadn't changed, but the sleepy expression had turned harder, more cop. "Yeah, I got that one for you. Player ditched."

"Sorry?" Jason shifted his attention to Noel too.

"C'mon. Things weren't so different back then. He and the girl are having a good time, then she turns up pregnant and starts nagging for all kinds of not-fun things. He arranges her ticket out of town, then accidentally misses the bus. What's she gonna do? Come back?"

"God, you're a cynic." Adam stared at Noel. It wasn't unthinkable that Valsin had second thoughts. The risk he'd taken had been huge. Adam just didn't want it to be true. "He gave her his *horse*."

Noel just shrugged. "So? Parting gift. It was just a horse."

"Yeah?" For some reason Noel's casual dismissal of the relationship got Adam's back up. "So when we split, do I get the Lexus?" Adam had been allowed to drive the Lexus exactly once when Noel had considered himself too buzzed to drive home safely and didn't want to leave his precious car parked on the street overnight if they called a rideshare. If anything could bring home the enormity of *gave her his horse*, invoking the Lexus should do it.

"Baby," Noel drawled, "if you catch pregnant, I promise I'll give you a lot more than a car."

"Okay," Jason cut back in forcefully, "I think we're getting a little off topic."

Adam gripped his tea glass and hoped his face wasn't as red as it felt. Okay, he'd done the bad thing and manufactured a committed relationship again, but Noel had taken it straight to the bedroom. Jason fussed with his napkin, obviously uncomfortable having his companions' sex life thrown in his face. Noel didn't seem fazed. He bestowed what looked like his first genuine smile on Jason. "What, you don't think Adam would make cute little professors? I can see them now, in their tiny horn-rimmed glasses."

Adam kicked him under the table.

Noel blinked innocently at him, but backed down. "Okay, Jay." He gave the name a subtle emphasis Adam couldn't interpret. "What do you think happened?"

"That," Jason said with commendable restraint, "is what we want to find out." He smiled pointedly back at Noel. "But for the record, I think you're wrong."

Noel shrugged, like it didn't matter, but he didn't take his eyes off Jason. "Prove it."

"Well, for one thing, in 1858, Valsin disappears."

"Define disappeared."

"After Ms. Davenport contacted me, my first

assumption was that history got the names mixed up and Valsin was never her lover, or at least not the one she left with. One of the first things I did was look for proof he was here after she left. So I looked for some kind of death record. It doesn't exist."

"That's not definitive," Adam felt compelled to point out. "We're talking right before the Civil War. Lots of people disappeared, or at least records of them did."

Jason scowled. "What, I'm an amateur? I backtracked to some of the references we do have, see if maybe he moved or something. All references to him stop around 1858."

"So he skipped." Noel shrugged. "Doesn't mean he went with her. Plus, what Adam said. It's not like we have every scrap of paper from back in the day." He hesitated, then glanced at Adam inquiringly. "Right?"

"Far from it." Adam backed him up without hesitation.

"True," Jason conceded. "But church records here are actually pretty well preserved. I expected to find marriage, children, death...something. Maybe I'm kidding myself. Maybe I'm too attached to the story too...but...I'm not liking that the legend is that wrong when we have two people who ought to fit perfectly into it. It feels like we're missing something."

But what? The conversation felt dead. Adam rubbed at his chin, frustrated. Noel would probably throw a fit if Adam volunteered them to spend the next day searching through old documents for anything new. So it came as a shock when it was Noel who revived the discussion. "What's the last thing you've got on him?"

Adam glanced over at him. Noel had moved out of his slouch. While still relaxed, he was actually sitting up in his chair. He hadn't gone so far as to lean forward, but his eyes were focused intently on Jason. One thumb tapped a rapid beat against his thigh, a sure sign his wheels were turning.

Adam never bought Noel's bored routine, any more than he did his snobby fashionista front. Okay, he maybe he was a little snobby. And he did like his designers. But most of the outside Noel was just something for the world to look at while the real Noel was busy underneath.

Ever since they got here, Noel had been all over the place—his energy spiking in all directions, wild and scattered. Right now, under the casual pose, he vibrated with the force of his focus, all of it turned on Jay. Adam frowned, but the next thought banished the spike of jealousy before it could fully form.

Noel's attention wasn't on Jay, but the case. Noel might think he'd moved on, but he was still a cop. Underneath that pretty exterior was an LA police detective.

"The last thing I... Oh!" Jason smiled triumphantly. "I left out the most important part. He cashed out. He was in negotiations to buy some land for a new home. The last concrete reference we have to him was the sale of his house in 1858. Presumably, he needed the money before finalizing the purchase of the new place, but instead of completing the deal, he just...disappeared."

Chapter Eight

Interesting. Valsin just up and disappeared.

Noel leaned against his chair's flimsy cushion, one finger tapping his thigh, his mind working double time. Brady's Diner looked exactly how he'd expected a diner in a small Southern town to look: red-and-white-checkered fabric on the chairs and in the windows, gray Formica tabletops with silver trim around the perimeters, and those upright napkin dispensers on every table.

His dinner companions were a lot less predictable.

Adam seemed to have recovered from his fit of pique on their walk over. Noel tried to feel guilty for his part in precipitating said pique, but couldn't. Instead, he swirled his straw through the ice at the bottom of his tall glass of Coca-Cola, taking stock of the situation.

"So you've got one historical figure—Marie—with a family legend but no lover, and another historical figure who sells his house and disappears. You're confident of Marie's family tree?" He directed his comment at Jason, because now that Noel's inner green-eyed monster had calmed down, he could behave like an adult. Or thereabouts.

"In addition to the scan of the family Bible, she sent

me a scanned version of something that had originally been typed out and mimeographed. There are some blanks, but overall, it's pretty complete." Jason spoke slower than he had when addressing Adam, as if he wanted to make sure Noel understood.

Noel stifled an eye roll. *These two, man.*

"You know," Jason continued. "The Marie and Valsin story speaks to so many issues that were integral to that time period. It's the kind of between-the-lines history we should be recapturing."

Noel couldn't argue with that. "So, here's another question. Do you think Ms. Davenport would take a DNA test?"

"What good would that do?" Adam leaned forward as if trying to draw Noel's attention.

Yeah, you don't want me paying too much attention to the foxy Asian dude, do you? "Not long before I left LA, we had a case with a victim, but no ID, which was a total bitch. Do you have any idea how hard it is to solve a murder when you can't identify the victim?"

Both Adam and Jason looked at him blankly. "If you don't have an ID, you don't have a motive, and you can't generate a list of suspects. All you have is a corpse and an identifiable pattern of injuries suggesting how they died."

"And the relationship to Marie and Valsin is...?" Adam had lost the blank look. His gaze sharpened, and he had his phone in his hand as if he was going to break into Google at any moment.

"There are a couple of different ways to use DNA to solve crimes. The most common is to test something left by the perpetrator at the scene, either blood or other body fluids, or maybe skin cells under the victim's fingernails, that kind of thing. You run the DNA through the national databank, and if you get a hit, you've identified your perp."

"Still not following you."

Noel gave Adam a baleful glance. "Patience, padawan. All will be clear in time."

Jason's laugh gave Noel a chance to reach for Adam's thigh under the table and give it a squeeze. His thick, firm thigh. As excellent as those meat pies had been, they hadn't completely taken away the taste of Adam's cock and his salty bitter cum. The taste that belonged to Noel alone.

Besides, Jason was kind of a cipher. Pretty to look at and shooting off subliminal sparks of attraction right and left, but Noel couldn't see him acting on the impulse.

"So here's the thing." Noel carried on with his story. "In the last couple, three years, there's been an expansion in the way we work with DNA. Instead of just comparing samples, looking for a match, now we can access a genealogical database, looking for familial relationships." He shifted in his seat, edging closer to Adam. "What I'm thinking is, if you had Ms. Davenport's DNA sample, you could expand her family tree, hoping to find a new branch that would lead back to Valsin."

Jason knocked his fist against his own forehead. "Aw, man, I read a paper about that not too long ago. That's how they found the Golden State Killer in California, isn't it?"

"Yeah." Noel gave his soda another twirl. "In part, it works because of how many people are having their DNA tested on sites like 23andMe."

Adam swiped his phone screen, his brow furrowed as if he was thinking hard. "So, we'd have Ms. Davenport send a DNA sample to 23andMe, and then what?"

Noel couldn't help but smile. For the first time since this whole adventure had started, he felt like he'd contributed something useful. "There's a separate database, GEDmatch, that's publicly searchable. I won't lie, this'll take some legwork. We put her data in and look for matches. Then it's a process of old-fashioned genealogical research.

"It'll take phone calls and looking through old records to identify all the branches of the family tree, while hoping to hit the one person, or maybe a couple people, who've heard of some long-lost relative. You mentioned Valsin had a cousin, but did you turn up any siblings?"

Jason and Adam gave each other a look that held all the heat of day-old coffee, making last night's jealousy-fest feel like a complete overreaction.

Of course, maybe the biggest difference is that tonight, I'm sober.

With a snort, Noel pushed that thought aside.

"I'd have to go back through the records," Jason said. He sounded eager, as if he was ready to jump right in.

"What difference would a sibling make?" Adam asked.

"Shared genetic material. The closer we can get, the more accurate it is." Noel had made a painful number of phone calls working the previous case. "And, I mean, we still might not find a match. Last time, it took a long while to sort through all the hits, build a partial family tree, and then get lucky enough to find a branch with a missing person who turned out to fit the description of our victim. Once we had her ID, we were able to put the rest of the pieces together."

"Did you figure out who killed her?" The admiration in Adam's eyes made Noel blush.

Noel rubbed at a tight spot in the back of his neck. "Yeah. Her boyfriend."

"It's always the boyfriend," Jason drawled.

Noel flicked a glance at Adam, as hot as he could make it. "You know how those boyfriends are."

"Hey, so now I want to start looking for Valsin's family." Jason sounded overly bright, and Noel had to turn away to hide his grin.

Adam nudged Noel's foot. "We should get back to the hotel. We're going to head home in the morning."

Heading back to the hotel sounded like a fine idea to him too. "If you get Ms. Davenport to agree to a DNA test, let me know, and we can start the search for real."

After a brief argument over the bill—which Noel won—they exchanged contact information. Jason promised to let Noel know if the DNA test was a go. Walking home in the twilight, Noel found himself holding hands with Adam, though hell if he could tell who'd reached for who's hand first.

His sense of relief was as intoxicating as any gin and tonic. Traffic was light, and nobody bothered the gays being boldly gay in public. Adam squeezed Noel's fingers, and Noel squeezed back. He didn't have the mental energy to get spun up about anything, not the question of whether the ghosties were real and not the game of does-he-or-doesn't-he that he and Adam were playing. *Or maybe I'm just crazy*. It could work either way.

He almost ruined everything by insisting they cross the street to avoid that cold spot again.

Adam didn't let go of his hand, but he gave a distinctly frustrated huff while they waited for the light to change.

"You're clearly not ready to talk about this." Adam's murmur was almost too low to hear. "But something's up."

Well, if that didn't sound like the first half of an ultimatum...

Waving goodbye to his momentary sense of peace, Noel gave Adam's fingers a final squeeze and let go of his hand. "It's...um..." God he needed a drink. "I'd rather not talk about it on the street." Or at all, really, but... "Let's go back to the hotel."

"Sure." Adam caught his hand again, and they walked the final block in silence.

Back in their room, Noel had to shout to be heard over the chorus of protest in his own mind. *You can't do this. He'll know you're crazy. He'll leave.*

Would he really leave?

The room had a small vanity with a bentwood chair, its padded seat covered in pink-striped sateen, and an upholstered wing chair near the window. Noel took the wing chair, and Adam spun the smaller chair around and straddled it.

"So..." Adam's blank expression did nothing to quiet the shrieking in Noel's head. His hands rested calmly on his knees, his full lips weren't curved in a smile, but his eyes weren't entirely cold either. There was a spark of ...something...Noel couldn't read.

Noel crossed his legs right over left, shifted in his seat, then switched to left over right. It was the only way he could keep his knee from bouncing two hundred beats a minute. Intimacy issues, remember? His nerves and sinews were straining toward the mini bar in the corner of the room. Gin, vodka, whisky, anything.

Dude, for once in your life, man the fuck up.

"So, you were right..."

Adam held his breath, realized he was holding his breath, then couldn't make himself breathe.

He tried to keep his expression calm while he waited for...whatever...Noel had to say. Not an easy task while a montage of the weekend's awkward moments played in his head. Everything from finding Noel curled in a ball on the porch, to the weird-ass way he kept wanting to cross the street, to his antagonism toward Jay to...Adam's insistence on claiming a relationship Noel hadn't acknowledged.

Something was bothering Noel. Maybe more than one something. The weird thing down the street... Adam would bet that had something to do with Noel's "superpower," as he called it. Though why Noel would keep a paranormal incident from him when it was the entire reason they were here was a mystery.

Adam wanted, really wanted, Noel to just admit he'd heard another voice or seen a ghost, or whatever might have happened. Maybe he was just scared and didn't want Adam forcing him into any more uncontrolled *experiments*. Because okay, maybe Adam had gotten a little carried away with the whole thing and needed to back off. Which he would do.

Absolutely, he could do that.

Or maybe this didn't have anything to do with ghosts at all. Maybe this had to do with Adam getting too clingy and trying to put a label on their relationship. Maybe this was *the talk*.

The meat pies, delicious half an hour ago, weren't

settling so great. Fried food, what had he been thinking?

Instead of finishing his sentence, Noel bounced up from his chair, took a few steps across the room, and then whirled back.

"I'm not good at this," he snarled accusingly.

Adam finally managed a breath. He stood up, took a step toward Noel, then thought better of it. "You don't have to do anything you don't want to do." *Talk* being the obvious thing that was problematic right now. More broadly...*trust me with your secrets, try to use your gifts... make a commitment.* All the stuff Adam wanted. He'd never thought Noel would be easy, though. He could wait. Or maybe Adam could make it a little easier. "Did something happen down the block?"

He tried to ask as gently as possible, but Noel's head snapped back, then shook sharply side to side.

"No? Okay, okay," Adam rushed to reassure him.

"That's not..." Noel went abruptly still, as though *no* hadn't been what he intended. "I was an ass about Jason, okay?" The words came out almost too fast to follow. "I was jealous." He waved a dismissive hand. "Sue me."

Then he clammed up and stood glaring at Adam as if waiting for...what?

"Umm...you were..." Maybe he had misunderstood. "But Jason's just..."

"Hot. And smart. And speaks your language." He scowled. "Obviously better boyfriend material."

Adam tried to wrap his head around the U-turn the conversation had taken. "I'm not interested in dating Jason." That was... Where did Noel get these ideas?

Noel just scowled harder. "Why not? You deserve someone hot and smart and not... He'd be way better for you than I am."

The little glimmer of happiness that had started to glow in Adam's chest winked out. So this *was* the talk? "You want me to date Jason?"

"Fuck no."

"But I'm not right for *you*?" The drive home was going to suck. Stupid thing to think about when he was faced with spending the night in a room with someone who didn't want him anymore. "What was that blow job this afternoon? A parting gift?"

"Jesus, Professor, what are you talking about? I just said I was jealous. I'm saying I don't want you to see anyone else. I know I'm fucked-up and selfish and high-maintenance. I don't know crap about history, and most days, I don't care. I'm definitely going to make your life miserable. If I were a nice person at all, I'd be flinging you at Jason for your own good. But I…" He clamped his lips shut. After a second, his chin came up. "I'm not a nice person."

Adam sorted through the barrage of words, trying to work out what Noel was and was not saying. "So, you don't want me to see anyone else?"

Noel flinched. "I'm not saying forever, just…while we're doing this thing."

While we're doing this thing? No clue what Noel thought *this thing* was. "And what about you?"

"What about me?"

"Maybe I'd be jealous if you looked at someone else."

Noel's gaze cut away toward the door, as if he literally wanted to run. "I'm going to fuck this up," he muttered. He shoved his hands into his pockets, slouching in on himself as if contemplating his options. When he met Adam's gaze again, his expression was fierce. He enunciated each word precisely, as though he didn't want any misunderstandings. "I haven't looked at anyone else since I met you."

Chapter Nine

The bass helped. The heavy thudding beat gave his unconscious mind something to fuss about, letting his conscious mind think.

Because damn, he needed to think.

Noel sat in a booth in a dark corner of Lafitte's Booty, a third-rate nightclub in the French Quarter. The stage was blessedly empty, but a couple of the dancers were sitting up at the bar waiting for paying customers to arrive. They knew Noel well enough to leave him alone.

Because Noel was better when he could be quiet. One reason he and Adam worked was that Adam liked to talk and Noel liked to listen, even if his lover sometimes veered into lecture mode. If Noel *had* to talk, alcohol eased the way, unfortunate side effects and all.

But right here and right now, he had a project and no one to interfere. His mind relaxed into the baseline, and he got to work.

He'd brought in one of those big tablets of Post-it notes, the kind that were a couple of feet tall. He'd set up his laptop on the chair beside him. He had a pencil tucked behind his ear and his bottom lip caught between his teeth. His laptop screen showed a list of Tisdales from all over the country, with an Excel workbook minimized at the bottom.

Jason had sent him the results of Angela Davenport's DNA test, Noel had texted back, and now, sending Jason quasi-flirtatious messages broke up the monotony of the research.

At the edge of his awareness, the light shifted. Someone had come through the bar's front door. Noel didn't react.

The part of his mind not complaining about the stereo's volume was ticking off names from a list. He'd waited the better part of a month, but finally he could contribute something. With the results of Angela Davenport's DNA test in hand—along with her permission—he'd gone to the GEDmatch website.

This was where things got real.

A shadow broke his concentration. No, not a shadow. Bergeron.

"Hey, wassup?" Bergeron had a baseball hat pulled low, his Nike jacket zipped up to his chin.

Noel scowled at the room in general. "Are you traveling incognito?

"Hell yes. I didn't want anyone to see me coming into this shithole. They'll think I got scabies or something."

Noel snorted. "Just don't touch anything, and you'll be fine."

Bergeron pulled out the chair across from Noel and straddled it. "Thanks, I'd love to join you."

"My dude." Noel shook his head. He didn't have time for distractions, he didn't want company, and he didn't want to have to talk. He wanted to plug the names he had into the family tree and run each through Google to see what he could come up with. He'd done just enough genetic genealogy to know it was boring AF, and he wanted to get to it.

Bergeron, however, had other ideas. "So, if they call strip clubs for heterosexuals titty bars, what do they call it when all the customers are gay? Dicky bars?"

Noel let a baleful stare answer for him.

"All right, then. You're in a can't-take-a-joke mood. I can roll with that." Bergeron made a sweeping gesture over the Post-it pad. "New project?"

"Sort of." Noel didn't bother hiding the mostly-blank page. "Can I do something for you? Because I'm busy right now."

"So you say. It's what?" He pulled a cell phone out of his pocket. "Three twenty-seven on a Friday afternoon, and you obviously started a while ago." He poked at the tall glass in front of Noel, empty except for ice and lime.

Noel blinked, even more annoyed. "It was soda water, dumbass." Because alcohol had developed some unfortunate side effects. "Seriously, what do you want?"

Bergeron settled back in his seat with his arms crossed, his grin making it very clear he was enjoying Noel's discomfort. "Can't a couple of coworkers have a drink on a Friday afternoon?"

"Not when one of us has work to do."

He craned his neck to get a better look at the Post-it. "Don't look like insurance work to me."

Noel liked Bergeron, he truly did, but right then, he wanted to pop him one. "I'm building a family tree for...well... Do you know any good plantation stories, the kind of things that get handed down in families?"

Some of Bergeron's good humor faded. "My people got stories all right, but they're probably not the kind you want to hear."

"Good point." The ghostly woman with the head scarf flashed through Noel's mind. Something about the reproach in her eyes made him more uncomfortable than the fact that no one else had seen her. He shook his head to clear the image. "It's like this. Remember when me and Adam went to Natchitoches?"

Bergeron nodded.

"We visited Magnolia Plantation, and one of the stories we heard had to do with a woman named Marie and her lover Valsin." He relayed the rest of the story as succinctly as possible, finishing with the TL;DNR summary. "So Marie made it to freedom, and Valsin disappeared. Now we've got this woman, Marie's descendant, and she wants to know what happened."

"That's wild. You think you can figure it out?"

"Don't know. I haven't made any progress since you showed up."

Bergeron gave an exaggerated laugh, pounding on the table with his fist. Noel flipped his head to clear the hair from his face and glared.

"Oh, all right." Bergeron stifled his laughter. "Have you heard about AfricaDNAdotcom?"

"What?"

"My Aunt LaShelle is all up in this stuff, and she told me they have a way of tracking the male line through the Y chromosome."

To cover feeling like an idiot for not having done better research, Noel gave Bergeron an impatient *keep going* twirl of his finger.

"That's about it. Since you're looking for Marie's presumed husband, maybe what you should do is see if the woman who contacted you has a brother."

"Huh." Noel pulled the AfricaDNA website up in his browser. "Huh."

One of the dancers sauntered over, his booty shorts

stretched painfully tight over his package. "Can I get either of you something?"

"I'll take a beer, a Budweiser," Bergeron said.

Noel flicked his glass. "Another one of these."

"The same, or you want me to put something fun in it?"

The dancer's bored expression was at odds with the invitation in his voice.

"Just soda and lime."

The dancer sashayed off, and Noel conceded defeat. He slid the Post-it pad off the table, put his laptop to sleep, and gave Bergeron something approximating a happy smile. "Did you hit your targets for this week?"

They could talk about work because it was easy, and next week, he'd try to do a better job of carving out time for this genealogy work. He couldn't do it at home over the weekend because Adam would be underfoot. They were "boyfriends" now, or some rough approximation of that word, although every time Noel looked back on that last night in Natchitoches, he got angry He'd wanted to tell Adam about the haunts, but somehow talking about *feelings* had been less scary.

That's fucked up.

And now that anger had him keeping petty-ass secrets from Adam, stuff like flirt-texting Jason or carrying around that damned gris gris, minor shit that had little meaning except for the weight he gave it by holding it close. Because that was the kind of thing a shitty boyfriend would do, and if Noel was good at anything, it was being a shitty boyfriend.

In the end, Bergeron wanted to leave after that one beer. Taking that as a sign, Noel packed up his gear and followed him out. He'd had a text from Adam:

<pre>
Adam: This shoot may never

    end. I won't be home

    till sometime tomorrow.
</pre>

They were in...Mobile? Somewhere in Alabama, trying to raise the ghosts in a three-hundred-year-old building that had been everything from a seminary to a brothel.

Noel wished him luck.

He passed on the opportunity to prowl the French Quarter with Bergeron and headed home. He wouldn't be able to crank the stereo to Lafitte's Booty levels, but hopefully, he wouldn't need to. Distracting himself with genealogy would keep him from getting hung up on other stuff.

The more time passed since their trip to Natchitoches, the stronger the memories became. If Noel stayed sober and had Adam around, he could manage.

Otherwise, I'm fucking insane.

He let himself into the house. Without Adam, the quiet echoed. The first creeping tendrils of memory reached for his mind with a cold, ill-defined fear.

Nope.

Noel shook them off. He could do this. He queued up last week's *Drag Race* and set the Post-it pad on the coffee table. The hairs on the back of his neck rose, as if he could sense someone watching. *No one is watching. You're in an empty duplex, dumbass.* Even the second unit was between tenants.

Adam was on the road, but Jay would talk to him. Noel whipped out his phone and shot off a text about the AfricaDNA website. Did he feel guilty for keeping secrets from Adam? Yes. Did he care? Not as long as

Jason responded.

He just couldn't stand to be alone.

Am I crazy?

Maybe.

Adam stared at the composition box on his phone. He fucking hated Twitter.

He did *not* swipe over to his messages, where his last text to Noel, *I miss you*, went unanswered.

Twitter waited.

What was he supposed to say? He did lectures. He did in-depth history on people who had been dead for a hundred years. He did not do the type of pithy commentary Twitter seemed to require.

But here they were, on-site and mid-shoot. Jim and Brittany, who both somehow managed to tweet *in their sleep* as far as he could tell, were in front of the camera. That left Adam to keep up the steady stream of promo the show demanded. The fans wanted updates. Happy fans meant more fans. More fans meant more viewers. More viewers meant better ratings. Better ratings meant—it had been made excessively clear to Adam— that he got to keep a second residence while he researched and wrote ghost stories. Even a tiny drop in ratings could mean a slashed budget.

Something about the current site seemed like the obvious answer for content, but so far, his attempts hadn't gotten any traction. Apparently, Twitter didn't find architectural trivia about the Wentworth building as compelling as he did. What next?

Jim and Brittany spent a lot of time on non-show chatter, which seemed counterproductive. Brittany was into birding and did a string of social media posts about local wildlife. She visited sanctuaries, took pictures with rescue organizations... Okay he could see how that might get some interest, and it was at least location-specific. Except he didn't know crap about birds, and that was her thing anyway.

Jim, who, as far as Adam knew, couldn't retain a date more distant than his own birth, had an obsessive fascination with old glass. Not the history surrounding it, just the glass itself. His accounts flooded out thousands of pictures of rippled, poured window panes, blown-glass ornaments, doorknobs, you name it. He got almost as many retweets as Brittany's birds and had a follower count over two hundred thousand.

Adam's own sepia image of the brothel ladies lined up along the bar had gotten a whopping two likes. No retweets.

"Be yourself," the social media girl from their PR firm had unhelpfully advised. Then, even less helpfully, *"Play up your Cuban heritage. The show could use a boost in the Latinx demographic."* He had bitten back several responses before deciding to pretend he hadn't heard her. He couldn't even attract the nerdy history buff demographic. How was he supposed to be responsible for an entire ethnic group with diverse geographic and cultural backgrounds?

His phone vibrated. Noel had finally replied. Grateful for the distraction, he swiped open the new message.

Huh. Noel had sent him a picture of... He clamped his hand over the screen. Not. Safe. For. Work.

After a quick check to make sure no one had noticed the weird behavior with his phone, he cupped his hand up and took another cautious peek. That was...artistic. Also stimulating. Also—he flattened his hand over the screen as one of the PAs hustled past on some errand— still not safe for work.

With some regret, he deleted the picture. No way was he taking a chance on having it accidentally scroll by at an awkward moment.

He couldn't suppress a little smile as he shot back, *Guess you miss me too?*

He waited for the reply and got...

...

...

The suppressed smile spread to a warm glow in his chest. Noel missed him. Being separated sucked, but they would get through. It was only a few days, and...

Noel's reply popped onto the screen.

Adam scanned it eagerly, then...clapped his hand back over the screen.

After a second, he risked lifting his hand enough to reply. *ffs. I'm at WORK.*

No response.

He felt like he had kicked a puppy.

A horny, X-rated puppy.

But he couldn't sext at work. Just...no. It wasn't like they were nothing but fuck buddies. They could have an actual conversation. Or maybe that hadn't occurred to Noel yet. Maybe he thought Adam was only up for the sexy stuff.

He wasn't. Not at all. Okay, yes. At all. The sexy games were amazing. But he didn't want nonstop play. He wanted...

He sent another text, hoping Noel would get the hint. *What have you been up to?*

Their physical relationship burned hotter than any he'd ever had, but he was greedy. He wanted...more.

He didn't follow fashion, but he wanted Noel's latest rant or rave on the designers he followed. He wanted what Noel had eaten for lunch, and how the receptionist at the firm had it out for him. He wanted the goddamn North Shore surf report, which meant nothing practical to him or Noel while they were based in New Orleans, but which Noel checked regularly anyway.

The reply took so long, he switched back to Twitter. He took a candid shot of Jim and Brittany hunched over their equipment and tagged them in his next post. The flash shot earned him a dirty look from the entire crew, but resulted in a stunning fifty likes and a few retweets over the next fifteen minutes. Still not an acceptable level per the PR goals.

Then he was back to staring at the composition box and trying not to notice that Noel hadn't replied. He was probably busy. Or had put his phone down in another room. Or...something.

Hours later, as they were wrapping up for the night, his phone finally vibrated.

```
Chandler: Had a drink with

Bergeron after work.
```

Nothing else.

The crew was heading out for a late dinner. Adam didn't stop to reply.

By the time he got back to the hotel, relaxed from a few beers and a little lonely after watching the younger members head off to find whatever nightlife Mobile offered, he'd lost the vague sense of dissatisfaction that kept him from replying earlier. A glance at the time told him it was past midnight. Noel wouldn't have work in the morning, but the office job meant his sleep schedule didn't include many late nights. If he hadn't wanted to chat about his day earlier, Adam could only imagine how he would respond to being woken up to answer a question about where he and Bergeron had hung out.

Adam's schedule wasn't entirely free in the morning either. He had a promo piece to do with a local news channel before he could head back to New Orleans, and two morning radio shows. Unlike Natchitoches, he couldn't rely on word of mouth and support from the local Historical Society. The largest Mobile group was firmly into *real* history and weren't thrilled to have a ghost show debasing their historical buildings with paranormal legends.

He set an alarm and climbed into bed, where his mind went immediately back to Noel.

Dirty pictures and a filthier text. At work.

Now that he wasn't worried about anyone reading over his shoulder, it was a little funny. Also, he wished he had kept both texts instead of panicking and erasing them.

He picked up his phone. Noel's sleepy bedroom eyes greeted him from the splash screen. It wasn't a great pic. A funky bit of light arced across one half of his face, and the angle sucked. Not exactly a porn pose. But he had caught Noel with a rare, genuine smile. No fronting or games. No posing for the camera. The good mood made it all the way to his eyes, softening the sharp gold glints to warm honey. Noel bitched whenever he caught sight of it, but Adam refused to pick a different background for his home screen.

He thought again of the picture he'd deleted. Definitely hot. And there were plenty of hot pictures on the internet he could access any time.

Or not.

Adam switched the phone to his other hand, stared into Noel's eyes, and employed nature's best sleep aid.

Chapter Ten

Jason: The Hysterical

Society wants an in-

person update.

Noel grinned at his cell phone. Jason had renamed the Historical Society, and oh, how it fit.

Jason: Can you pass the

word along to Adam?

Nah. If he was being a dick to Adam, he'd be one to Jason too.

Chandler: Maybe you better.

Not sure when I'm going

to see him.

Okay, yeah. He'd had a text from Adam saying he was thirty minutes out right about—he checked the time—twenty-five minutes ago, but hey. Maybe he'd be held up by a huge traffic jam.

On Saturday.

At noon.

Whatever.

Noel stuffed his phone someplace he couldn't see and went back to work. He'd spent the morning outfitting the study. He'd only renamed the back bedroom "the study" after he'd picked out a desk, rolling chair, and matching cabinet from the Jonathan Adler website. The furniture wouldn't be delivered for a week, and in the meantime, he'd set up a card table and folding chair and covered one wall with two-by-three-foot Post-it sheets, the kind used in team-building exercises at work. Angela Davenport's name was at the center, and as he came up with other names and relationships, he'd add them.

He'd started with the relatives Angela had identified, then added more from the GEDmatch database. The database was less specific, identifying third and fourth cousins, for example, but not showing the links in between.

Those links were Noel's to find.

"And why am I doing this?" he muttered, drawing a precise line from Angela to the name Byron Tisdale, her second cousin. "Because fucking Adam has a fucking hard-on for people who've been dead and buried for a hundred fucking years."

That and because Noel knew how to poke around birth and death records and census reports and all kinds of dusty old documents, and because filling in blanks gave him a weird sense of satisfaction.

He stepped back, surveying the Post-its. There was still way too much blank space. Angela had been able to take him back four generations on her mother's side. What he really needed, though, was her closest male relative. "Then we can give the nice people at AfricaDNA a shout."

The biggest drawback to the upstairs room in the rear of the house was the ambient temperature. *Heat rises.* And at already eighty degrees, the office would soon double as an oven. Pondering how much to spend on a ceiling fan, he changed from sweats to a pair of shorts he'd made by cutting the legs off a worn pair of jeans. He might have been wearing the same shorts last night when he'd sent Adam a couple of ill-advised texts.

What this guy does to me. Jesus.

Rather than ponder the intricacies of Adam, he jogged downstairs. He'd been a good sport for most of the last month, ever since their return from Natchitoches. With only one or two exceptions, he'd had nary a drink.

Nary a drink. He waved a finger at some invisible accuser. For a month.

He hit the freezer at a jog and scooped up a fistful of ice. Grabbed a glass. Scrounged a lime—only a little dried out—from the back of the veggie crisper in the fridge. Adam would be home all weekend, and Noel deserved a reward.

In just a very few moments, sweat beaded up on a glass filled with gin and a little tonic. The first healthy swallow smoothed over his roughest edges.

"Oh yeah."

Smirking at no one, Noel went out to the front room and flopped onto the chair closest to the window. The sun was too high to cast shadows, there wasn't the slightest hint of a breeze, and *where the fuck is Adam anyway?*

He resisted the urge to down his drink and pour another, settling for a moderately large sip. He already had the beginnings of a buzz, that melting sensation under his sternum that meant his brain might soon be rotating a few revolutions slower.

He wasn't stupid enough to try to sell anyone on that *I can quit anytime I want to* bullshit. He drank because it was a tool, a means to an end. It kept him from trying to crawl out of his own skin. After that...whatever had happened in Natchitoches, though, he wanted to stay right inside his own skin, thank you very much.

Because outside was scary as shit.

But with Adam home, he'd have a distraction. No, more than a distraction. A...a...what should he call it? If he closed his eyes, he could sense their connection, something unlike anything he'd known before. They were friends. Boyfriends. *Do I have to give it a name?*

Thank God his phone chirped before he went any further down that wormhole.

```
Adam: Ten minutes out. Are

you awake?
```

Fuck yeah. Noel headed for the couch by way of the front door, leaving it ajar. Then he settled himself on the couch, making sure he'd be the first thing Adam would see. A couple of quick rubs, and his cock escaped from his very short shorts.

```
Chandler: Come on in, babe.

The door's open.
```

Longest ten minutes on record. Finally—*finally*—a single knock made the door swing open. Adam stood in the doorway, one hand and both eyebrows raised. He needed a shave, and maybe a trim. Noel couldn't wait to run his hands through those thick curls and rub Adam's scruffy face all over his body.

"Hello?" Adam sounded oddly uncertain.

Noel raised his glass. "Welcome home."

Adam's gaze drifted somewhere south of Noel's chin.

"C'mere." Noel let his thighs fall open wider, the narrow stretch of denim hiding very little.

"Uh..." Adam raked his hands through his hair. "I thought we might go out to lunch."

"I got something you can eat right here."

Adam's short laugh had a wilting effect on Noel's confidence.

"What?" Noel shifted around to put a little less on display. "You've been gone all week, babe." Clenching his jaw, he forced himself to stop talking. *Whiny bitch is so not your best look, Chandler.*

"No, wait." Adam's suitcase thudded on the floor. "It's not that I don't like it"—he made a sweeping gesture that took in all of Noel's everything—"but the whole way here, I really just wanted to talk."

Noel bit down hard on his first six snarky comebacks, determined not to make any more of an ass of himself than necessary. "Hard week?"

"Some, yeah." Flopping onto the chair across from Noel, Adam raked his hands through his hair. "My social media presence is sorely lacking, we're probably going to be filming in Texas next week, and just now, Jay messaged me that the people from the Natchitoches Historical Society want some kind of update."

Oh yeah. The text from Jason. Years of working as a cop kept Noel's expression blank. "I wonder what they want to know."

"I guess the committee members are lining up in factions, with some who want to keep Angela Davenport's information a secret to maintain the community festival as-is, and others who want the full story, so they can...I don't know...change the reenactment or something."

That kind of talk had Noel soft enough to tuck back into his shorts. "All right, then." He stood and offered Adam his hand. "Since you don't want to fuck me, come see what I've been doing."

With their fingers intertwined, the sting of rejection faded. It was helped along when, halfway up the stairs, Adam caught Noel around the hips and ground cock to ass. "Where'd you find these shorts, anyway? You steal 'em off of someone at Lafitte's?"

"Don't tease the tiger, Morales." Still holding on to Adam's hand, Noel dragged him the rest of the way upstairs. No, he didn't feel rejected, which was...odd. He wanted to show Adam the progress he'd made. It'd give them something to show the hysterical...err, Historical Society.

Maybe he should even level up on another secret or two.

...nah.

"So this is the study." Noel flung the door open and stepped aside. Admittedly, it didn't look like much. He'd dragged the dusty card table out of the attic, and the Post-its on the walls were mostly blank. Still, Adam began a slow clap.

"Is this what I think it is?"

"If you think it's the beginnings of Angela Davenport's family tree, then yes."

Adam kept his arms crossed and his eyes narrowed. His body language made Noel's half-assed setup look even shabbier.

"The office furniture's coming the end of the week." Noel crossed his arms too, schooling his expression into something neutral, something confident, something that didn't look as defensive as he'd sounded.

Adam moved closer to the Post-its on the wall. "You

didn't tell me."

His cool tone of voice set off a spark of annoyance in Noel. "You were busy," he snapped, "and I wanted to make some progress before you got home."

"Cool." Adam glanced over at him. "Lunch?"

There was something sad in Adam's gaze, obvious enough that Noel wondered what the hell he'd missed this time. Whatever it was put a damper on his irritation. Made him sad too. "Sure. Just let me change into a different pair of shorts."

"I'll wait downstairs."

Adam lumbered off, leaving Noel more than puzzled. In the space of twenty minutes, he'd been cock-blocked, then angry, then sad.

That is too damned many emotions for one afternoon. He promised himself another drink and went to his room to change clothes.

Adam picked at his seafood platter, the extra-large fried version he'd been promising himself as a reward for sticking to a healthy diet while on the road. Funny, he remembered the oysters being better last time they had eaten here, when Noel kept insisting Adam *just taste* the ones from his plate.

In a culinary role reversal, Noel had gone for grilled fish with wilted greens. Looking at their plates, Adam had a weird moment of wondering if Noel had ordered the oysters just to give them away. Except, that was...was... He chased the thought around in his head for a while, trying to decide if the behavior should be classified as some type of sabotage or...or... He finally gave up because an extra-large side of fries to share was one thing, but the thought of Noel ordering a whole platter of food he knew Adam would like but wouldn't order for himself was...improbable.

The stuffed crab had definitely been better last time.

Or maybe he was just in a shit mood because, after days of being apart, who turned down sex with their hot boyfriend in favor of whining about work?

He jabbed his fork viciously into another oyster. Yep, he was the genius who not only turned down homecoming cock, but then got offended because the same hot boyfriend had shown an interest in his extracurricular project. Enough interest to set up a whole research space and spend what looked like a considerable amount of time poking at Jay's little mystery.

"Oysters okay?" Noel had put down his own fork. Instead, his hand rested at the base of his drink, one finger lightly tapping the side of the glass.

"Great," Adam muttered. "Fish?"

The finger stilled for a beat, then picked back up at a faster tempo. "Excellent."

Great. Excellent. Everything was perfect, then.

A discreet buzz alerted him to a new notification from his phone. Adam ignored it. He was taking the rest of the day off. Whoever it was could wait; he was too pissy to deal with them.

He should have gone with the sex. Right now, he could be enjoying his seafood platter in a haze of postcoital bliss instead of forcing down bite after tasteless bite. Noel had made one or two attempts at conversation, mostly about DNA research—something

Adam should have jumped on. Hadn't he wanted them to share some interests? They could be discussing theories about Marie and Valsin right now. So why was he in this *mood* instead?

His phone buzzed again.

"You need to get that?"

"No." It was probably Jay or someone from the show. Let them wonder if he had turned his phone off, or left it in another room or...just didn't want to talk to them about whatever common interests they might have.

"Look, if you don't want my input into Angela Davenport's story, just say so. I don't give a shit about some guy who went out for cigarettes a hundred years ago and didn't come back."

"Well, why are you doing it, then?"

Silence from the other side of the table. Noel's finger stilled again, then he curled his hand around his drink. "Bored, I guess."

Of course.

Noel picked up his drink, then sat it back down before taking a sip. "And it's a mystery, even if it's an old one. Kinda nagged at me."

Adam's phone buzzed. They both ignored it.

"And you care." Noel picked up his drink again. "You care who the baby daddy was, okay? Figured you were busy and I was bored." He took a healthy swallow of his drink. "But like I said, if you don't want me playing in your lane, just say so."

"No. No, I'm glad you're interested. I'm glad of the help." Adam blew out a breath, trying to tamp down his irrational irritation. He wasn't mad that Noel was dipping a toe in his pool, was he? Back in Natchitoches, the idea of Noel turning his sharp mind on the Marie and Valsin mystery had been hot as fuck. What changed?

His phone buzzed again.

A look of annoyance flitted across Noel's face. "Jesus, Professor, pick it up or turn it off. Never seen you ignore anyone like that."

No, he wasn't the one who ignored his messages. Adam's hand stilled halfway to the phone. Then he picked it up and changed the setting from vibrate to mute. He didn't look at Noel. "So... You've been working on this for a while. The DNA stuff?"

"I don't know if I'd call it working. Waiting, mostly. Just got the first results back."

"While I was in Mississippi."

A short silence. Noel wasn't stupid. "Yeah."

"You didn't mention it."

"Still not much to tell."

Maybe just the fact that he was interested. Maybe Adam would have liked to know that. He had *asked* Noel what he had been doing. All he'd gotten back was a sentence about drinks with Bergeron.

"I guess I didn't want you to get your hopes up if nothing popped. But today you were upset ,and I obviously wasn't enough of a distraction to cheer you up so...whatever."

"Whatever," Adam repeated. Jesus, he could never complain about Noel's lack of relationship skills again. He was being a total ass.

I obviously wasn't enough of a distraction to cheer you up.

Adam shot another glance across the table where Noel sat with his barely touched drink. He didn't really think that, did he? And it sincerely wasn't possible that he thought Adam would have blamed him if the DNA didn't pan out. It was more likely he had spent the time digging around in Davenport family history because he couldn't resist the mystery than he wanted to please Adam. And he had failed to mention it because he was more interested in dick pics than common interests.

Or, Adam sighed, because he was a secretive, mistrustful bastard who wasn't lying when he said he was shit at relationships.

"Those shorts could cheer up a dead man."

"Not how I remember it, Professor."

And now he had just sent the conversational equivalent of a dick pic. Maybe a little honesty was called for. He reached across the table until his knuckles just grazed Noel's on the side of the glass. "I like the shorts. I liked that you were waiting for me when I got off the road. The research is incredible. I'm glad you're interested."

Noel scowled at him. "Why do I hear a *but* coming?"

But it's been weeks. Why couldn't you talk to me? He couldn't say it. Maybe this wasn't about Noel keeping his distance. Maybe Adam was trying to move too fast. He skimmed his knuckles against Noel's again, wishing they were someplace more private, and settled for, "I missed you."

As a peace offering, the words felt both utterly inadequate and entirely too revealing. Noel's hand moved, lightning fast, to cover his on the table.

Adam looked up, sure Noel would demand a little more groveling. Instead, he met a dead-serious gaze.

"Yeah?"

Adam's breath caught because the tone wasn't mocking or teasing. He asked like he wanted an answer. "You know I did."

Noel's hazel eyes glinted gold, blinding bright, then he broke the moment by letting his eyelids droop into the sleepy expression that had driven Adam nuts from the moment they met.

"Maybe you can prove how much you missed me when we get home." His smile was all innocence. "Unless you want to talk."

Adam groaned. "I'm never going to live that down, am I?"

Somehow, in the past few minutes, the tension had drained out of his body. They were back on familiar ground, but maybe it felt a little more solid. Solid enough that Adam hoped a trip might come soon when Noel admitted he had missed him too.

A vibration against the table had him automatically reaching for his phone, before he remembered his was muted. Noel glanced at the screen, then swiped the notification away. "Bergeron being an ass. Sure you don't want to check yours? Thought it was going to vibrate itself off the table earlier."

He'd rather not, but...he'd turned off the social media notifications earlier, which meant someone who actually knew him had been trying to get through. Reluctantly, he picked up the phone and scrolled through the messages.

"Shit."

Noel's eyebrow twitched up. "Trouble?"

"I guess I should have paid more attention to whatever Jay wanted. The Natchitoches Historical Society has managed to get Annemarie in some sort of panic."

"Your ex?"

Why did Noel always insist on choosing that label for her? "My *producer*. And she's not the panicky sort. She wants to know what I've done to get the town of Natchitoches to mount a social media campaign against the show and how I'm going to fix it."

Chapter Eleven

Noel fiddled with his cocktail napkin, parsing possible responses. Quiet sympathy? *Meh.* Jealousy? *Mental shrug.*

Outrage? An overwhelming urge to fight Adam's battles? *That's the one.* "What the actual fuck? What's the hysterical society up to now?"

"Hysterical society." Adam smirked. "That's what Jay calls them."

Noel's jaw tightened further. The ex-girlfriend might not be an issue, but the hot historian could still make Noel want to knock their heads together. Like, he trusted Adam. He did, and he knew this reaction came straight out of high school, but still. Before he could dive too far down that wormhole, Adam spoke up.

"Apparently, the idea that I might be involved in the debunking of their local legend is not sitting well with them."

"You'd think they'd want the truth."

"Sure. As long as it involves Marie and Valsin riding off into the sunset, we're golden." His shoulders slumped. "That was a great group. They invited me to speak at one of their meetings while I was up there filming. Their president is the sweetest little old lady. I can't believe they're upset by this."

"Are they going to sue Angela Davenport for having a different version of her family's history?"

Adam's shrug spoke more of exhaustion than anything else. Noel had never seen him this discouraged. "Jesus, I'm sorry. You've probably worked seventy hours in the last five days. Let's finish up here and go to bed."

Adam stirred the mess of rice and oysters on his plate. "Maybe I should go back to my apartment. I'm not very good company right now."

Noel swallowed his initial protest. They didn't live together, and Adam had a right to ask for privacy. Except... "What's really going on?"

Adam blinked, his chin tucked against his chest.

"I mean..." Noel scrambled for a way out of this particular hornet's nest. "We're here because you wanted to talk, and whatever bee's flown up Annemarie's bonnet will keep till later."

The restaurant's tables were close together, and they both jumped when a neighbor's attempt to stand banged right into Adam's chair. Noel took the moment of distraction to flag the waitress and order another round of drinks.

"I don't want—"

Noel raised his hand. "Quiet. It's medicinal."

Adam propped both elbows on the table, his head in his hands.

"I'm going to get you drunk and take advantage of you."

Peering from between his fingers, Adam grinned, or at least his lips twitched in the general direction of a smile.

"I get the feeling this is bigger than a hundred-year-old mystery, and if you want to talk about it, I'm here."

Whoo boy. Look at me, being all grown-up and sympathetic and stuff.

Adam's smile grew more sincere. "Don't I look pitiful? I mean, it's not that big a deal. I'm just not sure I'm in the right place."

Right place? Right here, right now? With an effort, Noel bit back his initial response. Not everything is about you, Chandler. "Oh yeah?"

"Take this last week, for instance. I was on point with stuff for the camera, but every time I turned around, somebody from publicity wanted to know why I wasn't Twittering, I mean tweeting. I'm supposed to be feeding the fan base on social media, when all I want to do is, I don't know, dig through old records and reconstruct the past."

Relief made Noel even more sympathetic. Not that he'd really expected Adam would break up with him without any warning, but that whole "don't know if I'm in the right place" thing had sounded threatening.

The waitress brought their next round. Noel killed his old gin and tonic, handed her the glass, and took a deep swallow of the new one. The alcohol amplified his sense of relief, and he exhaled, letting go of the tension.

Adam's phone buzzed, and this time, he answered it right away. "Hmph." He blinked at Noel, his expression confused. "Jay wants to know how much progress you've made. He thinks we're going to need to present our findings to the Historical Society before things get any further out of whack." He blinked again. "Jay knew you were working on the DNA angle?"

"Well, yeah." *Damn it.* He'd only just talked Adam *off* the ledge. "He's the one who arranged for Angela to give a sample, right? He texted me to say he'd submitted it and again to let me know when the results were in."

"Oh." Adam rubbed his mouth with an open palm. "The way he said it, I thought… I, uh…sorry. I'm in a lousy mood today."

"It's okay." Noel rested his hand on Adam's, twining their fingers together. "Drink that"—he nodded at Adam's beer—"and let's get out of here."

He reinforced his desire to leave by catching Adam's calf with his foot and giving it a rub.

"At any rate"—Adam glanced at his phone again—"looks like I've got about two weeks to come up with something. Annemarie and Jay seem to think if I speak at the Historical Society again, I'll be able to smooth things over."

"Not *you*, babe. *We*."

Adam raked his fingers through his hair. "Are you sure you want to go back there with me?"

"Hell, no." Noel squeezed Adam's fingers. "But I will." He didn't know what to name the feeling, that warm, swelling sensation that reached from under his sternum to the pit of his belly.

Either he was going to have a heart attack, or he was falling…

Nah.

He didn't have a heart attack. In fact, after he and Adam finished their lunch, they headed back to Noel's duplex, where he was able to welcome his boyfriend home properly.

Boyfriend. Might be time to own that word.

With Adam back on location, Noel buried himself in work. Between the names Angela had shared with him and the results of her DNA, he made progress in filling in the blank spaces on his wall of Post-its.

Once his new office furniture had been delivered, he felt almost professional. The trick was, he needed to work both forward and backward to find the branch that led to Valsin.

From what he was able to reconstruct, Marie had given birth to a son shortly after she arrived in Pennsylvania. Her son had married, and his wife had borne five children, three girls and two boys. If he could find a male descendant of one of those boys, and if he could convince that man to give a sample to the AfricaDNA website, he hoped to then look for where else Valsin's DNA might have gone. And he wanted to be able to give the Historical Society as much information as possible. Nobody got to mess with his boyfriend.

Nobody.

On Saturday, some four days before he and Adam were heading back to Natchitoches, he got a hit. One of the people he'd cross-referenced with Angela's DNA on the GEDWeb page was a cousin several times removed. He was also a Tisdale, which made it likely he'd descended from Marie's son.

Yes. This gave him the juice, for reals. Noel plugged

the name "Byron Tisdale" into a page linked to the Hughes Wallace website—the one he was only supposed to use to search for work-related contact information. "What they don't know…"

The Hughes Wallace page coughed up the guy's email, mailing address, and cell phone number. "Well, well, well." Some of this shit was just too easy. He tapped the number into his cell phone. Tennessee address, but the area code was Houston. "Wonder if he's willing to chat on a Friday afternoon."

"Hello?"

The guy sounded distracted, as if Noel had caught him in the middle of changing clothes or something.

"Hey, I'm sorry to bother you." Noel spoke quickly, not giving the guy a chance to hang up. "This isn't a sales call. My name's Noel Chandler, and I'm working with your cousin Angela on a genealogy project."

"You're…what?"

The voice was gruff, with the kind of swing in the vowels that only came from growing up in New Orleans.

"Your cousin Angela Davenport has asked me to trace her ancestry, and I'm trying to find her closest male relative." That wasn't quite accurate, but close enough for his purposes today.

"Angela Davenport? You mean Angela Alden?" His surprise was palpable. "How'd you get my name?"

"Your sister, um"—Noel checked his Post-it—"D'Annette's name came up on a genealogy website, and I was able to look up the rest of her siblings online."

Noel had no reason to lie to the guy, and a fair amount of gratitude that he hadn't hung up already.

"Huh."

Noel waited to see if Byron had any more questions, rolling back and forth in his new padded office chair.

He spoke up before things could get awkward. "You do know Angela, right?"

"I do…" His voice trailed off. "To be honest, not all that well. She lives outside DC."

"Northern Virginia, yeah."

"We've met at a couple of family reunions, but that's about it."

"That's fine. This isn't a test." Noel tried for jovial and got somewhere close. "We know her fourth great-grandmother was a woman named Marie. Does that name sound familiar to you at all?"

Byron laughed loud enough to make Noel regret the question.

"Nah. Not that far back."

"What we're trying to do is find Angela's fourth great-grand*father*. No one knows who he was or what happened to him."

Another pause, but this one was more skeptical.

"Have *you* met Angela?" Byron finally asked.

"Not in person, but—"

"Because she's black, and I'm black, and you don't have to go back too many generations before nobody documented shit."

Noel was ready for him. "True, but there's a website that specializes in tracking Y-chromosome DNA, and it's aimed at African American men. If I can find a descendant of one of Marie's grandsons, I might be able to go back up the family tree to figure out what happened to Marie's husband." Another small white lie, but it'd have to do.

"You've got the wrong guy, then, because we're not actually blood relatives."

Noel smacked his pen on the desktop but kept his voice calm. "You're not?"

"Sorry to disappoint you, Mr. Noel Chandler, but I

was adopted when I was a baby."

The pen made soft thwaks on the glossy finish. "Well, damn. Google does have its limits." Noel laughed to cover his frustration.

"I guess so." Byron chuckled too. "But you know, you could talk to my great-uncle Richard Lafont. He's an actual relative of Angela's, and last time I checked, he was male."

"How do you spell the last name?" Byron spelled it out, and Noel made a note. "Do you have a phone number for him?"

Another chuckle. "He's about ninety-four years old. You're going to have to go see him in person."

"Uh, okay." Tap tap tap. "Where is he?"

"He lives in a home outside of Natchitoches."

Natchitoches. Of course. "All right, then. Is there anything you'd like me to tell your Uncle Richard when I see him?"

"Tell him he still owes me money from the Super Bowl. The old fool went and bet against the Saints."

"Wait. The Saints? What year was that?"

"Twenty-ten, but I got a long memory."

"I guess you do." Noel asked for the address, thanked the man sincerely, and ended the call. He made a box around the city name on the Post-it note. "Good ol' Nack."

Chapter Twelve

oel was driving—because of course Noel was driving. He had let someone drive the Lexus. Once. Only because he'd been too hammered, and he was too far from home to wrangle an Uber. Besides, Adam seemed to be okay with his copilot role. "Right?"

"What?" Adam gave him a sidelong glance from behind his Ray-Bans. Next birthday, Noel was going to buy him a pair from Oakley or Tom Ford or something.

"Nada, babe," Noel snapped back with the kind of grin that made a lie out of his words, nudging Adam with his elbow to reinforce the point. Even with the lure of Richard Lafont, he'd had to argue with Adam about making this trip. Adam might not want him at the meeting, but on some level, he knew Adam needed protection from the hysterical society, and dammit, Noel was going to be there for him.

Whether Adam wanted the help or not.

"In a quarter mile, turn left."

"Bossy bitch." Laughing, Noel eased up on the accelerator. They were on one of those two-lane country roads with a fifty-five mile-per-hour speed limit, which never made a lot of sense to him. Too fast with too little room for error for someone who'd learned to drive on the LA freeways.

They'd spent the night at the same chintz-tastic hotel as their first trip, and while Noel had been nervous about the possibility of haunts, so far, so good. He was less worried about being crazy and more convinced that good behavior was the key. As much as he hated to admit it, the ghosties and the gin seemed to go together.

He made the turn, and Siri almost immediately announced that they'd reached their destination. That was about the only thing they'd reached. On the right, a field of tall grass eventually ran into some trees. To their left was a long, low building, fairly new construction, with a wide porch under overhanging eaves.

The Cane River Home. A flat-black sign out front announced their destination. Grinning with excitement, Noel pulled into the circular drive. "Hmph."

"Now what?"

"Talk about being put out to pasture." He found a parking spot with no one on either side. *Fewer door dings that way.*

Adam laughed and popped the lock. "This was your idea."

On the way into the facility, Noel let Adam lead, the better to watch the way his black jeans cupped his ass. Once they were inside, though, Noel stepped up. A young woman sat at a reception desk across from the main doors, her makeup job doing its best to give her pale moon face some contour.

"Hi." Noel extended his hand to shake. "I called an hour ago. I'm Noel Chandler, and I'd like to see Richard Lafont."

Despite the phone call, Noel still wasn't completely sure Richard would be willing to talk to them. The woman's smile reassured him. "I do remember you, Mr. Chandler. Why don't you and your friend take a seat, and I'll call back."

There were exactly two chairs in the lobby, their hard surfaces and sharp angles clearly designed to keep people moving along. There were lots of windows, though, and the early afternoon sunshine took the edge off the refrigerator air that most Southerners seemed to need to function.

Noel and Adam had waited all of two minutes when a young man breezed through a set of double doors. He wore a scrub top, white pants, and a high-top fade, and with a wave, he led them down a long hall. At the other end of the building, they reached a wide doorway with a sign that said The Solarium.

Some thirty people were scattered around the room. Most of them were elderly, a few in wheelchairs, others seated at the small tables. A group was clustered around a flat screen on the far wall, watching a black-and-white movie, the volume turned to eleven.

The young man led them to a table near the corner. There were three people already there, playing cards. "Mr. Lafont, you have some company."

An old, old man looked up at them, the kind of old where his shirt hung off bony shoulders, his neck had a wattle, and his dark eyes were rheumy. He smiled, though, locking Noel into his sharply intelligent gaze. "Now, where did you come from?"

Noel shouted introductions, dropping Byron Tisdale's name. The young nurse patted Noel's arm. "Hang on a sec. Let me catch the volume." He strode across the room, and in a moment, the noise decreased to a manageable level.

"Anyway, Byron told me you were related to Angela Alden Davenport, and we wanted to ask you a couple of questions, if you're willing."

The old man flared his hand of cards. "You can see I'm right busy here, but I suppose if my rummy partners are willing, I could take a moment." He glanced from one friend to the other. "You okay with that, Delia? Curtis?"

The others agreed. The man, Curtis, wore an affable smile, but Delia regarded them with suspicion.

"Okay, then," Richard continued. "Now what can I help you with?"

Noel nudged Adam into the fourth seat at the table and dragged another chair from nearby, close enough for Adam's calm vibe to settle him down. "Do you know Angela, by any chance?"

Richard flicked his thumbnail along the edge of his cards. His skin was light tan, drawn paler by age. "I believe I have some Alden relatives somewhere, but to be honest, her name isn't ringing any bells."

Noel bumped his knee against Adam. "Did you grab the notebook?" Adam pulled it out of his leather binder, and Noel took a quick glance at his notes. "I think I tracked the connection. Your mother was Marinette Lafont, right?"

"That's right."

"And your sister was Terese?"

"Yes, sir."

Noel and Adam exchanged glances. Adam had been the one to dig up the family name in an old census, and from there they were able to track the birth records. Giving Adam an encouraging nod, Noel sat back.

"Your sister Terese was Angela's grandmother."

"Is that right?" Richard sat up straighter, his eyes wide. "I guess we are related, then."

Delia snapped her cards down on the table. "So what? Why you bothering us with this?"

This was sticky part. Their story was going to fly in the face of what the good people of Natchitoches had treated as gospel for years, and if the Historical Society was any indication, their new interpretation could get people real riled up.

"Angela came to us for help in digging into her genealogy—" Adam began, but he was interrupted.

"I know you." Delia pointed a crooked finger at him. "You're the one from the television, from that ghost show."

With an abashed smile, Adam nodded his agreement.

"That must be why she asked you, then." Delia leaned back and crossed her arms, apparently satisfied with his answer.

"Anyway..." Adam rubbed his chin. "You all know the story of Marie and Valsin, don't you?"

A chorus of agreement answered him, Richard Lafont's eyes sparkling with humor, like this was all a kind of joke.

"Angela told us she's descended from Marie."

"Oh ho, that means you are too, Richard." Curtis threw down his cards and laughed. "How come you never told us that before?"

Richard blinked his rheumy eyes. "I didn't know."

Delia's eyes narrowed again. "Seems to me you would if it was true."

Noel decided to bail Adam out. "Angela is able to provide documentation going back several generations, and we made a decent effort at filling in the blanks. I think her story is true."

"All right, then. This is very interesting, but..." Richard didn't finish his question, but Noel could guess where he was going.

"Why are we asking you about this?"

"Yeah."

Adam leaned forward, resting his elbows on the table. "So this might be harder to believe, but Angela's family story also says that while Angela was able to make her way to the north, Valsin didn't go with her. They were supposed to meet up, but he never arrived, so she went on her own."

Adam's announcement left the elderly people speechless for a moment, then they all started talking at once.

"That's not how it was." Delia's voice carried over the other two. "Valsin most certainly did go with her. My grandmama told me her great-granddaddy helped him that night."

She spoke with such conviction, Noel knew they'd never convince her otherwise. "What else did he tell you?"

"See, they needed horses, one for each of them, and great-granddaddy was in charge of the stables in town. He arranged for two horses to be saddled that night, and great-grandmama made up some bundles of food for them to take. You can tell that Yankee girl to take her foolishness and leave us alone."

"I'm sure you're right," Adam said, way more calmly than Noel could have managed. "But my friend Jason is doing some anthropological research over at Magnolia Plantation, and he's been unable to find any legal records mentioning Valsin Ferrier from the time they were supposed to have left."

Noel kept his mouth shut, letting the older people digest this new information. Finally, Richard heaved a sigh.

"Well, I can think of a few reasons a Black man

might have disappeared from the legal records. He could have changed his name." He paused thoughtfully. "'Course, we've always believed Valsin was a free Black, and no one in these parts would have gone up against his family to say otherwise. Still, he could have been jumped by slave catchers, I guess. They'd have torn up his papers and shipped him down to Florida somewhere."

Noel had read enough about plantation life to know that Florida was its own death sentence.

"But if he really, really disappeared, likely he up and got killed."

"He most certainly did not, and I think you young men are rude for even talking that way." Delia rose from her chair. "Maybe y'all should see yourselves out."

Curtis burst out laughing. "Settle down, pigeon. I still want to know why y'all came all the way out here bothering Richard with this."

Thank you for being sensible. Noel brushed the hair back from his face. "Well, I've done a bit of work in the area of forensic genealogy, and—"

"The what?" Curtis interrupted.

"There are computer databases holding people's DNA records. Our hope is that if we can find a close male relative of Angela, we'll be able take a sample of his DNA"—might as well lay it out there—"and see if we can track it back to Valsin by following the male line."

"So you want my blood?"

"Well, it's saliva, actually, but we'd like you to consider—"

"Oh, for pity's sake." Delia stalked off, leaving Curtis chuckling and Richard, well, Noel wasn't sure what Richard thought.

"It's certainly something we want you to think about first," Adam said, pouring on the calm, professorial energy.

Richard nodded without saying anything.

"You better do this, man," Curtis said. "I mean, Delia never gonna shut up if you turn out to be related to both Marie and Valsin."

Noel met Richard's appraising gaze, hoping his silence gave the man the time and space he needed.

"I tell you what," Richard said finally. "You go on about your day and stop by again, maybe Monday, and I'll let you know what I decide."

Noel and Adam both rose, hands extended. "Thank you very much. That's all we can ask," Noel said. After a round of handshakes, they headed back down the hall.

"Florida," Adam murmured, as soon as they hit the parking lot. "I doubt we'll ever find records if he ended up there."

Noel rubbed at the tight muscles running up his neck. He was torn between relief that they hadn't been kicked out, and disappointment that they hadn't left with a sample in hand.

They really did that?"

"Did what?" Adam asked absently, his thoughts still back at the rummy table. He'd love to go back and talk to the old folks sometime. Family histories could be fascinating.

Noel shook his head. "Tore up people's papers. Black

people. You know, back in the day."

"It happened. I take it you didn't see *Twelve Years a Slave*."

"That's…" Noel trailed off without finishing the sentence. "You think that's a possibility?"

"It's a possibility."

Noel let the subject drop, either tired of history lessons or to mull over the inhumanity of mankind. They had a few hours to kill before the Historical Society meeting, and he insisted they go back to the B and B and watch a movie. Adam didn't argue until he picked *Die Hard*.

"That's a Christmas movie. Choose something else."

"Yippee-kai-yay, motherfucker," Noel shot back. Adam eventually gave up, tuned most of it out, and woke up to the credits and the incessant ping of phone notifications, right about the time they needed to leave.

After their visit with Richard and the nap, he felt as optimistic as he had in weeks about locating Valsin. Maybe Noel was right. He needed some downtime.

With some dread, he picked up his phone to see what all the dinging was about.

"Shit."

Noel glanced at him from the driver's seat. "Baby, please don't tell me Annemarie is micromanaging this meeting. We got this."

"No." Adam scrolled through the notifications disbelievingly. "I…um…" He almost couldn't get the words out.

"Calm down and spit it out."

"I went viral," Adam said wonderingly. "I wasn't even trying. It was just an offhand remark about that shoot in Mobile. Someone called @fakecatmem with almost a million followers picked it up. People are *engaging*."

"There you go, baby, I knew you could do it." Noel maneuvered the Lexus into an open parking spot. "Now let's get in there and knock them dead."

The board meeting was held in the Natchitoches Parish Library, the kind of building that looked like it had been modeled after a pile of children's blocks. The meeting room was bright and clean, with one wall of glass that looked out over the bookshelves below. Adam had only been in the building once before, but he'd been in hundreds of libraries, and they all had the same effect on him. Libraries were places of refuge and discovery. He let the familiar sense of calm cool some of his jittery excitement over his Twitter success.

He was actually starting to look forward to this event. He did a lot of publicity appearances, but amateur history groups were his favorites. His presentation last month had gotten a warm reception, maybe thanks to Jason laying the groundwork for the importance of folklore. The group had followed the logic to ghost stories as folklore, and his hour had ended in a lively discussion. Adam couldn't imagine much had changed.

Jason met them outside the door of the meeting room, wearing pressed khakis and a button-down shirt instead of his usual shorts or jeans. Nothing in his manner conveyed tension or unhappiness, which Adam found additionally reassuring. Annemarie and the PR department were freaking out over nothing.

Adam spotted the wispy white hair of the president, Camille Williams, in a group down the hall. When she saw him, she hurried toward him with open arms. He'd been right. Camille couldn't possibly have anything to do with any threats to the show.

"Adam, everyone is so happy to have you back again to speak."

Adam let her hug him, bending over slightly to pat her gently on the back. She smelled of Aqua Net and flowery old lady perfume. Underneath her sweater, her shoulder blades felt small and brittle, like she might crumble to dust if he gave her a proper hug.

When Adam introduced them, she looked ready to give Noel the same welcome. Noel's face betrayed a flash of panic, and somehow, he managed to scoot out of arm's reach without making it look like he was dodging her.

Camille's eyes twinkled at Adam, as though she knew exactly how prickly Noel could be. "You were so busy last time you were here. You didn't get a chance to meet many people. At least let me introduce you to our board members before we get started."

Adam relaxed a little more. Camille was definitely on his side. And these were his people, fellow history nerds. He would be able to talk about what they were doing and explain the importance of recording the truth when they could. He made a mental note to give out his Twitter handle.

Afterward, maybe he would take that downtime and spend the weekend doing touristy things with Noel, just the two of them.

"This rascal here is our treasurer, Harrison Whitney." Camille led them over the group down the hall. The gentleman who extended his hand had curly gray hair and a pair of aviator glasses he had to have bought in the seventies.

"Pleased to meet you." The man enveloped Adam's hand in a thick-fingered grasp. "Welcome aboard."

"Nice to meet you too." Adam let the old dude win the power squeeze. Noel submitted to a brief shake, offered a bland smile, then settled into the social version of his cop face. This involved looking idly rich and pretty until people forgot to take him seriously.

Randi Crenshaw, the vice president, was up next. Maybe forty years old, she had dark skin and thick braids pulled back and twisted in a knot. Like the other members, she had dressed casually, but her manner was corporate. The look she gave Adam was friendly enough, if a bit reserved.

"Our secretary, Darla, isn't here," Camille said. "Which is a shame because I think you two would hit it off. Bless her heart, she has her hands full with a new baby and a death in the family."

Camille herded them into their meeting room, where another two dozen or so people were milling about. Everyone hurried to take a seat in one of the folding chairs set up in neat rows. It was quickly obvious there weren't enough chairs, so more milling ensued while Randi and a few volunteers collected extras from other rooms.

Finally, everyone was seated except Camille, who stood at the front of the room.

"Gracious," she began. "We have a full house today. I wonder what the draw is."

She waited for the smattering of laughter to subside before she continued. "I'd like to thank Dr. Pham and his associates for joining us tonight. Most of you know Dr. Pham, and many of you were here for Professor Morales's talk in April. I know you are all excited that they're both here today. Since we've got most of the Mayhaw Days planning wrapped up, I move we defer the business portion of our meeting to give more time to our speakers. The officers and committees can post their reports on the group forum."

Randi typed notes on a small laptop. "I second the motion," she said without looking up from the screen.

"All in favor?" Harrison said.

There was a resounding "aye" from the room, and Camille smiled at Adam.

"Thank you. Now, Professor Morales..." Camille's smile sent a spray of fine wrinkles out from the corners of her eyes. "We all enjoyed your talk last time you were here. As you know, there have been a lot of wild rumors and attempts at revisionist history flying around since then. We're so glad you and Dr. Pham have taken the time to come put them to rest."

Adam, who had started to make his way to the front, almost tripped. *Revisionist history?* Did Camille think that? Or was she just repeating rumors? His confidence evaporated, and he glanced at Jason, who also looked troubled. Noel's affable cop face hadn't shifted, but his gaze followed Camille as she yielded the floor

Adam tried to put his misgivings aside and focus on the talking points he'd prepared. He threw Noel a smile as he explained how historical research was like detective work. A lot of it required tracking down evidence from different sources to get the full picture. He emphasized that he and Jason were "in the middle of an ongoing investigation" and that no conclusions had been reached yet. He ended with a strategy he hoped would make allies out of the group. "I know many of you have your own family stories about Marie and Valsin. I hope you all will consider compiling those histories and working together as history detectives to enrich our understanding of this pivotal event in your town's past."

He got a polite burst of applause at the end, but chickened out on pimping the social media accounts. The last thing he needed was anyone telling his new followers how he was undermining history. Still, he felt like most people were reserving judgment.

Jason took the floor next. He talked about some of

the research he'd been doing at Magnolia, touched briefly on the science of using DNA as a tool, and reiterated Adam's requests for family stories. "As you know, my specialty is folklore. Through these stories handed down over time, we see what's important to people. Many of them change through the years to reflect contemporary concerns and values. No matter which version of the Marie and Valsin legend is real, all your stories are valuable pieces of the town's lore. I welcome you to share them with me for potential publication in a paper I'm writing. Although"—he laughed self-deprecatingly—"not many people read *my* work. Perhaps we could convince Professor Morales to publish them in one of his travel guides."

Adam snorted. But the line got a stronger round of applause than he had managed, so he let it go.

Camille smiled approvingly at them both as she joined them at the front of the room.

"We only have the room for a few more minutes," she said. "Let's go ahead and adjourn so we can start putting the chairs away. If any of you have questions, I'm sure Dr. Pham and Professor Morales won't mind staying."

They were immediately mobbed.

The questions were about everything, but a disturbing number seemed to circle around to why they were "destroying" the Marie and Valsin story.

"I heard the show paid Ms. Davenport to say those things," one woman accused.

Adam held on to his temper. "That's not true at all. Shooting had already wrapped before Ms. Davenport contacted Dr. Pham."

"Then why did you come back around here? Seems like all these rumors started when you showed back up." That was one of the younger men.

"Exactly," another woman said. "It's all a publicity stunt."

Adam faltered. How did he counter something that insane?

"I asked to come." Suddenly, Noel was at his side, giving the woman one of his lazy smiles. "Sorry to bust your conspiracy theory, but I wanted to see the park and do some antiquing." He slid an arm around Adam. "Right, babe?"

It was a bald-faced lie, but the distraction gave Adam a chance to catch his breath.

"But you think her story is true?" The woman wouldn't stand down.

"We haven't corroborated the story yet. We're still researching." Jason broke in smoothly.

The board members joined the group as he spoke. Camille beamed at Jason like he was a star pupil. "Exactly. Miss Davenport's story is just that. Dr. Pham just said he collects any old version of history. That's why we don't want Adam putting the wrong one on national television."

"Oh for fsss—"

Adam squashed whatever Noel had been about to say with a sharp elbow to his ribs. He appreciated the support, but he did not need Noel either lying or attacking little old ladies for him.

"I understand your concern," he told Camille. "But the show focused on the voodoo legend associated with the plantation. The Marie and Valsin legend was just thrown in for some local flavor and because it's a story a lot of people have heard of. There wasn't a paranormal element for us to explore."

"Is that right?" Harrison drawled rather than spoke. "If it's nothing to do with Haunts and Hoaxes, why are y'all asking questions all over town, then?"

"Jason mentioned Angela to me because he knew I'd be interested in the story as a historian. Noel and I offered to help him fill in some of the blanks." Adam kept his voice casual and willed Harrison to let it go.

"And how do you define *blanks*?" Harrison asked.

"Well, the four or five generations between Marie and Valsin and today, for starters."

"What can you tell us so far?" Randi asked. Adam still wasn't sure which side of the fence she was on.

He tried to summarize their search. "As you know, in Angela Davenport's version of the story, Marie reached Pennsylvania, but Valsin did not."

Everyone nodded, although a lot people looked like they wanted to argue.

Adam continued. "Angela shared her family Bible with us, and with that information, we were able to start constructing a branch of her family tree. While we're here this week, we want to obtain a genetic sample from a male relative, to see if we can track it back to Valsin in some way."

"A male relative of whom?" Randi snapped.

"One of Angela's relatives, a man named Richard Lafont, who lives over in the Cane River Home."

Randi straightened, her lips pursing tighter. "You can't be invading someone's privacy like that."

Adam had to respect her forthrightness. "Noel spoke with Richard and asked his permission to obtain the sample. He's thinking about our request."

Harrison gave a disgusted huff and focused his attention on Noel. "And what will you do with that sample?"

"I'll send it to a website that specializes in genetic tracking using samples from Black men," Noel responded. "I'm hoping that between Angela's family tree and the information from this genetic report, we'll be able to meet in the middle somewhere, describing Marie and Valsin's family trees from both ends."

The group around them had grown now that the chairs had been stacked away. One of the other members called out, "But if Valsin didn't arrive in Pennsylvania with Marie, what did happen to him?"

Harrison waved a hand in the air dismissively. "Valsin carried Marie out of Natchitoches, and I know that's the truth because my great-grandfather helped them escape."

"Sure," Randi shot back, "yours and mine and everyone else's." From her tone, Adam couldn't tell if she was an ally or just not Harrison's fan. "Look, in those days, Black men sometimes disappeared. There's no mystery about that."

Adam hated to disagree with her. "But Valsin wasn't just any free Black man. On his mother's side, Valsin was related to the Rousseaus, one of the wealthiest families in the state. If he'd met up with Marie and they'd been captured hundreds of miles from here where no one knew him, I would buy it," Adam said. "But anywhere within a few hours' ride? No one would have wanted to take the chance of being caught kidnapping him. His family was too powerful."

"So you're saying he wasn't caught." Randi's single raised eyebrow told Adam she was still skeptical.

"If he was, there's no record of it," Jason said.

"Look," Adam continued, "I think it would have taken strong incentive for Valsin to leave the area if he didn't go with Marie, but at the same time, I can't figure out any reason for Marie to lie to her children. Angela didn't grow up knowing her Marie was *the* Marie. She just wanted to trace her roots. In fact, Dr. Pham was the one who made the connection for her because the facts support that conclusion."

"But?" Harrison prompted.

"But nothing. We have evidence supporting both stories, but they can't both be true." Adam felt his shoulders tightening. This line of questioning pointed out everything they *didn't* know. He must look like an idiot. "None of it makes sense. Even if we include the kidnapping theory, what are the odds of Valsin coincidentally getting kidnapped at the exact time he's supposed to leave with Marie?"

Camille interrupted before he could finish. "I really don't see how we resolve this. As far as we know, Valsin's family didn't look for him because they knew he ran off with Marie. Angela Davenport didn't even know about Valsin until Dr. Pham told her." She patted Jason's arm. "Honey, I know you have all those fancy degrees, but you're mistaken, that's all. You've got poor Adam chasing a wild goose."

Adam opened, then shut his mouth. She'd just swatted away all their work like some kind of annoying fly, and he didn't want to be responsible for anything he might say.

"Seems to me," Harrison said, "that y'all don't have any proof one way or the other. However, if you try to disrupt Mayhaw Days, I guess I'll see you in court."

"Now, Harrison, there's no need to go that far," Camille soothed.

Noel huffed a laugh, and Adam's lips twitched before he could stop himself. He couldn't actually laugh, even though the guy would have nothing to support any kind of legal action.

"On what grounds?" Noel asked. "Unearthing the truth?"

Harrison Whitney's hearty façade faded away. "Don't get smart with me, young man. I've got ways of making your life quite miserable if I put my mind to it."

Against Adam's side, Noel tensed. Adam leaned into him, hoping he would keep his mouth shut. This was exactly the attitude they were here to try to defuse.

"Harrison!" Camille looked distressed. She turned to Noel next, maybe sensing he was less likely to back down. "He's got a point, though. Mayhaw Days is a major event in this town. Businesses stand to lose a lot of money if the tourists don't show up. And they don't just come for meat pies and mayhaws. Marie and Valsin have been the topic of two feature films and I can't count how many books. People want to see where they lived. They want to take part in historical reenactments. They want to see where Marie and Valsin met and courted."

Adam bit back the observation that no one actually knew where they met.

Camille continued, "They stay in our local inns, eat in our restaurants, book tours of the park and other historical sites, and buy lots and lots of mayhaw jelly, just like Marie used to make."

"I thought Marie was a seamstress," someone complained. "My great-great-aunt told me…"

"You're wrong," Harrison butted in. "Marie was a cook. Everyone knows that. She was famous for her mayhaw jelly."

"Seems to me she became a cook about the time you rebranded Mammy's Mayhaw Jelly," someone from the back pointed out.

"That stupid movie got it wrong," Harrison argued. "She was a cook. And Valsin met her down by the Cane River while she was picking mayhaws."

"You mean that spot on your farm where you take the tourists for pictures?" Randi sounded incredulous. "Harrison, just admit you made that one up to sell tours."

"She was a cook," Harrison insisted stubbornly. "And I rebranded because Mammy is a racist caricature offensive to African Americans. Marie's Mayhaw Jelly reflects our proud multicultural heritage."

"Or because the boycott was tanking your sales." That was Randi again, but under her breath.

Harrison either didn't hear her or pretended not to. "Cost me a bundle. I'm not going through that again."

"I'm sure it was the right thing to do, and we're all proud of you, Harrison." Camille smoothed the moment over. She turned to Adam, "You see how it is? Harrison isn't the only one who stands to lose money if you discredit the legend. Without Marie and Valsin, Mayhaw Days is just another fruit festival."

"I'd like to put forth a motion," Harrison said.

"We're adjourned," Randi started. But Harrison cut her off.

"All this confusion is bad for business, so I move that we declare the story of Marie and Valsin to be true and valid, and any other interpretations of said events will be declared lies and untruths."

What's the difference between a lie and an untruth? Adam wondered.

"Seconded." Conspiracy Lady apparently didn't have a problem with it.

"I said *we are adjourned*." Randi didn't shout, but her voice carried around the room. "May I also remind everyone that we are the Historical Society, not the town's PR department. We're not going to make any blanket statements until Dr. Pham finishes his research and we can review it in its entirety."

She locked gazes with Harrison, who had gone red in the face and started puffing up indignantly. The room around them went uncomfortably quiet.

"Oh my," Camille said faintly. "I didn't... Oh dear.

Harrison?"

Harrison's gaze shifted to Camille. His face got redder. "Fine." He glared at Adam and Noel. "This isn't over. I'm calling an emergency meeting of the Merchant's Association."

He stormed off. Adam noticed that at least half a dozen other members felt compelled to leave at the same time.

His heart sank. So much for an easy win.

They answered a few more questions, but within a short time, a librarian approached to remind them that another group had the room booked.

They were almost free of the building when a voice stopped them. "Professor Morales? Doctor Pham?"

Adam turned, Noel at one shoulder and Jason at the other.

Randi walked up quickly, as if she didn't have much time to waste. "I heard you two were asking some of the Rousseaus for genetics samples."

Jason nodded. "We did, yeah."

She stood with arms crossed, her chin lifted. "Story goes that my fourth-great-grandmother was Marie's half sister."

Adam hesitated, not sure how to respond if he wasn't willing to ask the logical question. Angela saved him by answering it anyway.

"No, I don't have any proof. Just a lot of family stories, same as everyone else around here."

"Are you here to ask us to stop researching Angela's story?" Adam hoped the defeat didn't sound in his voice.

"I'm not Harrison Whitney," she said with a little heat. "You probably noticed Harrison and I don't see eye to eye on much. I'll give him one thing, his motives are pretty straightforward. There are a few other

Harrisons in town, and if you can come up with a marketable new spin on Angela Davenport's story, you'll bring them around."

Adam stared at her. At his side, Noel wasn't as slow. "What about everyone else?"

"You know, whether I'm related to Marie or not, I have roots here. My family has lived in this area for generations. No one forced us to stay. This is our home, and we love it. But living here, in the shadow of the plantations, and learning the history... Sometimes that's not easy to sit with.

"I imagine it's not easy for a lot of people. Not a comfortable thing at all. So we have these stories. If you put all the stories together, Marie wouldn't have had to escape. Her owners would have packed her a lunch, and the whole town would have turned out to see her off and wish her well. I bet most of them imagine her being sheltered by one kindhearted abolitionist after another as they smuggled her on up north, where she was welcomed with open arms."

Adam ducked his head. "When I was little and heard about the Underground Railroad, I thought it was an actual railroad, or at least a series of tunnels. It's a catchy phrase, but the term glosses over the reality of what people endured on the journey north."

"You said you might be related to Marie. Does your family have any stories about helping her escape?" Noel asked.

"No." Randi's tone was flat. "Those aren't the stories my family tells. We have all kinds of theories about how she did it. How *she* did it. She emancipated herself. Any help she had came from Valsin, a free man who loved her enough to give up everything and go with her."

She gave Jason a significant look. "People remember Valsin Ferrier, but you say he was a Rousseau. So there's a Rousseau right in the middle of it all. Funny how everyone seems to have forgotten that."

"All those stories," Adam said. "Don't you want to know the truth?"

"Maybe," Randi said. "Angela Davenport certainly deserves the truth. But this isn't her history alone. Folks here have a lot invested in the traditional version of things, and many won't be well pleased to have that taken away from them."

Noel and Jason exchanged glances, and Adam nodded. "We'll keep that in mind."

"See that you do." With that, she turned on her heel and strode back to the meeting room.

Chapter Thirteen

Once she was out of earshot, Noel turned to the other two. "So...you've been asking around for samples? No luck with that?"

Adam sighed. "It's complicated."

"What's complicated? I spent a month tracking down one guy. You're telling me you already know dozens of Rousseaus, and you couldn't get one vial of spit?"

"First of all, they go back a hundred years before Valsin, and they've been intermarrying to the point where the roots of the family tree are almost too snarled to make heads or tails of."

Noel grunted, because any words that came out of his mouth would be laced with snark.

"For what it's worth, I did talk to some of them," Jason said.

"And?"

"And you have to understand the Rousseaus were plantation owners."

"Wealthy. Got it. What's that got to do with anything?"

Adam picked up the baton. "Most of the people we talked to don't know a lot about their family history except they've been in this area for generations. It's like Randi said, they grew up with these stories, and that's their truth. Whenever we brought up Valsin, we got some interest. Everybody knows his story. But when we started poking into how they were supposedly related..."

"From what I've heard, everyone and his uncle helped those two escape. What was the problem?"

"The Rousseaus were what people around here call Creole." Adam started moving toward the Lexus. "Technically, it just means they were from somewhere else, France or Spain. But for families like the Rousseaus, it meant they were mixed race, French and African."

"Okay?" Hurrying to catch up, Noel kept his hands in his pockets so he wouldn't smack Adam upside the head.

"We're in the deep South and...it's complicated." Adam waved a hand, as if Noel was going to pick up understanding out of the air.

Jason stepped in to clarify things. "So the first few people I talked to were about evenly split. Half wouldn't admit to having any African heritage, because they were *French*, thank you very much. The rest wouldn't admit to being descended from enslavers unless it was on the wrong side of the sheets, like Valsin. Then word got around within the family that someone was questioning the Marie and Valsin story. After that, they didn't want to talk story anymore."

"Huh." Noel hit the key fob, and the Lexus chirped back. He waved to Jason and climbed in. Adam took a few more minutes, long enough to give Noel a flash of jealousy, one he quickly squashed. Jason and Adam were not a thing. *Grow up, Chandler.*

They were almost back into Natchitoches proper

before he came up with a question. "Did all this come up before or after the show started getting complaints?"

"All what?"

"People shutting you down."

"I don't know."

Despite the weariness in Adam's slumped shoulders, Noel pushed on. "You could tweet about it."

"What?"

"Send a tweet about the meeting tonight, maybe thanking the members for considering an alternative to the traditional narrative."

Adam raked a hand through his hair. "Are you trying to get me fired?"

"I mean, you just want to wait around until Monday, then we go home and wait on the DNA? That could take weeks. You're happy with that timeline?"

"If you like, we can do a little more sightseeing while we're here."

"You mean there's something we missed last time?" Because, boy howdy, did Noel love hanging out with dead people's stuff. Right up there with *oh, by the way* moments.

Oh, by the way, we're probably surrounded by members of the Rousseau family, who were distantly related to Valsin.

Seriously, Noel hated *oh, by the way* moments almost as much as he hated chasing down witnesses and filing reports. He wanted as much background as possible before he started working a case, and when others on his team held back pertinent information, it pissed him off.

But this wasn't a police investigation, and Adam and Jason weren't some patrol unit he could smack around. Still, this new revelation made him wonder what else they might be hiding.

Okay, hiding might be a little strong.

"There are some hiking trails." Adam had never sounded so depressed.

"I didn't bring the right shoes." Yes, he was being a princess, but damn. Adam's half-assed offer made Noel want to shake him. Digging into people's private stuff pissed them off. Nobody liked talking to cops either, but Noel had never let that stop him.

Adam straightened his shoulders as if he'd sensed Noel's irritation. "We could visit Valsin's house. Well, sort of."

Not much of an olive branch, but Noel gave him points for trying. "What do you mean *sort of*?"

"His actual house was demolished years ago, but the current owners of the property are huge fans of the legend. They've collected a bunch of Civil War-era artifacts and set up what they call a museum. They actually reconstructed his workshop and have some of his personal effects. That's where Jay found the family correspondence I was telling you about. He had a fit because he wanted the letters and such donated someplace where they could be properly preserved and protected, but the family won't part with them."

"You've seen Valsin's stuff?"

"Just a few photos Jay took."

"Just photos, huh?" Noel smirked at Adam's obvious sense of loss. They were old letters, fer crissake. "Might be kinda fun to go fondle them."

Adam's eyes narrowed as if he was suspicious of Noel's intentions. "Might be."

After that fucktastic meeting, Noel figured Adam needed indulging. "Okay, Professor. Museum it is. Which way are we headed?"

Adam gave directions while trying to tweet and

cursing the spotty broadband. The farther they drove, the thicker and darker the clouds became, as if the sky was building up to a storm. Noel shrugged against the tension building in his shoulders. Yeah, he needed to start treating this as a real thing, not some effing game. Which meant the three of them—Noel, Adam, and Jason—needed to sit down and put everything on the table, so there'd be no more *oh, by the way* moments.

Which could include that damned cold spot in front of the Steel Magnolia house and possibly that near-ghost experience at Magnolia plantation.

Which meant Adam would be pissed off at Noel for keeping secrets.

The bands across Noel's shoulders tightened. He hated being too clever for his own good, but he hated the ghosties even more.

"In two hundred feet, turn left."

Grateful that Siri interrupted that train of thought, Noel hit the turn signal and slowed down some more. They were in the middle of bumfuck nowhere; no cars on the road, and only the fields with their orderly rows of corn and soybeans proved there were other humans around.

Maybe he should just start talking now and get things out in the open.

"Turn left now."

Yeah, he'd start talking, as soon as he could unlock his jaw.

They still had another six or seven miles to go, which took about five minutes given that Noel was unable to drive the speed limit even when he was on a two-lane country road. Adam finally gave up on Twitter, stuffing his phone away with a huff. The clouds reached a new level of purple, weighing Noel down.

Siri saved them with a well-timed "Destination in

five hundred feet."

Noel slowed the Lexus. "This is the place?"

Adam's shrug held none of Noel's surprise, like he knew all along they were going to end up in Hicksville. They pulled up in front of a rickety old house that looked like it should have blown down in the last hurricane. The yard was a cemetery where old iron tools had gone to die: pumps, tillers, claws, and abstract pieces of bolted-together iron rusted away in the sparse grass.

There were two smaller buildings nearby. One might have been a barn at some point in the past, its double doors now padlocked shut. The other must have always been a tool shed. The open half of its Dutch door showed shelves and racks stocked with a range of smaller hand tools.

For all its disorder, the yard was surrounded by a sturdy chain-link fence. Tossing a glance at Adam, Noel flipped open the latch. "Didn't tell me we were heading onto the set of *Deliverance*."

Adam rolled his eyes.

Humming the banjo-picking tune, Noel headed up the path—a worn-out stretch of grass under the glowering sky—that led to the front door.

The growl stopped him before he saw the dog. The low-pitched, vicious sound froze him in his tracks. He held out a hand to stop Adam, who bumped against his shoulder. The front door swung open, and the growl pitched lower.

"Someone must be home," Adam murmured in his ear.

The door opened another few inches and the dog came into view. Well, Noel could see a muzzle and a set of bared teeth, anyway. "I thought you said it was some kind of museum."

"Cut it out," someone snapped, a female someone whose voice carried an impressive level of command. The growling stopped. "Can you try not to be a dumbass, dumbass?"

The door opened on a young woman who could have stepped right out of Beverly Hills, or maybe some high-end shop in Miami. Her sleek blonde hair was pulled back, leaving her sculpted cheekbones bare. Her skin was flawless, and every detail—from her jeans to her shoes to the delicate band of diamonds on her wrist—added up to money. She had the dog by his collar, and she gave them a flashy smile.

"Sorry about Dumbo here." She shook the collar, but the dog's attention never wavered from Noel and Adam. "He's been kind of a mess since my uncle died. Hang on a sec, and I'll put him in the back room."

Noel used the time she was gone to take an inventory of the stuff in the yard. "We need those guys from *American Pickers* to check this place out."

Adam snorted. "Not if my crew gets here first."

"You think this place is haunted?"

"Haunted by the spirit of a hoarder."

"No kidding." There really was a lot of stuff. The woman had left the door open, and from Noel's angle, the piles of boxes in the front room were either being packed up or had never been unpacked in the first place. From far behind them, thunder rumbled, just loud enough to be threatening.

The dog yelped, a door slammed, and their hostess returned. Whether it was a conscious decision or not, Adam hung back, leaving Noel to deal with Miss Gucci. "I'm Noel. Noel Chandler." Now that the dog was gone, he strode forward, hand extended.

"Hi, Noel. I'm Spring Whitney." They met up by the front door and shook hands. "If you're looking for

Uncle Chas, well, he passed on about two weeks ago. I'm just"—she looked around at the chaos on the yard—"trying to figure out what to do with all this stuff."

"Was it your Uncle Chas who owns the Valsin Ferrier museum?"

Adam moved up close to Noel. "We understood you had some of Valsin's original possessions."

Spring's pretty blue eyes widened. "You look familiar." Shaking one of her manicured fingers at them, she giggled. "You're from that ghost hunters show, aren't you? My aunt's all spun up because y'all are saying that old legend isn't true."

Noel figured he better do most of the talking. "We're not trying to ruin anyone's legend. I'm an insurance investigator, and—"

"Well, shit. You couldn't even let an old man get cold in his grave before you started poking around." She gave another innocuous laugh, but her gaze turned skeptical. "Take a look around. Do you see anything remotely valuable? Just go away and let me get stuff done."

Maybe skeptical wasn't the right word. There was something...off about her. Something that pinged. "Hang on." Noel was damned sure not leaving. Who would have sent one woman in—he glanced at her feet—four-inch heels to organize a lifetime of possessions? Something about this scene didn't feel right. The dog had responded to her, but for all they knew, Spring Whitney had been out there feeding it treats every day for a week. "We just want to talk. We won't slow you down too much."

Her grin faltered and her brows lifted as if she was truly surprised by his persistence. "I'd invite y'all in for tea, but I'm pretty busy right now. Maybe come back in a week or so."

A flash of lightning gave the scene a surreal cast, and Noel shot a glance at Adam. His slight shrug was either permission to continue or an admission of defeat.

Noel wasn't quite ready to give up. "I am sorry we're bothering you." He laid on the charm. "I mean, you're right. We have heard that the story of Marie and Valsin might have had a different ending, but we don't really have an agenda for our visit. We mostly wanted to talk to the person who'd put all this together, to see if we could learn anything new."

Another bolt of lightning hit, along with an immediate clap of thunder loud enough to make Noel jump. Right on cue, the heavens opened up, dumping rain.

"Shit." Spring flinched against the onslaught, already turning toward the house. "Not going to stand out here and argue with you. Come on in."

With Adam at his heels, Noel followed Spring to the house. He took a single step over the threshold and yelped when the gris gris in his pocket came alive. The floor dropped out from beneath him. He fell, spiraling down into darkness.

Chapter Fourteen

Voices. He stands in the shadows, quiet, barely breathing. Men. On horseback. They know. They know, and she's in danger.

He eases his way around the corner, his pulse thrumming with anger. Silent as a ghost, he fades into the trees. Once he can no longer hear them, he runs.

He runs.

Hands grip him, and he fights them off. No. He can't stop. Not now. "No." The sound of his own voice startled him, as did the sudden specter of a figure with white-blonde hair leaning close to his face.

"Noel? Noel Chandler?"

Who was that? Another voice called out, deeper and more masculine.

"Come on, Noel. Mi rey, wake up."

Noel stopped running, had never really been running in the first place. He screwed up his eyes against the pain. Everything hurt, all his muscles cramping at once. "Ahh God. What the hell?"

"Noel." This time, Adam got right up in his face. Noel pried an eyelid open. With blurred vision, he traced the familiar contours of Adam's cheekbones and chin, clinging to the mix of warmth and fear in his eyes.

"Wake up, Noel. What's going on?"

Noel tried to talk, but choked on a mass of spit in the back of his throat. Another wave of cramps had him curled into a ball. "Adam." He managed to gasp out his boyfriend's name. "What the hell is this?"

"Is he, like, diabetic or something?"

Memories flashed through Noel's mind like a reel of old-fashioned film. *Who was the girl again? Autumn? Summer? Something like that.*

"No." Adam's terse response didn't invite follow-up. The logical question, *why is your friend curled in the fetal position on my living room floor*, wouldn't lend itself to easy answers.

Rain pounded on the roof, water dripping down between the rafters. *Where the...? Oh, we were at Valsin's house.* Relief at connecting those dots made Noel giddy. "I'm okay," he managed to whisper. "Everything will be fine."

He could only hope he wasn't telling a lie. Part of his soul was still running through the dark.

Jesus. The irony made him laugh. Except he couldn't, because every damned thing hurt.

"Do you want something to drink? Is there running water in this place?" Adam directed the second question at the woman, who knelt nearby, getting dirt all over her $500 jeans.

"I've got some bottles in the car."

She was up and gone before Noel could stop her. "Wait." His whisper had a little more force, and he nudged Adam's knee. "Don't let her leave."

"She's just getting water." Despite his protest, Adam crossed to the door. Rain still hammered down, hard enough to spray the floor. "Wait. What?"

Headlights sliced a path through the rain. Noel managed to force himself into a sitting position even though it made his head swim. "She took off, didn't she?"

"Son of a bitch."

On cue, the dog began to whine.

"Do you suppose the owner really is dead, or did he just run to town for some groceries?" If Noel kept both palms on the floor, he could maintain his balance. Mostly.

Adam shook his head, somewhere on the far side of exasperated. "Let me go see if I can find food or water for the dog. Hell, for all we know, he doesn't even live here."

"'Spose we should bring him with us?"

Adam blinked once, slowly. "No, I don't think we should adopt a damned dog."

"I didn't say adopt him."

Under other circumstances, the blankness in Adam's expression would have made Noel miserable. Right now, he'd use anything—even the source of the scratching and whining from the other room—to keep from talking about what just happened.

But they were going to talk about it. Adam radiated determination from every pore.

And Noel was running out of excuses.

Adam took a final glance out the door as Spring's Ford, sporting Enterprise Rental plates, made it to the end of the long driveway and fishtailed out onto the highway. As if he knew she'd left the property, the dog gave one final whine and went silent. Something about "Spring" seemed familiar, but he couldn't place where he had seen her before. Frankly, he didn't give a shit right now.

He turned back into the house, where Noel still sat cross-legged on the floor looking pale and spooked. The fact that he hadn't gotten up to chase Spring himself scared Adam as much as the actual seizure. He squatted down so they were on eye level and cupped a hand around Noel's jaw. Finding cool, clammy skin under the scruff did nothing to reassure him. He leaned a little closer, until the herby aroma of overpriced personal care products superseded the oppressive miasma of humidity and old grime. "Hey, wanna tell me what happened?"

Noel's chin came up, and he got the stubborn look that said he wasn't about to admit any weakness. "I fell down."

"Like hell."

Noel gave him bland cop face, as if Adam were some passerby off the street who had gotten too personal.

Worry took a temporary back seat to a strong urge to drop his hand lower and wrap it around the man's neck. He tried a different approach. "*Are* you diabetic?" Not likely, but it would be just like the little shit to hold something like that back.

"Fuck off."

"Hypertensive? Prone to seizures? Maybe you're coming down with the flu?" Adam waited a beat. "No? Just clumsy, then?"

The clumsy comment hit pay dirt. Noel twitched away from him, then picked a spot on the far wall to address his comments to. "Something happened."

I know, mi rey. He dropped his hand down to Noel's

arm and stroked gently instead of pulling him into an embrace the way he would have anyone else. This was Noel. Vulnerable Noel was...tricky. So Adam just stroked his arm, listened to the rainfall, and waited.

"It was like falling into a hole. I was here then...nowhere." His voice caught a little on *nowhere*, and a chill rippled through Adam despite the Louisiana heat. "Then I was somewhere but I...ummm... I wasn't me."

Adam looked around. The house wasn't new, but it didn't exactly reek of ghostly atmosphere unless you counted the scent of moldy cardboard and dust. In terms of possible ghost habitation, it didn't have near the history of someplace like the plantation. Unless Spring had axe-murdered Uncle Chas before she hightailed it.

The random thought incited a second dump of adrenaline on top of the one he'd gotten when Noel collapsed.

He took a frantic glance around the room before his rational brain reasserted itself. Mostly. He gave the clutter another once-over. What could have happened here that would have pinged Noel's radar when the quarters at Magnolia hadn't warranted as much as a blip?

Then again, you never knew what went on behind closed doors. Maybe Uncle Chas was some sort of psychopath who had abused his wife and kids. The place was set back from the highway with no close neighbors. *Isolated.*

He tried to reign in his overactive imagination. They were only a few minutes from downtown Natchitoches. But *something* had just hijacked Noel.

"Any idea who you were?"

Noel mustered a half-assed shrug.

He should probably drop it. Noel still looked like a ghost himself and obviously wasn't ready to relive the experience. On the other hand, he *never* wanted to talk about it. Not the psychic stuff, not his feelings, not...anything that mattered.

The leftover adrenaline soured into something bitter and nasty. "Fine."

Noel flinched away and scrubbed a hand through his hair. "Just give me a sec, okay?"

Great. Now he was a bully. Before he could muster an apology, Noel rolled to his feet. He didn't quite stick the landing, or at least the stumbling step at the end of the maneuver didn't look exactly planned. Adam scrambled up after him, worried there might be a replay of the earlier collapse.

Instead of letting him offer support, Noel turned away from him. He shoved his hands in his pockets and looked around the room as though assessing his surroundings. "Jesus. This place is a mess. Not as bad as a few I saw back in LA, but getting there." He toed one of the boxes littering the floor. It didn't budge, but the cardboard bowed out a little, inciting a frantic rustling from inside. Half a dozen silverfish skittered out of a crack at the side and disappeared into the surrounding clutter.

Adam shuddered, but Noel seemed unconcerned. He wandered over to inspect one of the stacks of magazines covering the coffee table. "They all have the same smell. Decay and bug spray. Like the bug spray is going to make anything better. At least the dog here seems housetrained. The ones that include feces are the worst."

The magazines were apparently of no more interest than the box on the floor, because he continued his circuit of the room, picking his way between boxes until he was as far away from Adam as he could get and still be in the same room. "I think I was Valsin. Wanna get dinner?"

Adam opened his mouth. Realized his brain hadn't caught up. Closed it. Tried to process.

Noel glanced back over his shoulder. "Well?"

"What?"

"Dinner? Evening meal? Maybe that meat pie place again."

"Back up. Valsin? That's..." Not possible.

Because ghosts in general are so *possible*, the nasty little skeptic in his head mocked. But he had wrapped his head around ghosts. Even embraced the idea. In general. For Noel. Because he believed Noel. Except this...

He had the sudden, absolute conviction that Noel was fucking with him. "Bullshit. What the fuck, Noel?"

Noel clamped his lips together and glared.

"You know Valsin didn't live in this actual house, right? This place can't be more than sixty or seventy years old. So why would Valsin jump you the second you stepped across the threshold?"

"I don't know, Professor. You're the one who's all hot to document these fun little episodes. Why don't you tell me?"

Adam didn't even bother to answer. There was *no reason*. That's why. He could expand his mind to include the existence of ghosts, or psychic residue, or whatever the fuck happened to Noel back in New Orleans. Whatever had happened to both of them. But there still had to be some logic to it. There had to be a reason.

"Is that what this is about? You think I'm too invested in your...your..." They didn't even have a *name* for it. "Superpower," he finally spat out, even though he hated that phrase. Hated the mocking way Noel tossed it around.

Noel had stopped glaring. The cop face had returned, cold and watchful.

Adam hated that too. Hated that Noel could just turn off whenever the emotions got a little inconvenient. Hated to be frozen out.

"You think I'm too invested in ghosts and too invested in Valsin so you, what? Just made something up?" The colder Noel looked, the hotter Adam burned. Thunder rolled outside, echoing the chaos eating him within. He knew he was close to crossing a line, but the knowledge didn't stand a chance against the rage. The hurt. Why couldn't Noel just *talk* to him?

Their whole relationship had started with one honest conversation. and Noel had spent every moment since trying to pretend it hadn't happened.

"So no meat pies?"

Twin lightning strikes flashed so bright, the dingy room lit up from the outside in. Before the afterglow faded, a crack of thunder shook the house and startled a frightened yelp from the back room. In the aftermath, everything felt unnaturally quiet. Adam's words fell with crystal clarity into the silence.

"Did you make it all up? Everything? From the beginning?"

Chapter Fifteen

Noel didn't stop until he hit the Lexus's driver-side door. Rain poured as hard as if the entire Gulf of Mexico was coming through a fire hose over his head. By the time he'd crossed the overgrown lawn, he was soaked through, hair plastered to his head and water trailing down his spine from his neck to the small of his back. He hit the key fob, and the door chirped.

And...nothing. He stood there with water running into his eyes and a chill settling into his bones, and he couldn't make himself open the door.

Because if he opened the door and left Adam in this backwater shit hole, that'd be it. There'd be no way back. Lightning flashed, followed by a low rumble of thunder. He needed to make absolutely sure he wanted to end things with Adam before he got into the Lexus, because once he did, *terminado. Aloha* and *mahalo* for your *kokua.*

The. End.

Christ on a cracker. If Noel left, Adam would probably call Jason to come pick him up. And didn't jealousy just add a layer of shit to this fucked up situation? Noel clamped his jaw to keep his teeth from chattering. What had Adam just said? That Noel had made it all up? "Fuck him."

Adam and Jay deserve each other.

Keys clutched in his hand, he pounded the window. *This is such bullshit.* As if he'd make up...all that. His mind flinched from reliving that awful drop into darkness. He hit the window one more time, anger fueling his fist. "Like I'd seriously...no, you pompous academic jackass. I wouldn't make it up."

He took one more swing at the window, pulling the punch before he smashed the glass. Water splashed into his eyes, and he blinked. A swipe with the back of his hand was useless. He gave a growl of disgust and stalked back toward the house, trying to pick words out of the angry churning in his head.

He couldn't figure out what made Adam different. If this had been a fight with Stephen the hissing sissy, his ex from LA, Noel and the Lexus would have been down the road well before his shorts got soggy.

"Fuck me," he mumbled. He jerked the door open and stumbled into Adam, who stood at the threshold, as warm and solid as home.

Face-to-face, Noel couldn't come up with any words, angry or otherwise. For a moment, neither of them spoke. The hipped roof kept the rain off Noel, and from the other room, the dog whined.

"I know you didn't accuse—"

"I'm sorry. Seriously—"

They talked over each other, then both stopped. Adam's curls were a mess, as if he'd been dragging both hands through his hair. *Yeah, it's time to man up, Chandler.*

"Here." Noel extended one hand, palm up.

"What?"

He gave a peremptory shake. "Take my hand. The last time I came through this doorway, I fell into the void.”

“The void?” Adam’s fingers twined with his, thick and strong and sure.

Noel took a step inside, pausing to see if the crazy came back. Nope. He was in the same shitty cabin with the slightly leaky roof and the wild beast in the other room.

And Adam.

“Okay.” Noel took another step inside, crowding Adam. *Damn.* Pissed as hell and he still wanted to drop to his knees in front of this man. He had to fight through a surge of heat to make himself heard. “This is not some Hallmark chat, right? I don’t play that way.”

“Look, I really—”

“You really talk too much, is what you do.” Noel took another step, forcing Adam to choose between taking a step back or standing belly to belly.

He chose the latter.

“I don’t like this.” Noel emphasized the point by squeezing Adam’s hand. Hard. “But I would not”—another squeeze—“bullshit you. I might not tell the whole truth”—ever, because secrets were fun—“but I don’t lie.”

They stood close enough for Adam’s breath to brush Noel’s cheek. “You’re soaked,” Adam murmured.

“Came damned close to smashing the Lexus’s window too.” The dog pawed at the door. “I wonder if that chick is going to come back here for her pet.”

“I’d just as soon not stick around to find out.”

The storm gave a half-hearted thunderclap, as if ready to wrap things up for the day. Noel’s anger faded with it, leaving him chilled and nauseous. “Let’s get out of here. We need to sit down and figure out what we know and what we don’t.”

Adam took hold of his shoulders. “On one

condition."

Noel fought an overwhelming urge to roll his eyes. "What?"

Giving Noel a sharp shake, Adam lifted his chin. "I want to know what happened, and why you think Valsin was involved."

"Wasn't Valsin."

Adam dropped his chin to stare at Noel over top his glasses. "What made you change your mind?"

Noel shrugged, or he would have if Adam wasn't pinning his shoulders in place. "I...don't know. I stepped into some kind of ...black space, thinking someone else's thoughts." The rush of borrowed fear sent a shiver through him. "We just spent all day talking about Valsin, you know? He's the first name I grabbed."

Adam nodded slowly, gazing into some middle distance that let Noel see the wheels in his head turning. The man was smart, dangerously so.

The dog gave a frustrated yelp at the same time Adam's phone beeped. He took a step back, giving Noel an apologetic smile. "It's Annemarie."

Noel let him go, taking the opportunity to try to wring some water out of his hair. He wasn't keen on the impending conversation, but keeping his mouth shut had come very close to ruining things with Adam. Time to bite the bullet. Take his medicine. Try for honesty for a change.

Because he wanted this thing he still couldn't name. Well, that he didn't want to name. Because scary words might be involved.

Whatever.

"They what, now?" Adam yelped. "Arrested him?"

The magic word. Noel poked his arm. "Who?"

"There's no way. At the risk of sounding like a total

cliché, there must be some mistake."

"Who?" Another poke, this time accompanied by a foot stomp. *Arrested* put the situation into Noel's wheelhouse.

"Hang on, Anna." Adam covered the phone with an open palm. "Jason's been arrested for trafficking in stolen artifacts."

A burst of laughter escaped before Noel could stop himself. "That's a joke, right? Captain America couldn't possibly be a thief."

Adam held up a finger and went back to his phone call. Noel shook more water out of his hair and wondered if the hysterical society had the kind of extremists who would try to frame an innocent historian for disrupting their civic mythology.

A flash of blue lights through the window distracted him. Blue lights? Like, the cops? He moved closer, and sure enough, a black SUV with a flashing lightbar across the top pulled to a stop in front of the house. He glanced at Adam, who made his excuses and stuffed his phone away.

"Does it count as trespassing if we were invited in by the dead guy's niece?" Adam asked.

Noel snorted. The odds of her story being true were slim to negative numbers. "She's the only one who knew we were out here."

"I don't suppose we can sneak out the back."

The memory of running hit Noel with a full-body tremor. "No. Just...keep your mouth shut unless they ask you something directly."

Opening the door, he watched the pair of cops walk through the grass. The rain had mostly given up and they were hatless and in shirtsleeves. One was a light-skinned Black man and the other was a ginger.

The Black man's name tag identified him as Bolden.

He did the talking, while the ginger—MacLeod, according to his tag—tried to look threatening. "We got a call about a break-in. You two know anything about that?"

Noel stepped out onto the little porch. Adam followed, and somewhere behind them, the dog growled.

"My friend and I heard this place was some kind of museum, and we came to check it out. The deceased man's niece let us in."

The cops shared a glance, and MacLeod grinned. Bolden's eyes were light enough to be disturbing. "And what was the young woman's name?"

"I didn't say she was young." Noel let that simmer for a couple beats. "She introduced herself as Spring Whitney."

"I know a lot of Whitneys, but none of them are named Spring." Bolden looked at his partner. "You recognize her?"

MacLeod's grin widened. "Nope."

Noel shook his head, ready to bet cash money Spring Whitney – whoever she was – had made the call in the first place. "Fucking *Deliverance* all over again." He tried to keep his voice down and might have failed.

Bolden's glare sharpened, but MacLeod pointed at Adam, his grin a shade more sincere. "Hey, you're that guy from the ghost show."

Giving Noel a side-eye, Adam took a step forward. "Yeah. I'm Adam Morales, and we're just scouting locations. If it's a problem, we'll go."

"It's a problem." Bolden looked significantly less impressed by Adam's claim to fame. "My wife's aunt says y'all are trying to prove the Marie and Valsin story is some kind of fake."

"She a member of the hysterical society too?" Noel

muttered, earning a hard stare from Adam. They didn't need to say a damned thing to a couple of beat cops from Hicksville, but letting Adam talk might be faster than demanding a lawyer.

"I liked that episode where y'all found the voodoo graveyard." MacLeod had stars in his eyes. "You should do that again."

"We've got some good stuff coming up." Adam fished around in his pocket and brought out a business card. "Do you follow us on Twitter? That way, you won't miss anything."

"I don't, but I will." MacLeod took the card. "Y'all should probably head out, though. If you're really interested in the museum, you got the wrong drive. The place you want is about a quarter mile back toward town. I think the Parsons family took the sign down since the old man passed. Doubt any of the kids are interested in keeping the place going, but his granddaughter is handling the estate. Darla might be willing to give you a tour if you catch her at a good time."

"Thanks." Adam shook the cop's hand. "I'd love to touch base with her. If she's not interested in the collection, Dr. Pham at the university can help her rehome the artifacts."

"I'll let her know. In the meantime, you boys watch the property lines while you're *scouting*." Noel could practically see the air quotes. "Folks here keep an eye out for each other. Try not to wander into any place else you don't belong."

Noel closed the front door, giving the house one more thoughtful look. "Did Mr. Parsons own a dog?"

The cops glanced at each other.

"Nope," MacLeod said. "Never heard of him having a dog out here."

"There was one here when we got here. Ms. Whitney shut it in the kitchen before she left."

With that parting shot, he strolled to the Lexus, Adam right behind him. The cops might have headed for the house; Noel didn't stick around to see what they got up to. As soon as Adam shut his door, he put it in Drive.

"Well, that was awkward." Adam rubbed his temple as if a headache was brewing.

Noel smiled, then chuckled, then gave a full-on laugh. He'd gone from spiritually highjacked to damn near single to bullied by a couple of local cops. "Hey, at least we didn't get arrested."

Adam's laugh was less enthusiastic, but since he'd missed out on the spiritual hijacking, Noel understood. "Shall we try to work our magic and bust Jason out of jail?"

Head tipped toward the sky and his eyes shut, Adam gave a tired sigh. "Sure. What could possibly go wrong?"

What could possibly go wrong?

Sarcasm to disguise his very real dread. At this point, Adam would be happy with even one thing going *right*.

His experiment to verify Noel's abilities had failed. Possibly as a side effect, their relationship was teetering on the edge of a precipice. His job...aside from the occasional private grumble about not being exactly intellectually fulfilling, he hadn't even *thought* this much about his job in years.

He got paid to research and could more or less pick his topics. He wasn't getting rich, but how many historians were? Aside from a few minor annoyances, the job had been a thing he didn't *have* to think about. Now suddenly, his career seemed like it might be on the precipice too.

He snuck a sideways glance at Noel. He should apologize again. He had been out of line.

But Noel had come back. He seemed calm enough now, whereas who knew how he would react if Adam brought up anything sticky? The last thing he needed was to find himself on the side of the road in the rain, miles from the nearest Uber.

Yes, they needed to talk, but talking with Noel required so much effort, like picking his way through a briar patch. No, he didn't lie, or Adam didn't think he did, but he raised withholding evidence to an art form. Adam didn't know if he had it in him right now to tease out whatever truths Noel hadn't seen fit to share. Anyway...

Nothing like this ever happened before you met him. Are you sure he's worth it?

And wasn't that a shitty thought?

Okay, he doesn't lie, but is he delusional?

Adam squeezed his eyes more tightly shut, as if doing so would block out the thought. No. He didn't believe that. He wasn't that poor a judge of character, and nothing about Noel screamed delusion. Anyway, it wouldn't just be Noel. Unless delusions were transmissible by touch, he had experienced a little bit of whatever Noel had seen in Lafayette cemetery.

Wait until the academic community finds out you

actually believe in ghosts. If you weren't a laughingstock before, you will be then.

Which shouldn't be a consideration. Truth was truth. Weighing the opinions of people who already didn't take him seriously against his relationship with Noel was... He couldn't believe he was that guy. But if the show dumped him, and no one in academia took him seriously then...where was he going to be when Noel got tired of hiding out in Louisiana and went back to his real life in California? The tension hovering just on the fringes of discomfort since their fight blossomed into a full-blown headache.

"How did your girlfriend know about Jason, anyway?" Noel's voice interrupted his spiral of negativity. Maybe if he focused on conversation, he could ignore the pain.

"She has an intern who monitors local social media around all the shoots. Apparently, Facebook and Twitter lit up." Probably something he should have noticed if he were any good at social media. "And don't call her my girlfriend. She's my producer."

"Producer, whatever. Why call you? She worried you're going to wind up in jail next?"

After the last half hour, the possibility didn't seem all that far-fetched, but there was no way Annemarie could have known that yet. Distracted by the coincidence of both them and Jason having almost simultaneous bullshit run-ins with local law enforcement, he answered without thinking. "She doesn't think I'm selling stolen antiquities, if that's what you're asking."

Of course Noel latched on to the thing Adam wanted him to let go of. "But she's worried you might be in some other trouble?"

"She trusts me to clear up the Valsin thing." *I think.*

"Adam, she's been on your ass constantly since we got here. If she thinks you can handle the locals, what's the problem?"

"She didn't understand why we came back up here in the first place after the shoot was over. Apparently, I'm behaving out of character. She's...confused." And maybe slightly worried about his career.

Noel chewed on that for a minute. It seemed he didn't have nearly the same trouble reading Adam as Adam had reading him. "She doesn't like me."

"I didn't say anything like that."

"I'm right, though."

"She doesn't know you. There's no reason for her not to like you." Adam considered leaving it there, but he could hardly blame Noel for not sharing and then keep things back himself. "She thinks I've been...different...lately, and you happened at the same time."

"Different. Since I *happened*?"

Noel's tone said he found some significance in that, but for the life of him, Adam couldn't figure out what. *Happened* was said with definite amusement. Before he could pick through the nuances of the rest or think of a way to ask, his phone rang again.

"Let it go to voicemail. Whatever it is will keep."

Adam ignored him. "It's Jason."

Chapter Sixteen

Jason apparently had a good lawyer or, more likely, the charges were bogus because he hadn't been held at the station. The situation was a PR nightmare for all of them, though, and Adam immediately suggested they join forces to assess the damage.

He didn't know why he was surprised Jason lived on the river. In a house. Well, of course a house. But...a real house.

From outside, it looked like pretty much any nice-sized ranch. Big yard, azaleas for days, surrounded by other mid-century homes in a neighborhood right outside the historic district. But inside, it was so very, very *Jason*—soft lighting and minimalist décor, with lots of gleaming wood floors and clean lines. Shades on the windows were pulled up to showcase the view of the river. One whole wall of the living room was glass— floor-to-ceiling windows and a pair of glass pivot doors. A few strategically placed large plants mirroring the profusion of greenery on the deck back gave the impression of an open-air pavilion, even though the chill of central air gave lie to the illusion.

Jason met them at the door, barefoot and wearing a pair of white mid-calf pants and a loose linen shirt. Despite the casual clothes, tonight he didn't look like a student. He looked like a professional. A successful professional. Which he was. And why had Adam expected anything different?

Maybe because his own digs were rented apartments in LA and New Orleans, both decorated in Pell Grant Undergraduate. There was a reason he went to Noel's house more than he invited him over.

Jason lived more like Noel. Who, Adam noted with irritation, was eying the place with something that was either approval or suspicion or both as he toed off his shoes and left them next to Jay's by the door. Adam reluctantly removed his own Nike's and peeled off his socks. His feet looked oversized and hairy, and he felt vaguely naked. Noel and Jay both looked as comfortable with the situation as if they were on the beach.

Despite the tension around his eyes, Jay greeted them in full host mode. "I'm so glad you came. Either of you want a beer? Because I am definitely having a beer."

"I wouldn't mind a beer," Adam agreed.

"Got coffee or something?"

Jason's eyebrows twitched up at the same time as Adam's, but he nodded. "Of course, my dude. I've got Lion. I'll start some brewing."

Adam's irritation ratcheted up a degree, because now Noel was giving Jay the same look as the house. Approval. Or suspicion. Or both.

Maybe Jay noticed, because he suddenly blurted out, "Look. I didn't steal anything."

"Of course not!" Adam rushed to reassure him.

Noel, in direct contradiction to his earlier

comments, just shrugged.

"Noel." Adam knew he was turning red, and the headache, which he had forgotten, reasserted itself as a painful tightness in his temples. "Tell Jay you don't think he stole anything."

Noel blinked at him and finally dredged up some words. "Gotta admit, I can't see it, but then again, my job would be hella easy if I could just look at someone and know if they were guilty."

"Noel."

Jason snorted out a laugh. "Adam, let him be. Always a cop, huh? You guys make yourselves at home. I'll be back in a sec. We need to talk."

By the time Jason came back out with the beers, coffee, and a tray of crackers and cheese, Adam had settled into a chair. He had picked the chair deliberately rather than settling on the couch next to Noel, who was obviously in a mood to be difficult. His own feelings were too complicated right now to add physical closeness to the mix. He preferred to be able to look both men in the eye.

As it turned out, his fears were mostly unfounded. If not exactly chatty, Noel behaved himself—sipping his coffee and munching his way through more than his share of the snacks.

Unfortunately, Jason dumped a completely new set of worries on them. The charges against him weren't completely bogus. Someone *had* stolen some rare Civil War-era letters on loan to the Norton Gallery in Shreveport. The authorities had been stumped until one showed up on the internet recently, supposedly for sale by Dr. Jason Pham.

"Jesus." Adam ran a hand through his hair. "How did you convince them to let you go?"

"The listing and account were deleted. By the time

the local guys picked me up, the team up in Shreveport had already decided it was bogus. The pictures weren't new. They were pulled from the internet, and the account was obviously a fake. Plus, I don't have access to that collection. Or rather, I have access, but through the current curator. I couldn't just waltz in and take anything. If someone was trying to set me up, they didn't do their homework."

"And why would someone do that?" Noel asked. "Try to set you up?"

"I thought maybe someone from the Historical Society got a little carried away."

"Sending someone to jail is more than a little carried away," Adam protested. "I know the Historical Society is riled up right now, but I can't believe any of them would stoop to this level."

"That's because you're too trusting," Noel said. It didn't sound like a compliment, especially when combined with the accusatory look he sent Adam's way. "Usually. But in this instance, I agree."

"Why?" Adam and Jason said in unison.

"So you pulled off a sophisticated heist leaving no clues, then you posted the most recognizable piece up on the Internet? Please, you're not that stupid." He gave Jason a sardonic look, "We *assume*."

Jason grinned. "You believe me."

"*Assuming*," Noel continued, "you had nothing to do with this, the attack was obviously personal. I hope the locals weren't stupid enough to charge you."

"No." Jason didn't look happy. "No charges, but I'm still a person of interest. I'm stuck paying a lawyer, and my grant committee's not happy. Guys, we've got to clear up this Marie and Valsin thing. I can only afford one PR nightmare at a time."

"I don't like to pile on," Adam said, "but my producer

says the Historical Society, the Merchant's Association, and the Friends of Cane River Parks are all threating a full-scale social media campaign to discredit any claim the Marie and Valsin legend is false. According to them, we're distorting the historical record and impugning the character of local heroes as part of a cheap media stunt. I'm sorry, Jay. Without us here, I doubt anyone would have ever gotten wind of this. I thought the show would be great exposure for your work. Instead, I've brought you nothing but trouble." He didn't add that his own career might be in just as much jeopardy as Jason's.

Noel polished off the last cracker and his coffee. He'd gotten an intent look while Adam was talking. "If I'm right, Jay was a pretty easy target since he's already been the subject of gossip lately. Either of you think it's a pretty weird coincidence we both had a run-in with the police today?"

"What?" Jason's jaw dropped. "What happened? Why didn't you say anything?"

"It was nothing," Adam said. He summarized their run-in with Spring and the sheriffs, leaving out both Noel's collapse and the following fight. "A weird misunderstanding."

"Maybe," Noel said. His foot had started tapping, a dead giveaway he was focused on something. Or maybe the coffee had been too strong. "Funny, we got blamed for something we didn't do too."

"Or didn't meant to do," Adam said. "If Spring wasn't a member of the family, we really were trespassing."

"It's a shame about Charles Parsons," Jason said. "We disagreed on a lot, but he was a real history buff. The sheriff was right. Except for one of his grandkids, the family won't have any interest in the museum. The best we can hope for is they'll make sure the artifacts are preserved."

Noel hadn't said anything while Adam filled Jay in on their afternoon, but his foot was still twitching. "Are you really worried about the Historical Society? I thought any publicity was good publicity. You don't have a producer breathing down your neck like Adam does."

"The park won't suffer," Jay said. "The publicity either way will be good for it. But there are always more researchers than grant money. If I get a bad rep in the community, it's likely someone else will get their research at Magnolia funded."

"Same with TV," Adam muttered. "It's not like I'm indispensable to the show."

"Fuck's sake." Noel looked between the two of them. "I guess just dropping the whole thing and letting Ms. Davenport find her own ancestor is out of the question."

"Are you kidding?"

"You want us to *lie*?" Adam sputtered over Jay's exclamation.

"Fine, fine." Noel flapped his hands at them. "Just saying it would make things easier on both of you to let the locals win. What does it matter at this point anyway?"

"Angela Davenport has the right to know the truth about her family's history," Adam said. After all the bulletin boards and DNA research, he couldn't believe Noel could just walk away. He had thought the investigation was one place their interests intersected. "If you aren't interested, we don't need your help. We can do our own research."

"Calm down, Professor," Noel snapped. "I didn't say I wouldn't help. I just don't see it being worth two careers. If you're sure this is what you want, let's lay out what we've got and get serious with it."

They spent the next two hours doing exactly that, hashing over every detail they could think of. The problem was, the facts remained stubbornly the same. None of them had found anything that proved the story either way.

"Our best bet is the DNA," Jay finally concluded.

"What I've been saying," Noel grumbled. "Sorry to break it to you, but that's going to take some time."

Adam sighed. "You can bet the locals aren't going to go into Mayhaw weekend with a cloud over their precious legend. They'll use the festival to launch their social media campaign."

The evening ended on that unoptimistic note.

Back in the Lexus, Adam slumped in his seat. "Maybe it won't be so bad."

"Hey." Noel twisted in his seat, leaning over the console until he was in Adam's space. "You really think Annemarie would replace you?"

Adam sighed. "I don't know. I mean, she wouldn't like to, but if she thought I was a liability, yeah. She's pretty ruthless."

"Fuck that." Noel put his hands on either side of Adam's face. He looked about to say something, then he shook his head. His hands tightened in Adam's hair, pulling him forward until their lips met.

The kiss was unexpected. Soft. Un-Noel-like. Until it wasn't and there were teeth and tongues everywhere. Until for once, it was Adam who felt taken in hand, overwhelmed, and mastered. Until it was over and Noel still had his hands clenched in Adam's hair.

"Listen to me," he said. "That's not going to happen."

Fierce, his cop. But, "You don't know that. We'll have to hope for the best."

Noel sat back and turned on the ignition. He looked grim. *Intense.*

"You're probably right," Adam tried to reassure him. "Noel, whatever happens, it will be okay. Anyway, I'm probably overreacting."

"You're a shitty liar, baby." He backed the car out onto the street. "But don't worry. Something will turn up."

Noel thought he'd seen all sides of Adam: grumpy, stuffy, salty, and sweet. Drama-queen Adam was new and different and not entirely pleasant.

"This is all so much bullshit." Adam fiddled with his phone, his whole body vibrating with stress.

Noel squinted into the setting sun. They were only about half a mile from the Calico Nightmare Hotel. "We'll get some dinner, babe, and maybe have a drink." Because apparently, the spirits could grab him whether he was drunk or sober. "Things'll look better when we're not hypoglycemic."

And if they didn't, Noel would figure out a solution. He hadn't said anything out loud, but he was one hundred percent committed to saving Adam's gig, and Jason's too while he was at it. He just needed to figure out an angle.

The fine people of Natchitoches were rightly protective of their own history, although it was hard not to ascribe an ulterior motive to the vague threats that had come their way. Jason's arrest was the first direct move their opponent—or opponents—had made.

It was almost like someone knew what had happened to Valsin and didn't want them to find out.

Noel snorted. For a guy who'd grown up in LA, he didn't have much time for The Industry, but that line had come straight out of some scriptwriter's nightmare.

With Adam busy tweeting, or thereabouts, Noel turned the current conundrum around in his mind, seeking a way in to unravel it. Better that than fretting about the conversation he'd promised Adam they'd have. It pissed him off that Adam had accused him of faking...whatever it was that had happened, which was added incentive not to bring up the subject.

He found a parking spot in the small lot next to the hotel. "Want to go up to the room before dinner?"

Adam shrugged, uncharacteristically morose. "Sure."

Oh, hell no. Clearly Adam needed a blow job, the sooner the better. Noel took his arm, glancing all around to dare anyone to mess with the queers. "Come on, princess. We'll grab a quick shower and get some food."

Despite the storm that had blown through, the air was heavy with humidity. Noel's jeans had dried from their soaking, but they clung to his body like a sticky second skin. He pushed open the door to the hotel and was halfway across the lobby when someone called Adam's name.

"Mr. Morales? Adam Morales?" The young woman at the front desk waved them over. Her light hair and plastic smile reminded Noel of Spring Whitney, another piece of the weird puzzle they were stuck in.

"Yeah? That's me." Adam headed to the desk, Noel

right on his heels.

"I'm very sorry, Mr. Morales, but there was an electrical incident in the room next to yours, and we have had to vacate both rooms until the repairman gets through."

"A what?" Noel shifted his weight to stand a little in front of Adam. He didn't mean to sound like a dick, but he had no fucks left to give.

"I am sorry, y'all." She barely blinked at Noel's antagonism. "We don't have any other rooms, but I've taken the liberty of making you a reservation at the Best Western over on University Parkway."

Noel shot a glance at Adam. "The Best Western?" Yes, he was a snob, and no, they would not be staying at some fifty-dollar-a-night slum. Another couple had come up behind them, their doughy Midwest cheeks flushed from the heat.

Britney—okay, her nametag read "Lucinda." but she was a Britney through and through—tightened her smile another notch. "That's the best we could do on such short notice. The doorman collected your things and is holding them behind the bell desk. If y'all will step over here, I've settled up your bill."

She placed a sheet of paper on the counter between them. Noel covered it with his hand. "You're fucking kidding me. You're kicking us out *and* you expect us to pay for the pleasure? I think you ought to comp us last night to make up for the hassle."

"It's all right, Noel. Just leave it." Adam slid his credit card across the counter, but Noel snatched it up.

"Nope." He handed the credit card back to Adam and glared at her. "Your Yelp average isn't going to like a one-star review for kicking us out on our asses." The other couple took a step back, their stares pressing on Noel like a pair of hands on his shoulders.

Britney tapped the counter with a single long nail, flicking a glance at Mr. and Mrs. Midwest. "I do see your point of view, Mr..." She gave Noel an expectant nod.

"Chandler. Noel Chandler, and if you see my point of view, you'll understand why we're going to go get our things now, look through them to make sure nothing is missing, and then go back to the car without leaving your fine doorman a tip."

"Noel." His name came out more like a groan.

She exhaled heavily, her smile as plastic as when they'd started. "Thank you very much for choosing the Judge Porter House. I do hope you'll visit us again."

Noel let his smile explain how long it would be before they'd return. Holding Adam by the elbow, he stalked past the Midwest couple to the bell desk, breathing deeply to keep from going off on someone. Bags in hand, they headed for the Lexus.

He hit the key fob, the rear gate opened, and he tossed the suitcases in. He didn't bother opening them. Adam's mortified silence said they needed to get on the road.

Only after they were belted in did Adam use his words. "I know it's irrational, but I'm pretty convinced the Historical Society has connections."

"You think they faked an *electrical incident*"—Noel gave the word air quotes—"because the hysterical society wants us gone?"

Adam's laugh was tinged with exhaustion. "Maybe."

Shaking his head, Noel pulled out his phone. "I hope you're not disappointed that I turned down the Best Western."

Another laugh, this one with more humor. "I expected nothing less."

"Are you implying that I'm high-maintenance?"

Still resting his head on the seat back. Adam grinned at the roof. "It's part of your charm."

"Hmph." Noel sent a quick text to Jason. "Let's see if Captain America can recommend a place for us to stay."

Adam's phone rang almost immediately. "Oh hey, Jay. Yeah, the hotel claimed there was an electrical problem or something. They offered us a room at the Best Western, but..."

Why did he call Adam when he could have just returned my text? Noel gave himself a mental slap, about out of fucks, especially for the ones labeled jealousy.

"Nah, we can't... You don't have to... Okay, hang on." Adam covered the phone with his hand and gave Noel a tentative glance. "Jason wants us to stay at his place."

"That's"—Noel blinked—"unexpected." *Unwelcome? Fucking awkward?* He shrugged, lost in a sea of frustration. "I'd like to stick around until Monday to talk to Mr. Lafont."

Taking that as assent, Adam worked out the details. He was still on the phone when Noel pulled the Lexus into the closest grocery store parking lot. Twenty minutes later, they were well supplied with a super-sized box of hot fried chicken, a couple of pounds of jojo potatoes, three kinds of chips, a bag of those stupid baby carrots to feed Adam's guilty conscience, two six-packs of Coors Light, two liters of tonic, and a bottle of gin.

A large bottle of gin.

And three limes.

On the way back to Jason's house, Noel decided they'd both sleep better if they hashed out what happened that afternoon. He hated bringing it up, didn't want to talk about it any more than they already had, but… "You made me promise I'd tell you what happened out at that Parson's house."

Adam jerked upright as if Noel's words had caught him dozing. "Uh, yeah. I guess I did."

"So…" *Now what, genius?* They got caught by a red light, and Noel drummed his fingers on the steering wheel. "Like I said, I stepped through the door, and things went dark." The memory crowded around him with a suffocating presence. "I didn't… I wasn't… I think I relived someone else's memory." And while that someone might have been Valsin, Noel wasn't ready to admit it. Yet.

"And this has happened before."

Fuck me. "Yeah, it has." The admission cost him something. Every time he said the words out loud, they got more real, and if Adam didn't believe him, then he really was crazy. *Sit with that a minute, Chandler. You might really be crazy.*

"Lafayette Cemetery?"

"And LA." And one or two other times that weren't worth mentioning. He'd never felt more exposed in his whole damned life. *Fucking naked.* The light turned green, and he had to force his fingers to stop drumming so he could grip the wheel. Hands busy, feet busy; all he had left was grinding his teeth, waiting for Adam's reaction.

When none was forthcoming, he started talking to fill the void. "The first time scared me enough that I had to take a leave of absence. The second time…" Another red light. *Damnit.* "For a while, I figured it only happened when I had a buzz on, but today proved that wrong."

"So you're just on a leave of absence from your job in LA?"

"What? Um, I guess. I don't know. By now they

might have dropped me." Noel scraped his fingers through his hair. Whatever product he'd put in it had long ago washed out, and it flopped into his face.

"Interesting. I guess I knew you'd be taking off at some point."

The light turned green, and Noel slammed his foot on the accelerator, rocketing them out into the intersection. "Fuck you, Adam. You asked me what happened, and I told you. I have no plans to leave New Orleans, and no plans to leave you, unless you want me to go. Do you want me to go?" If the answer was yes, Noel might just run his fifty-thousand-dollar vehicle right off the damned road.

"Don't be stupid."

Noel didn't know how to respond to that, and Adam followed it up with a silence that went on for long enough Noel thought he'd dozed off. *Unbelievable, man.*

Siri warned him that the final turn was coming up, and Adam stirred. "So, if Mr. Lafont doesn't want to donate any DNA, we're SOL, right?"

"You said you and Jason had interviewed descendants from Valsin's side of the family, right? I mean, there are ways of obtaining DNA samples without consent if you really need to."

"What do you mean?" The shock in Adam's voice made it sound like Noel had suggested kidnapping or chloral hydrate or something.

"Dude, people throw shit away, you know? It's called dumpster diving. All we'd need to find is a wad of hair they pulled out of a hairbrush or some tissue they spit into or something."

"Oh. Good."

Noel turned left at Siri's command. Jason's house was a block or two farther down.

"Because I don't think I can ask you to use your, um, superpower."

Pulling into Jason's driveway, Noel brought the car to a stop before he spoke. He needed the time to compose a response. "Adam." He turned to face his friend, his lover, his... "I'm either crazy, or when I'm in the wrong place at the wrong time, random spiritual entities can jump my consciousness. I seriously don't see how that helps us figure out what happened to Valsin."

"But you said today—"

"Dammit, Adam. I was fucking freaked out. Who knows what the hell I said?" He rubbed the back of his neck where a band of muscle had turned into a solid knot, no longer in the mood for true confessions. "Anyway, it's not like I can control it."

There was something speculative in the silence that followed, something Noel really didn't like. Rather than wait around, he hopped out of the car, filling his arms with suitcases and as many of the provisions as he could carry.

Well, he grabbed the bottle of gin, anyway.

Chapter Seventeen

You were willing to go yesterday." After the endless series of unfortunate events on Saturday, Adam woke up the next morning with the realization they had a full day to kill before meeting with Richard Lafont and nothing useful would be open on a Sunday. Then he remembered the museum.

"Yesterday, you just wanted to see some moldy old letter." Noel scowled at Adam as he headed toward the coffee maker for a second cup.

"And I still want to see it."

"No, today you want *me* to see it. The same way you wanted me to *see* that cabin out on Magnolia."

"Jason's already arranged things with Parson's granddaughter." And yes, maybe he had let Jason do that before springing the expedition on Noel. He wasn't sure why he couldn't let go of the idea that Noel's gift was the key to the mystery of Valsin. "Until the estate is settled, we don't know what will happen to Valsin's things. And we can try one last experiment before we leave."

Noel put his cup on the counter. Instead of filling it, he stared at the cabinet in front of him, back tense. "It's never worked like that before. It doesn't happen because I touch something or open my inner fucking eye or whatever. There's no effort on my part. There's no warning." He turned around. His voice was low but clear. "The heebie-jeebies hijack me."

Adam swallowed.

"And even if it did work," Noel continued, "what would it prove? The DNA is tangible evidence. For all we know, my little *episodes*"—he made air quotes—"are a chemical imbalance."

Adam shook his head. Noel couldn't believe that. Adam couldn't let him believe that.

"It won't hurt to try."

He thought Noel would refuse, but instead he heaved out a sigh. "Fine."

Adam tried not to notice how not-fine Noel sounded about the outing. It would be worth it if they learned anything. The truth was worth it. By the time they finished their coffee, showered, and made the drive, he'd convinced himself it was true. By then, the tension between them had settled into something resembling a truce.

The real Valsin Ferrier Museum was less than a quarter mile from Mr. Parson's home, close enough that a faint trail marked the route he'd walked between the two every day. Only a small copse of trees and brush separated the museum from the house, but in terms of visual impact, they couldn't be further apart. The yard at the house had been overgrown with weeds and littered with junk. By contrast, the grass surrounding the museum was perfectly trimmed. Adam had no idea what Valsin's actual workshop looked like, but the pine building with the porch along the front and barn doors on one side seemed as likely as anything else. He wondered if Parsons had found images from the period or if he'd let his imagination and handy building materials inform the construction. Either way, Adam would bet the roof didn't leak.

"This is a waste of time." Noel had already made two trips around the building. It was locked up tight and featured a very non-nineteenth century security system. He hadn't spared a glance down the trail toward the decrepit house. In fact, his gaze seemed to shy away from it. Instead he stopped to stare at a tree bursting with small red fruit. He reached up and plucked one off. "Look at this. I wonder if those are mayhaws."

"Probably." Adam didn't care. He was sick of hearing about mayhaws.

Noel took an experimental bite, which he immediately spit out. "Damn, that's tart. Maybe it's not ripe."

When Adam still didn't show any interest, he tossed the remaining fruit into the trees and started another trip around the building. He'd dressed for travel in shorts and a black tee with a fit just snug enough to show off the definition in his shoulders. To the casual observer, he probably looked relaxed. Adam knew better. His cop was practically vibrating with energy. Nerves, maybe. Or maybe whatever the thing was that meant he sometimes saw ghosts.

Adam pulled out his phone. They were on time. Parson's granddaughter was late.

He snapped a picture of the museum, then suppressed a strong urge to throw the phone at the building. The on-again-off-again country cell signal was off again. No tweeting while they waited. He'd thought the Twitter response yesterday would make everyone happy. Instead, he'd gotten a note from PR asking him to *engage consistently* to keep followers interested and *refrain from posting anything controversial.*

"Hey." Noel appeared at his side. "What's wrong?"

"No connection." He meant to stop there, but his mouth apparently had other ideas. "Fans are upset. Show is upset. We barely mentioned Marie and Valsin. I would have loved to do a show on the legend, but we're the *ghost* show. So...whatever."

Noel stared at him.

"It's fine."

Noel stared at him some more, shifting on his feet and looking uncomfortable. "Hey, it'll be okay. We'll work it out."

"Sure."

More staring. "Baby..." He trailed off.

"What?" The word came out snarly and Noel threw him a sharp look.

"Look. Are you sure you even want this job? It's stressing you out, and all I've heard since we've been here is how much you hate being 'the ghost show guy.'"

It was his turn to stare.

At Noel.

The fitted black tee probably cost more than Adam's second-best suit.

Noel drove a Lexus he'd gotten as a birthday gift. He lived in a house he didn't have to work to afford and Adam couldn't afford at all. He could change jobs on a whim because he didn't need to work at all.

"Yes," he enunciated. "I want to keep my job. It's not like I'm going to waltz into another gig like this."

"You could go back to teaching. Get your PhD. Publish a paper like you keep talking about."

Adam laughed derisively. "The only thing worse on an academic résumé than 'ghost show guy' is being the historian who got canned from the ghost show."

"What about your books?" Noel didn't seem willing

to drop the subject.

"Without the publicity from the show, my books bring in about enough to cover my car insurance. Not the payment. Just the insurance."

Noel didn't get it. Adam didn't have a trust fund to fall back on if his career crashed and burned. He couldn't ditch a perfectly good job and run halfway across the country to fuck around at another job he didn't really need. Anyway, if he quit now, what did he have to show for the last decade of his life?

"What about you? Still loving Hughes Wallace?"

Noel's face closed down. "You know I can't be a cop anymore."

Adam knew no such thing. Noel was made to be a cop. One day, he was going to wake up and realize that, then he would head back to Los Angeles.

He tried to imagine following Noel back to LA and meeting the rest of the Chandlers. His imagination balked. Sure, the unemployed cable ghost show guy from North Florida was going to meet Noel's high-society mother. They probably had tons in common.

He raked his hand through his hair. If he kept taking his frustrations out on Noel, impressing the family wouldn't be an issue. "Sorry. I'm all over the place lately."

The sound of tires on gravel drew their attention before Noel could respond.

A blue Ford Focus pulled into the parking lot. Noel wandered up to join Adam as the door opened and the woman inside popped out.

"I'm sorry. I'm *sorry*, y'all. I know I'm late, but it's been a day." She was wearing yoga pants, a maternity shirt, and off-brand running shoes. She pushed the car door shut with her foot and headed their way talking a mile a minute. Or as close to that as a north Louisiana drawl could get. "The baby's got colic, and I've got a pile of paperwork for the estate, and…oh Lord. Y'all don't care about any of that. I'm Darla."

"Adam Morales." Adam extended his hand. "I'm sorry for your loss. We didn't mind the wait."

"You're Dr. Pham's friend, Professor Morales. You're on TV."

For now. "Call me Adam. And this is Noel."

Noel gave her one of his lazy smiles, the kind that made him look like he never thought about anything more important than the next wave. "How do you know Jason?"

Darla had already started toward the door, pulling an extra ring of keys out of her bag as she walked. "Historical Society, mostly. Plus he and Pappaw were…" She threw them a look. "You ever hear the term frenemies?"

"Jay said they didn't always see eye to eye," Adam said.

Darla rolled her eyes. "To hear Pappaw tell it, all they did was disagree. But they disagreed *regularly*, you know what I mean? The last couple of years, about the only time I saw Pappaw get worked about much of anything was when Dr. Pham's name came up. Well, and Miss Cookie, but that was a different kind of thing."

"Miss Cookie?" Noel broke in. Adam gave him credit. He didn't think Darla had caught the gleam in Noel's eye that meant he was suppressing laughter.

Darla gave him a funny look. "How have you not met Miss Cookie? Anyway, Pappaw always said they were fellow history buffs, but between you and me, I don't think they spent every Thursday night discussing the Gettysburg address."

"Go, Pappaw," Noel breathed.

Darla unlocked the door and disarmed the security

system. Adam moved closer to Noel. There was no reason just stepping inside the museum should trigger a psychic event, but he would have said the same at the house.

As they stepped over the threshold, goose bumps broke out along Adam's arm. But other than the transition from muggy Louisiana heat to aggressive climate control, nothing unusual happened.

The inside of the building was one large room. Parsons had devoted most of the space to recreating a nineteenth-century woodworker's shop. The museum had an impressive collection of antique tools hanging on the walls and displayed on shelves and cubbies. Large items hung from a rack near the ceiling.

Adam found himself irresistibly drawn toward the focal point of the room, an antique lathe. A set of balusters was stacked nearby with one, half-finished, still on the lathe.

"That's the actual project Valsin was working on before he ran off with Marie," Darla supplied.

"Really? How do you—" Adam caught himself. He was a professional, dammit, not a tourist. "Amazing," he finished wryly. "I suppose this whole workshop is exactly the way Valsin Ferrier left it?"

Darla snorted out a laugh. "To hear Pappaw tell it. He could make you believe it too." An expression of sorrow settled over her face as she looked around the room. "I miss him something fierce."

"He did a good job with the workshop," Adam found himself saying. "The lathe alone is worth the visit."

"After Mammaw died, he poured all his energy into this place." Darla blinked away the moisture in her eyes. "Thank you. He would have loved to show you around. Was there something in particular you wanted to see?"

"Jason said he authenticated a ledger and some letters that belonged to Valsin. We'd love to see those."

"Is this about the research you're doing for Ms. Davenport?"

Adam tensed, but Darla's tone was merely curious.

"I've seen the pictures Jason took, but there's something special about the real thing, isn't there?"

She nodded understandingly. "It's the reason Pappaw wouldn't let Dr. Pham take them. They're over here." She showed him to a counter running along the right side of the room. On top sat a row of museum cases.

Adam stepped over to into the first case, which held a ledger. His breath caught. Unless both he and Jay, who had already authenticated it, were wrong, this was the real deal. This was Valsin's business ledger, income and expenses recorded in neat rows. Most casual buffs were less interested in these types of mundane historical records. Personal correspondence was sexier, but business and household accounts told their own stories of life in the past. Adam had already pored over Jay's photos of this one and he was still captivated by the original.

Noel, however, had moved on to the next case. "What's this? Valsin kept a diary?"

Jay hadn't said anything about a diary. Adam frowned over Noel's shoulder at the elegant script covering the page.

"That one wasn't Valsin," Darla said. "That was Miss Emily's diary. The story goes that Miss Emily was the one who helped Marie and Valsin escape."

Another one? Adam suppressed an eye roll. He couldn't keep the skepticism out of his voice. "I suppose she wrote it all down in her diary?"

"I wish." Darla laughed. "Miss Emily really does

mention Marie several times, though. She used to hire her from Magnolia for various things, usually as a seamstress. I don't know why everyone thinks Marie was a cook.

"Anyway, Miss Emily lived in one of those big houses over in the historic district, and she had brought Marie to stay with her for a week or so to help out. Marie didn't escape from Magnolia. She disappeared from right in the middle of town."

Adam stared down at the glass, mind churning. He thought he'd heard every story about Marie this town had to offer. "I never heard of anyone called Miss Emily."

Darla must have picked up on the skepticism in his tone. "Well, she was Miss Cookie's great-however-many-times aunt, and Miss Cookie is just as crazy about Marie and Valsin as Pappaw was, so I suppose it's likely she embellished a little."

More than likely. Adam leaned over to get a better look. If the book was a fake, it was good enough to pass muster on first glance. Adam got the same buzzing feel he had with the ledger, the sense of *history* reaching out to him. He scanned the text hungrily. Sure enough, Miss Emily's entry for the day was about sending her brother to Magnolia to fetch the *girl who did the fine needlework for the christening gown last fall.*

Marie wasn't mentioned specifically, but the date was the same month bounties had gone out for her return. "Has anyone authenticated the diary?"

"I think so?" Darla pursed her lips. "Honestly, I don't know. I thought Pappaw was bad about hanging on to things, but Miss Cookie barely let this thing out of her sight. Only a few members of the Historical Society have been invited to view it, and it took Pappaw forever to get her to let him display it. I've never been allowed any closer to it than you are right now. The one thing I know is that Miss Cookie absolutely believes that diary has been in her family since before the Civil War."

"I wonder why Jay didn't mention it?"

Darla laughed. "I'm sure Pappaw was going to spring it on him at some point. He wouldn't have been able to resist gloating that he had it and Dr. Pham didn't."

Adam shook his head. He wished he could be surprised that no one else knew about the diary, but he'd been around collectors enough to know that they could develop all sorts of paranoia over their prized pieces. Most were eager to show them off, but some went exactly the opposite direction.

"I'd love to read whole thing, if you can arrange it." He held his breath, hoping Darla would offer to open the case.

"I'd let you do it now," Darla said, "but I can't find the key to that case. I hope Miss Cookie knows where Pappaw stashed it."

Adam exhaled a sigh of regret, but reminded himself they weren't really here to read diaries of forgotten young belles, no matter how interesting. He resolutely moved on.

The final case held a single piece of paper. His breath caught. This was the letter. Personal correspondence in Valsin's own hand. Ledgers built a world out of notations and numbers, but a letter was a focal point pulling him in to a moment in someone else's life.

Beside him, Noel frowned at the scratchy writing, then peered closer. "Is this a letter about *hogs*?"

Adam nodded absently, already drawn into the past.

"Oh my God, I can't believe you're getting all mush faced over a hog letter. Gross."

"Look." Adam touched the glass reverently. "It's to Valsin's cousin. He's asking if he was able to get a fair price for the hogs he just sold, and he promises to send over *a few curiosities I have turned my hand to. They may distract little Jessie, who I know is sore tried being kept abed.*"

"Huh?"

"He made some toys for one of his cousin's children who was bedridden for some reason. I wonder if he was sick, or hurt."

"Hogs and sick kids. Fascinating. You get turned on by some weird shit, Professor." But Noel sounded more indulgent than disparaging. He stood close enough to Adam that their shoulders pressed together as he stared down into the case, apparently trying to figure out what was so interesting.

"It's continued on the back. Would you like me to open the case so you can read the rest?" Darla's tone was hushed. Adam glanced up. For a moment, they shared a glance of complete understanding. Darla might pretend she only cared about the shop for her grandfather's sake, but Adam could spot a fellow history buff. At his nod, she dug out her keys and opened the box.

Adam froze. "I haven't washed my hands."

"I'd send you over to the house, but the water's off. Just be careful, okay?"

Minimal touching, then. He leaned forward. The closer he got to the letter, the more the present receded and the closer the past seemed, as if he were standing over Valsin's shoulder watching him write. He wiped his hands on his jeans, hoping to remove as much of the oil as possible, and then turned the page.

"Anything interesting?" Noel's voice seemed to come from far away.

"Just more family stuff." Nothing to interest Noel, but Adam couldn't force himself to look away. Keeping his hands to himself was a major act of self-control. Touching an old document always gave him a sense of stepping back in time, a visceral connection to the writer. Unlike Noel, it was all in his head. Any impressions he got of the past were based on studying the period and knowing how it probably looked. It wasn't fair that Adam had devoted his life to studying the past and Noel was the one who got to experience it.

"It's signed," he finally said. Which expressed exactly none of what he felt.

Or maybe it did, because Noel bumped their shoulders together softly and refrained from making any more comments about hogs.

Some incessant buzzing from her phone had taken Darla back across the room, where she was muttering to herself and texting furiously. Adam waged a brief internal battle with himself about the importance of *not touching*, then bent his head closer to Noel. "Do you want to touch it?"

"Why would I..." He broke off as understanding dawned.

"Just the corner." Adam forced the words out. Noel had clean hands. The Lexus was climate-controlled, and God knew Noel had it detailed often enough. He tried not to think about Louisiana humidity and natural skin oils.

"I...uh." Noel's lips thinned. "Yeah, sure. Why not? What we're here for, right?"

Adam snuck a glance behind him to make sure Darla was still occupied with the phone, then angled his body to better conceal what they were about to do. "Just the corner," he repeated. "Hurry up."

Noel's hand shot out, hovering over the delicate paper in the briefest pause. Adam drew a breath, but before he could rethink, it was done. Noel's hand dropped, one finger tracing the corner of the page in what was almost a caress.

Adam sucked in a breath as he watched, reliving the thrill of his own brief contact... He imagined allowing his own finger to linger on the same page Valsin Ferrier had touched over one hundred and fifty years ago. He could almost hear the nib scratching across the page, smell the ink, see his sleeves, rolled up from laboring in the shop or to keep them free of any ink stains. And if he could see all that... He edged closer to Noel, ready to steady him if the visions were too much or if some foreign entity took over his body.

Then it was over, and Noel took a step back.

Adam shook his head, not sure what had happened. The past had been so close, like seeing something out of the corner of you eye. As if all he had to do was turn his head at the right angle and he could step into 1857. Surely Noel had felt it. He had to have seen something.

He swept his gaze over Noel, looking for any signs of disorientation, but Noel took another step back and gave a tiny shake of his head.

Adam frowned. "Nothing?" He didn't realize he'd said it out loud until Noel scowled. He gave a more vigorous shake of his head and cut a glance significantly toward Darla, who had finished her texting and was heading back toward them.

"I'm sorry." Vexation replaced her earlier grief. "I'm going to have to leave sooner than I thought. Was there anything else you particularly wanted to see?"

Adam shook his head and followed Noel to the car. *Enough already.* The letter and ledger were well documented. He didn't really need to be here viewing the originals for any legitimate research. As for their other motives, Noel's talent, once again, had refused to cooperate.

Chapter Eighteen

Adam had anticipated some awkwardness while sharing space with Jason, but it never materialized. In fact, by Sunday night, Jason and Noel were bonding over DVRed episodes of *Drag Race*.

Because of course they were. Why had he expected anything different? Their list of common interests seemed endless. They liked the same brands of coffee and artisanal kombucha. They discussed the merits of beaches with names like Rubber Ducky and China Walls. Right before the *Drag Race* marathon, they'd fallen into an almost tearful memorial to a long-closed food truck both agreed had the best plate lunches on the North Shore.

Adam hunched over his phone and tried to ignore the ruckus on the television as he dredged up another inane tweet to keep PR and his new followers happy.

And why was he annoyed, anyway? He *wanted* them to get along. The surfing he'd expected to be common ground. Plate lunches and kombucha...okay, that could all be lumped under "Hawaiian shit." But *Drag Race*? He hadn't seen that one coming. Just like he hadn't seen the nice house with the swank interior coming. What else was he missing?

Now Noel was sitting on the sofa next to Jay, close enough that their elbows rubbed occasionally when one of them reached for his beer. Adam's chair faced away from the TV, so he could focus. Or so he could have a perfect view of Noel's normally sleepy bedroom eyes as they crinkled in amusement at something Jason said.

He wasn't flirting. So Adam wasn't jealous, precisely. Except somehow, he was bothered by the *way* Noel wasn't flirting. Noel flirted by default. He even flirted with Porter Bergeron, who was a work associate and straight and should have been off-limits.

Noel flirting with Porter didn't bother him.

But this...beers and *Drag Race* with Jason... Noel going from barely veiled hostility to friendly banter, *"Assuming you're innocent"* being less of a dig and more of an inside joke... Every *"brah"* tightened the screws of tension in Adam's neck until his shoulders were almost touching his ears. He consciously forced them back down and stretched his head from one side to the other, trying to loosen the knots.

"Where were you this afternoon, anyway?" He hadn't meant to ask in front of Jason, but the words slipped out.

Noel left off an explanation of why Jason's favorite queen was destined to lip-synch for her life to blink at the interruption. "Me?"

Adam just stared at him. He'd asked a perfectly reasonable question. They were here together. As a couple. And they were working on a project together. Yet Noel had seen fit to take himself off alone for half the afternoon.

Noel narrowed his eyes at him. "Had a few errands." The same non-explanation he'd given before he left. "Why?"

Jay glanced back and forth between them, then turned pointedly to the TV, tactfully staying out of it.

"No reason," Adam mumbled. They had spent a lot more time together this trip than either of them were used to. Noel was entitled to some alone time, which he'd obviously needed. But he could have just said so instead of disappearing for hours, then showing back up without a single shopping bag to show for the *errands*. Adam knew he should let it go, but the secrecy seemed so pointless. The more he tried to ignore it, the more it irritated him. With Noel and Jason getting so chummy, and Noel unwilling to explain, it felt like the disappearing act was more an attempt to escape Adam than the awkwardness of playing houseguest.

At the next pause between episodes, Noel excused himself for a restroom break. Adam waited a few minutes and then followed to loiter in the hallway and listen to water run in the sink.

"Shit." Noel stopped just short of barreling into him as he came out, obviously in a hurry to get back to a show Adam had no interest in. Noel shifted gears quickly, stepping back to let his gaze wander up and down Adam's body. A slow grin spread across his face. "Well, *hello there*."

Flirting.

Forget this.

Adam headed down the hall to their bedroom. Now he needed space. He needed *quiet*.

To tweet.

Instead of rejoining Jason in the living room, Noel trailed behind him. Inside the bedroom, he shut the door and made a deliberate show of setting the lock. "Finally ready to get rid of some of that tension?"

Adam turned to stare at him incredulously. "Jason's in the other room waiting for you."

Noel shrugged. "He's a big boy. He can wait a few minutes, maybe turn the sound up." His smile slipped a bit at whatever was on Adam's face. "Or we can be super quiet. That'd be hot too."

"I'm not having sex with you while Jason's sitting right down the hall."

All the humor left Noel's face. "And you wouldn't let me get you off last night while he was sound asleep either. Jesus, princess. This level of stress isn't healthy. Something's going to have to give eventually."

Adam wasn't sure how he had suddenly gone from professor to princess. Professor had always broadcast more undertones than he could parse, but princess sounded like something Noel would call one of his exes. The last thing he wanted was to be lumped in the same category as the guy with the cats or the one before, who had managed to burn a pile of Noel's designer wardrobe on his way out.

"Maybe what should give is you tell me exactly what errands you were running in a town where you don't live." *Fuck.*

Or maybe Noel just brought it out in people, because Adam had never said anything like that to one of *his* exes. He was the grounded guy, the stable one who didn't throw fits or stress over the little things.

Except right now, he didn't know who he was. His life had turned upside down. He needed something to be okay. He needed *them* to be okay. And he was going about it all wrong. He tacked on a belated and surly, "Please."

The please shouldn't have worked, but for once, Noel's aversion to relationship norms worked in their favor. "Okay, calm down. I just wanted to talk to a few people on my own." His eyes darted down for a second, then back up, almost challengingly. "I got a few

Rousseaus to donate some DNA."

Adam stared at him stupidly. "You what?"

"Look, don't get your hopes up. It will probably take forever to get results back, and even then we'll have a lot of work to do to connect the dots."

"You were out collecting DNA samples?" *This* was supposed to make him less tense? "Why the *fuck* couldn't you just say that? Why couldn't you have said that this afternoon when you left?"

"I just told you I didn't want to get your hopes up."

"We could have gone together."

"No."

One word. *No.* Adam clamped down on his immediate hurt reaction. *Why?* Because Noel obviously hadn't wanted him to tag along. Because he hadn't wanted to share his time with Adam. Because when it came down to it, they had nothing in common.

"Jesus, baby. Don't look at me like that. You and Jay struck out on this one. I thought a fresh face might be better." He spoke slowly, as if explaining something to a child. "And I didn't want to get your hopes up if I struck out too."

"You could have told me."

"Fuck's sake. I'm telling you now."

Except telling him this afternoon before he left, even if he hadn't wanted Adam to come, would have meant more. They could have discussed it. They could have shared ideas. Instead, Noel had gone off on his own. Adam still wouldn't know a damn thing if he hadn't pushed the issue.

His stomach hurt. His head hurt. His neck hurt.

He wasn't thinking logically. He massaged his neck, hoping to get some increased blood flow to his brain.

The silence stretched out.

A million thoughts chased themselves through his

brain. Not one made it past his lips.

Noel's expression went from frustrated to calm. Cop face. Public face. The pretty rich-boy face that hid all his secrets. He turned the lock. Turned the knob. Opened the door.

The words caught behind Adam's lips formed a logjam until his throat ached and his vision blurred.

Noel walked away.

The door of the Lexus slammed with the finality of the coffin's last nail. Yeah, Noel had fucked this one up but good. He mashed his fingertips into his temples, pressing hard, then harder, desperate to release the vise clamped around his head.

Am I going to do it this time?

He'd almost cut out on Adam after that misbegotten trip to Parson's cabin. Maybe he should have left then. Put them both out of their misery.

Noel turned the engine on and leaned back against the headrest, forcing his shoulders to relax. Did he really mean to leave? *It's time.* Putting the car in gear, he backed slowly out of Jason's driveway, wheels crackling on the gravel at the edge of the road. He drove an entire block, pulled the car to the side of the road, and turned the engine off.

He inhaled, imagining the air swirling through his lungs. Some therapist along the way had tried to teach him to calm himself by breathing. Fat lot of good that had done. His lungs were made of Styrofoam, and the air was the color of smoke. Be easier to visualize the swirl of a hefty shot of gin poured over ice.

Because when it came right down to it, he didn't want to leave Adam. He liked Adam. Maybe more than liked him. He liked his pompous-professor teaching voice, and the way his hair curled over his ears, and his habit of laughing whenever Noel popped off with the most inane garbage. Even more, he liked being with someone who let him be quiet.

But Noel had run. *Again.* He made fists, gently punching his thighs. Noel ran. That's what he did. He'd run from his family, he'd run from LA, and before that, he ran from...

His mind shied away from a memory steeped in shame.

If he was digging that deep, he really must be up shit's creek. "With no paddle, my dude."

No paddle and no place he'd rather be.

Noel sighed. Okay then. He wouldn't be going any farther. That didn't mean he was going back inside. Not yet. He reached for the lever at the bottom of the seat and reclined it to the fullest. If he went back in now, their fight would just start all over again. They both needed time to cool off. Besides, it was spring in Louisiana. He could sleep right here and wouldn't even need a jacket.

Noel's resolve lasted till about three a.m. He'd amazed himself by actually falling asleep, until a pair of cats had had a duel to the death somewhere between him and the river. After that, every snap and scuffle had him convinced...well, never mind. Adam wouldn't be coming out to check on him. Adam thought he'd left for good. The only time Noel's phone chirped had been an email inviting him to a preview of the fall line at the

BOSS Shop in New Orleans.

He deleted it.

To pass time, he imagined them both in bed, asleep, Adam lying on one side with a protective arm across Noel's chest. All that did was highlight his current discomfort. The Lexus's leather seat didn't quite flatten, the steering wheel limited where his legs could go, and after a while, a layer of chilling dew coated everything.

Meanwhile, Jason's guest room had a queen-sized bed. "With a damned perfect mattress." Somehow, the memory of the mattress made the SUV's seat even less comfortable.

Using the steering wheel for leverage, Noel dragged himself up to sitting. This was stupid. He'd walked out before saying anything he couldn't take back. *Right?*

Something landed on the front hood of the Lexus. Noel jerked upright, heart pounding. A cat glared at him through the windshield. "What is with you?" The creature didn't answer, leaping up to the SUV's roof, a fluid shadow in the darkness.

Snorting, Noel started the Lexus and put it in gear. *That cat better watch itself.* "If I find footprints in the morning, you're toast."

In less than a minute he was back in Jason's driveway. Crossing the dew-damp lawn to the front door put an interesting spin on the walk of shame. With luck, they hadn't locked him out. Noel might well possess the skills to pick just about any lock, but it felt weird using them on a friend.

The handle turned, and the door opened silently. "Hmph. Solid construction." He felt a touch of something like disappointment, not because he wanted to leave, but because now he would have to face Adam and—*gulp*—apologize.

With any luck, he'll be asleep.

Adam was awake.

Noel knew it as soon as he opened the bedroom door. Adam lay still, but his breathing was too quiet to hear, not the deep, regular snoring breaths of sleep. "Hey," Noel said, keeping his voice low in case he'd guessed wrong.

"Hey," Adam answered.

"I, uh..." Noel cleared his throat. *Ball up, Chandler. Get it over with.* "Owe you an apology."

Adam waiting to answer, long enough to make Noel wonder if he should have stayed outside.

"I can't even remember what we were fighting about." Adam sounded more amused than the situation called for.

"Go ahead and laugh." Noel spun on his heel and had the door open before Adam stopped him.

"Come on, Noel. Or leave. Fuck." Adam sat up in bed. "I mean, can you honestly tell me what we both got so pissed off about? Because I'll be damned if I can remember."

Noel crossed his arms, his back to the bed. "It started out when you turned down a blow job."

"You took off because of that?"

"No, I took off because you were fucking furious with me after I'd collected DNA from a couple of people without asking your permission first." Noel was surprised by his own bitterness. "It's like you don't trust me at all."

That soft scratching sound must be Adam raking his fingers through his hair. When he didn't say anything, Noel felt obligated to fill the silence with his own word salad. "I mean, I get it. I'm a shitty boyfriend. You're probably right to be angry with me, and I apologize for not saying anything ahead of time. I just..." He exhaled, letting go some of his frustration. "I just didn't want to disappoint you." *I just didn't want you to be disappointed in me.*

"Shut up." The mattress didn't squeak, exactly, but there was a rustle of fabric against fabric and the sudden warmth of Adam's body close to his.

"We're both tired." Adam's hand closed over Noel's shoulder. "And I'm sorry too."

Noel covered Adam's hand with his own. "I'll try. I will." He didn't quite know what he'd just promised, because keeping secrets was his real superpower. "You might have to remind me sometimes, though."

They stood there for a while. Adam slung his arm around Noel's waist, and Noel sank into his strength. "Let's go to bed," Adam murmured.

"I'll race you."

Noel skimmed out of his jeans and tossed them onto the suitcase at the foot of the bed... Adam was already under the covers when he got there, and in a matter of moments, they were in the same position Noel had imagined: Noel on his back, and Adam on his side with an arm draped over Noel.

Except unlike in his fantasy, Noel wasn't asleep.

Adam's breathing deepened, and for a few moments, Noel debated whether to say something else, to make some kind of claim on Adam. Their exclusivity agreement had felt like such a huge step a month ago, but now it wasn't enough. Noel needed Adam to know he could count on Noel, that they could refer to each other as boyfriends without blushing.

He just didn't know how to say it, and by the time he figured out, Adam had started snoring. Noel slept too, but not for as long as Adam. The sun had warmed the cellular blinds to a pale gold by the time he woke up, and for a while, Noel was content to listen to Adam breath. At least if he was asleep, he wasn't stewing about work or whatever. Adam gave a muttered groan, lifting his hand from the bed and letting it fall again. *Nope.* That cloud of anger was still there.

Noel had no doubt last night was all his fault. He was crap at being a boyfriend. Adam's job was giving him hell, and Noel had walked right into it. He should have left the Rousseaus alone. He should have had less to drink...or maybe more to drink...or something.

Hell. I don't know.

Frustrated, Noel stretched out, the sheets dragging on his skin. He'd had his hand slapped for playing lone wolf, and whatever happened next, Adam and even Jason would be invited along. Adam let loose something close to a snore, and Noel gazed at him from the corner of his eye, the rising sun had brightening the room. With any luck, Noel's cell phone wouldn't bother him.

He swiped the screen and brought up his notepad app. Back in the day, some academy instructor had written "the five Ws" on a blackboard: what, when, where, why, and who. It was one of those basic lessons that had embedded itself in his mind, and after running hard from his years on the force, he only remembered the basic stuff. He started a new note.

What: pattern of harassment, including social media campaign against H&H, Jay's arrest, possibly hotel shenanigans.

When: since H&H filmed here? Since Angela Davenport told Jay about her family history? Since he & Adam had started looking into what happened to Valsin?

Where: Natch.

Why: ...

Who: ...

The last two were always the hardest, although finding why would lead to who, and vice versa. And really, none of what happened rose to the level of crime. Harassment, yeah, and potentially damaging to Adam's career, and to Jay's.

But nothing illegal.

Adam coughed, drawing Noel's attention. He pressed the phone against his chest, blocking the light. Still asleep. Okay, he didn't know *who* or *why*, and the *what* and the *when* were pretty vague. The one solid he had was *where*. Natchitoches. If they went back to New Orleans, all the other Ws would fade away.

Good thing that was where they were headed.

Noel shut down the phone. It wasn't as if they'd planned to stay here indefinitely. They would go by the Cane River Home and get an answer from Mr. Lafont, then head on home. He'd drop Adam off and force himself into the office, and things would return to normal.

And then maybe Adam would calm down.

Noel really needed Adam to calm down.

And with any luck, it'd be a good long while before Noel stumbled over another haunt. Long enough that he could convince himself he wasn't going crazy.

Chapter Nineteen

oel gave Adam a confidence-boosting grin. "In and out and on the road, right?"

Adam balled up his napkin. "Sure."

Locking his grin in place, Noel climbed out of the car. *In, out, and on the road.*

They were early enough that most of the residents were still at breakfast. Richard Lafont sat alone at a table near the window. The comb marks made lines through his thinning hair, and he wore a gray sweatshirt despite the warmth of the day. On Noel's approach, he raised his mug. "Well, I've just had all kinds of visitors today."

"That right?" Noel tugged on the two chairs across from him. "Mind if we sit?" Adam had followed him in, his silent reproach beginning to really chafe Noel's nerves.

"Make yourselves at home."

"You're a popular guy." Noel took a seat and, after an awkward beat, Adam did too.

"You know it." Richard grinned, but something serious lurked in his affable gaze. "And the interesting thing is, my last visitor wanted to talk about y'all."

"Really?" Noel shrugged at Adam's quick glance.

"That's right. A friend of mine, more of an acquaintance, I guess, came in right after they brought me my eggs. He said he'd heard y'all had asked me about a DNA test, and he was pretty convinced y'all are up to something fishy." His smile faded. "He tried very hard to discourage me from going along with your little plan."

Something fishy? Sounded like a line from an episode of *Batman*, the Adam West version. "Huh." Noel straightened in his chair, hands flat on the table. "I don't know what to say."

Adam leaned forward on his elbows. "We don't know too many people in town."

"We don't," Noel said. "And we're happy to answer any questions you have. The important thing is whether you think we're trying to cause trouble or not."

Richard rubbed a knuckle along his chin, making a soft rasp. His gaze shifted from Noel to Adam and back again. "To be honest, I don't know. Your song and dance about me being related to Valsin Ferrier is a little bit hard to believe. Maybe it'd be better to let the dead stay quiet."

Adam gave a frustrated snort. Noel slid a hand along his thigh, under the table where it couldn't be seen. The muscle was taut, his leg vibrating. Willing Adam to keep quiet, Noel gave Richard his best witness-calming smile. "I hear you, man. If Angela Davenport hadn't brought us her family Bible with all the names penciled in, I wouldn't have believed it either. If you're willing to help us, that would be great, but I understand if you don't want to."

"Hang on." Adam shifted in his seat, moving out from under Noel's grasp. "History is important. The truth has value. I don't want to ruin anybody's Mayhaw Days, but damn." He exhaled hard. "There has to have been a reason why Valsin Ferrier's name didn't appear in Marie Tisdale's Bible, and why her family says she arrived in Pennsylvania alone."

Adam gave Noel an apologetic smile. "Like you said, it's just a matter of posing the right question to the right person, but if we could have your help, Mr. Lafont, we'd have that many more people to ask."

"See, the thing is..." Lafont's frown was thoughtful rather than unhappy. "Y'all might be here to cause trouble, but I have the feeling it's the right kind of trouble." His smile broadened. "So you can have my blood or my spit or what have you, and I'll just tell that Harrison Whitney to go bother someone else."

Harrison Whitney. Bad hair and seventies glasses. Noel glanced at Adam and, with a subtle nod, let him know that they'd be discussing Mr. Whitney later.

Leaving Adam to listen to Lafont's stories, Noel jogged out to the Lexus for the DNA kit. Collecting the sample should take less than five minutes, and, allowing time to jet back to Jason's to grab their stuff, they should be on the road within an hour. He'd text Bergeron as soon as they headed out so—

A woman stands next to the Lexus. A Black woman, wearing a long gray dress and an apron, her head wrapped in a faded red scarf. Her eyes are large and dark, and she holds her hands clasped in front of her belly, her knuckles blanched with tension.

Noel's mind took in those details, along with the knowledge that he could see right through her. The air turned chill, and gooseflesh crawled up the back of his neck.

She looks right at him, and though he cannot hear her, he knows she has a message. A message for him alone.

Please.

Please.

Noel stood alone beside the Lexus, head down, hands gripping the back of his neck. The vision, now vanished, chilled him to his core.

So either the ghosties are talking to me now, or I'm losing my fucking mind.

Had Marie Tisdale appeared in the middle of the damned parking lot and pleaded with him to do something?

Aw, shit. Now I'm naming them.

His head throbbed, and he could feel his own pulse in his throat. *Get it together.* He'd come out here for a reason. Oh. The DNA test. With shaking hands, he unlocked the Lexus, grounding himself in its familiar leather-and-new-car smell. Before bringing the test into the Home, he sent Bergeron a text.

Cover for me.

Then he opened the note he'd started the night before and added a name to the *who* line: Harrison Whitney. Because apparently, the only way to prove he wasn't fucking insane was to figure out what happened to Valsin and why someone didn't want them to know the answer.

Which meant staying in Natchitoches.

Convincing Adam to stay would take some finesse, and if at all possible, Noel wanted to do it without mentioning Marie. Just because he'd told Adam about his last ghostly encounter, didn't mean he had to cough up every little episode. Maybe, sometimes, on a very good day, he could say *I see ghosts* without wanting to hurl, but he was deeply ambivalent about the feeling that Adam agreed with him. He had to believe Adam saw more in him than his superpower.

Aw, man. He gouged a thumb into his temple where a headache had set up shop. He could do this. He just had to go back inside and act like a professional without letting anyone see that his hands were still shaking.

With that in mind, he made short work of testing Lafont. As soon as he and Adam were back in the Lexus, Noel offered the opening salvo in the great *let's stay in Nack* debate. "What do we know about Harrison Whitney?"

Adam glanced up from fiddling with his phone. "Besides being on the board of the Historical Society, he runs a small empire of tourism-related businesses. Wonder if that Spring Whitney is related to him at all?"

Another name to add to the *who* list. Assuming that *was* her name. "The cops didn't recognize her. Anybody could have picked a local family name to try to blend in."

"Sure. Sure." Adam's vague response hinted that he wasn't paying much attention.

Just as well. "I mean, what was a well-dressed young lady doing on the set of *Deliverance* anyway?" Noel murmured the question, mostly asking himself. "And what was up with that dog?"

Adam gave his phone a disgusted swipe. "Maybe Camille knows what Harrison was up to. They seemed to be on pretty friendly terms."

"Good point." Noel let out a breath, grateful for the yank out of the Spring Whitney wormhole. *Time to sell my plan.* "You know, I'm wondering if we should stick around another day or so...talk to Camille again, maybe talk to Harrison himself."

Adam looked at him like Noel had threatened to shave his head. "I thought you couldn't wait to put old Natchitoches in your rearview mirror?"

Noel faked a laugh, his chest tight with tension. "Well, yeah, but that's before I had a name for the *who*."

"The who?"

His laugh turned more sincere. "The *what* is harassment, the *when* is since we starting threatening the local mythology, the *where* is here, and, if we assume Harrison Whitney is the *who*, the *why* becomes his financial stake in preserving the myth as it stands." The joke was on Noel if all he could come up with was Policing 101.

"So what do you think?" Noel continued. "We'll do another twenty-four hours of on-the-ground investigation, and then we head home."

Adam's expression was unreadable. "You really think it's worthwhile?"

The words were right there. Noel just had to open his mouth and they'd come tumbling out. I saw another ghost, and not just any ghost. I saw Marie, and she wants me to find Valsin, and we can't leave until we do.

He just wasn't ready.

And maybe he'd never be ready. Secrets were his default, and running was his preferred coping strategy. If that made him a chicken shit, well cluck cluck cluck. Somebody ought to give him a medal for even debating whether to tell the whole story to Adam.

Baby steps, Chandler.

Noel still hadn't managed to pry open his mouth when Adam gave a disgusted snort. "Whatever. We're not on location until next week. Let me call the production manager and make sure there's nothing unexpected in my queue. I can research here just as well as in NOLA."

Siri gently encouraged Noel to make a left-hand turn, and he exhaled with relief. At some point, he'd have to fess up, but for now, he'd take the reprieve.

As long as Adam could take time off work, Noel had

another day to figure out what had happened to Valsin. Adam's scowl would have shut Noel down, but apparently, the person on the phone was not intimidated.

"I thought we were doing Hummel Park next. I've spent the last month trying to unearth the origins of the ghostly farmer stories." He paused. "Uh-huh."

Adam looked pissed, or even a step or two beyond pissed, effectively distracting Noel from his own drama.

"I said I would call her, and I will."

Following Siri's directions, Noel pulled the Lexus into Jason's driveway. Jason's Leaf was gone, but he'd left them a spare key.

"I know she's upset. I'll work it out with her." Adam hung up without saying goodbye. The look he gave Noel came from a place of deep unhappiness. "Annemarie wants to talk." He put air quotes around the word talk.

"That's not good."

Adam squared his shoulders. "It'll be fine. What's the worst she can do?"

Fire you?

Chapter Twenty

Inside, Adam went straight back to the guestroom, where their bags sat open on the bed, ready for the final packing they weren't going to do. He stared at them blankly before picking them both up and dumping them back into the closet. Nothing in his life made sense right now. He didn't mind staying; he just didn't see the point. Noel had been hot to leave this morning. So why were they still here?

His brain was stuck on a hamster wheel. Noel's abrupt about-face. Marie and Valsin. Social media. The Historical Society. Mayhaw Days. DNA. Noel's visions. Annemarie. Around, around, around. He couldn't focus on any of them.

"Enough already." Suddenly, Noel was right in front of him.

Adam took a startled step back and stopped when he realized he was up against the bed.

Noel did something with his foot at the same time he gave a sharp shove. Adam let out a yelp as fell backward, and another *oomph* as Noel landed half on him.

"*Shhhh.*" Noel clapped a hand over Adam's mouth. He moved his hand to land a hard kiss, then moved lower to suck on his throat. One hand was already busy on Adam's fly. Straight to the point.

Adam stared at the ceiling and tried to collect his thoughts. "Noel, we can't..."

"Shut up. We can."

His fly popped open.

Adam wriggled, trying to move away, but Noel clung, barely seeming to notice the movement as he got the zipper down. Adam's stomach still hurt. His head, his neck. The fall had knocked him off the hamster wheel, though. The only thing left in his head to chase around was Noel and a ball of fear he didn't know what to do with.

He needed to think.

"Noel."

Noel's hand landed on his cock. The oxygen deprivation in Adam's brain reached the level of spots in front of his eyes.

"Noel, stop."

Noel went utterly still. "Really?"

Adam couldn't make himself say anything else. Suddenly, he had the quiet he wanted, the space to think.

All he could think about was Noel, warm and solid against him, his soft curls tickling Adam's nose. He smelled of rosemary shampoo, parsley facial cleanser, clove deodorant, lemongrass hand soap—a whole herb garden of designer scents mingling with his own spicy-sweet fragrance and the hint of hops on his breath to create a smell that hooked right into Adam's brain and drove every other thought out but Noel.

He wanted to wrap himself in that scent. He thought if he got enough of it, he might finally be able to breathe again.

As if he'd heard him, Noel finally moved. He rested

his head alongside Adam's, temple to temple, not looking him in the eye. "You really want me to stop?"

Yes. Rosemary, tickling his sinuses. Clove. *Noel.* "No."

Then Noel did raise his head. His heavy-lidded eyes met Adam's. Tonight, the amber was dominant in the hazel, and his gaze was more serious than usual. "Stop thinking. I know I'm a shit boyfriend, but this I can do."

Noel shut off any protest he might have made by touching his lips to Adam's. The kiss started surprisingly gentle, almost comforting. Before Adam could appreciate the fleeting sweetness, it turned urgent and nasty and...*no*... A little part of him mourned the loss of that sweetness.

Noel's hand moved back under his shorts at the same time his tongue made a particularly aggressive sweep and...like flipping a switch, they were on familiar ground.

Adam arched up into his hand, thought pretty much obliterated except for *yes* and *there* and *more.* And how did Noel know exactly how to touch him?

Rosemary. Parsley. Hops. Breathe.

He sucked in air as Noel kissed and bit his way down his torso, then let it out on a groan as Noel wrapped his fingers around the base of his cock.

"Shhhh." A finger over his lips as Noel's breath ghosted over his cock. Then the whole hand as he began sucking a hickey on the side, leaving the head leaking and deprived.

Lemongrass. Breathe.

But he couldn't breathe. The air was trapped in his lungs, and he was tense, so tense.

Noel left off the hickey. His tongue flicked up, teasing the frenulum before circling the glans. Then he...

Madre de Dios.

Maybe that wasn't completely in his head, because the hand over his mouth tightened.

Clove. Noel. Noelnoelnoel.

Overload. Everything tightened, tightened, tightened until he thought he would shatter.

Breathe.

He couldn't. His lungs would burst.

So he shattered.

He exploded into a million shards of sparkling glass.

Bright. White. Empty.

Rosemary and...

He breathed.

Noel.

He opened his eyes.

Noel was curled into him, one arm over his chest, one leg hooked over him.

Adam's phone was ringing.

"If you pick that up, I'm never blowing you again."

Adam closed his eyes and breathed.

Noel climbed out of bed, moving slowly because he didn't want to wake Adam. They'd both needed that. Noel huffed a soft laugh. *Should have knocked him down and sucked him off last night and saved myself six hours in the Lexus.*

At least now they could both focus.

He threw on his jeans and carried his laptop out to the dining room. Something had been bugging him, a detail that he'd missed earlier.

He'd come to Natchitoches because Adam wanted to test his superpower. Cool. Check that off the list. He'd gone into the old slave quarters and heard...crickets. Even yesterday, when Adam asked him to give that letter a sneaky touch, he got nothing. It was almost like when he tried to use his superpower, it hid from him. It only jumped him when he wasn't looking.

So maybe he hadn't been trying in the right places.

Opening a browser, he typed "rules for ghosts" in the search bar. The hits were pretty much gibberish. *Damn it.* The wood slats of the dining room chair were cold against his skin, and he drummed his fingers against the keys without typing anything. *What am I missing?*

Noel stared out across the dining room, as if A Clue would drop from the ceiling. Jason didn't believe in clutter, obviously, but above the credenza, he'd hung a set of photos, all eight-by-ten, in identical wooden frames. *Probably koa.* Jason standing with his arm around a woman, both wearing cap and gown, with leis hung thick around their necks. Jason with what had to be his whole family, a crowd of Phams of all ages and sizes. Jason with a man, their body language telling tales of possession even though there was space between them. They were all safe behind their glass.

"None of you want to help me either," Noel muttered, then glanced around, afraid someone might have heard him. He rubbed his arms against the gooseflesh. The pictures weren't staring at him. Should have put on a damned shirt. AC was always colder than it should be.

He'd rather open a window and let the trade winds cool things off.

Okay. *Focus, Chandler.* Time to lay everything out. He opened a blank document and began to type.

Point #1—assumption: the ghostly woman is Marie, and she's appeared on the plantation and in the parking lot of the Shady Acres. She wants me to find Valsin.

Point #2—assumption: I'm not crazy. Since coming to Natchitoches, I've had two uncontrolled spirit interactions, for lack of a better description. The first happened outside the Steel Magnolias house and the second was at the old Parsons house. After the second, when Adam asked me what had happened, I said it was Valsin, then backtracked.

But...

What if it had been Valsin? What if both the takeovers had been Valsin? According to Miss Emily's diary, Marie had been working for her in town, which gave Valsin a reason to be nearby. "For all we know, Miss Emily lived at that Steel Magnolias house."

Miss Emily, the woman who had borrowed Marie from her owner. Borrowed. Like she was a damned cup of sugar. Noel tapped a rapid rhythm on the table.

"I am batshit crazy."

"I don't think so."

Adam's voice made Noel jump a good country mile. "Fuck, dude. Don't sneak up on me like that."

"Sorry."

Between the rumpled hair and the sleepy eyes, Noel wanted to drag Adam right back to bed. "I was, uh, just trying to figure things out."

"Cool. I called Annemarie." Adam rubbed his temple, an expression of pain on his face.

"Oh crap. What'd she say?"

"She wants me to fly out to LA. I've got tickets on a flight out of New Orleans tomorrow afternoon."

Shit. Noel tapped double time. "When do you want to head back?"

"Soon, I guess."

Noel nodded, calculating time and distance and comparing it with what he wanted to do They had a little time to play with, maybe an hour. "Sure, but on the way out, I want to make a stop, maybe two."

"Where?"

Steeling himself, Noel started talking. "Look, I want to try one more thing. We've gone to places we think might trigger me, but we haven't done any repeat visits to places that did. Like the cold spot in front of the Steel Magnolia House."

Adam raised his eyebrows but didn't say anything.

"And if that doesn't work, then the old Parsons house, the place that tripped me up when we first went there."

"The place where you said Valsin jumped you?"

Noel's cheeks heated. "Yeah, that one."

"And we hope to find...?"

"Whatever it is Marie wants."

"What?"

Shit. He'd stepped right into that one. Adam's expression cycled through more emotions than Noel could keep up with, finally settling on anger. Noel had about ten seconds to defuse the situation, or Adam would be catching a commuter flight to New Orleans.

"I saw her. Marie." Cold started in his fingertips, winding its way up his arms and around his heart. "Outside Shady Acres this morning. She wanted... She asked me..."

Adam's expression hadn't changed. He just stared at Noel, the intensity of his gaze drying up the flow of Noel's speech. The silence between them grew into a barrier so high and wide, Noel wondered if they would ever cross it.

"You know, you can talk to me."

Adam's comment reached further than just this incident, and for a moment, Noel could only stand there like an asshole. His jaw worked, and finally the words came. "If I talk about the ghost, it makes them real."

"Keeping secrets doesn't make them any less real." Adam shook his head. "I thought you wanted to know the truth."

"I do." Daring to take a step closer, Noel put a hand on Adam's arm. "I want to try again...a do-over. You know?" *Give me a do-over on all of it. Please.*

Adam's gaze narrowed. "You're not trying to humor me, right?"

"I'm not humoring you, no."

"Because you haven't seemed very invested in..." Adam paused as if searching for a word, or maybe biting back whatever word almost tripped out. "I just feel like I've had to push you to make an effort every time we had an opportunity to test your abilities."

Push? Noel rolled his eyes. "For fuck's sake, Adam. I'm doing the best I can here. If I'm not crazy, I'm psychic, and both options suck. I don't see how I win."

They stood staring at each other for a moment, until the awkwardness reached a tipping point. Noel rubbed a hand through his hair, and Adam cleared his throat. "Ready to go?" Noel asked.

"Yeah." Adam shifted his weight but he didn't move. "You never told me what happened in front of the Steel Magnolia house."

"Later. Let's move."

They loaded the Lexus, and in twenty minutes, they parked in downtown Natchitoches. Good thing it was a short ride. The silence in the car was all about truce and not forgiveness. The midafternoon sun had a firm grip on the day, and Noel had a firmer grip on the gris gris in his pocket.

"Let's walk down past the Calico Catastrophe," Noel murmured. He took off, and, after a step, Adam followed.

"I can't believe you just referred to the Judge Porter House as the Calico Catastrophe."

Noel raised a single eyebrow. "It was clean, at least."

"You're such a snob."

Noel smiled and kept walking. "Yup."

In another block or so, they were close to the cold spot. "Maybe it's the wrong time of day," Noel said. The words came out weak because nerves had a stranglehold on his throat. His mouth was dry. The last time he'd walked down this sidewalk, he'd...well, something had happened. Something he couldn't remember, except to know it had been...not good.

Approaching the spot, Noel had to fight to keep from turning around or crossing the street or running the other way. Anything to keep from having his senses jerked out from under him again.

"This doesn't seem like the kind of area a ghost would haunt." Adam's observation dragged Noel back to his surroundings. The road was lined with trees, their roots buckling the sidewalks, and the warm air rising up from the river wrapped everything in its sticky weight. "If you think Marie was trying to tell you something, shouldn't we go back to Magnolia? Or even the Cane River home?"

"I don't know, man. I mean, something happened the first time I walked along this sidewalk."

"If Miss Emily's family stayed in town at least some of the time, then it's reasonable to think Marie might have been with them."

"Which would give Valsin a reason for being here too, yeah." Noel kept walking. The conversation had brought them right up to that cold spot. Heart hammering, he willed his muscles to keep moving, his legs to keep walking.

And passed through the spot without a flinch.

"Well, shit." He kept going till they reached the end of the block. "That wasn't supposed to happen."

"What wasn't?"

"Nothing." Not a damned thing had happened, which meant Noel was going to have to go through this again. *Fuck.*

"It's okay. You can tell me."

Noel kept moving, the sound of his hammering heart slowly fading from his ears. "Nothing happened. I mean, something was supposed to happen, and it didn't."

Deciding he'd rather walk all the way around the block rather than pass that cold spot again, he steered them to the right. The shade was denser on the side street, cooling the air. Someone hollered, "No!" or maybe "Noel!"

Noel glanced over his shoulder in time to see a shadowy figure fade away. "Marie?" Adam's hand lost its grip on his elbow, and in another step, he plunged into a dark and freezing space. No cars, no sun, no Adam.

But someone was coming—a pair of men shouting his name.

Chapter Twenty One

Finally. He *knew* Noel had been lying to him about whatever had happened their first night in Natchitoches. The fact that it might actually be relevant to Valsin seemed like a stretch, but Adam wasn't going to argue if it meant Noel was ready to embrace his talent.

He pushed aside a flicker of worry over exactly what form *embracing* might take. Marie and Valsin were just the start. He wouldn't have to guess and wonder anymore. Noel had a ticket straight into the past. Who knew what they might learn?

He wouldn't just be "the ghost show guy" anymore.

"Do you need me to do anything?" he asked a little breathlessly. How could he help? What did he know about this street aside from some unsubstantiated rumors about the Steel Magnolia house?

Next to him, Noel made an irritated noise and jerked away, his face set into a frown as he looked back the way they had come. Adam shoved his hands in his pockets and clamped his lips together, trying to undo whatever he'd done to annoy Noel into canceling the experiment.

It took him a minute to realize it wasn't something

he'd said. Noel was staring down the street, head cocked as if listening.

Adam turned back too, searching for whatever had distracted Noel.

The street was deserted. He caught the faint sound of muted music as a car drove through the intersection at the end of the block and the rhythmic whoosh of an oscillating sprinkler. Nothing out of the ordinary.

Since Noel still hadn't moved, Adam took another step forward, adopted the same head tilted listening pose, and strained his ears for...whatever. He kept listening, not taking his eyes off the street as he half whispered, "What's up?"

Noel didn't answer. Adam finally had enough of the game, swinging around to demand an answer and maybe an explanation about what they were doing out here and...

He stopped.

Took a step closer.

Stopped again, afraid to talk, to touch, to breathe.

Noel wasn't listening, at least not to anything Adam would be able to hear. His gaze darted back and forth, tracking something down the street—a street Adam had just verified was deserted except for themselves. Like the last time Adam had watched this happen, his pupils were contracted to pinpoints. A faint sheen of sweat stood out on his brow, but Adam would bet Noel's skin would be cold and clammy to the touch. They had stopped under a giant oak. Sun filtering through the leaves of the tree danced over skin so pale, the light looked like something moving under his skin.

Adam blinked away the harrowing impression—the idea that it wasn't Noel standing next to him anymore. Or not just Noel.

Okay, okay. Just Noel doing his thing. He didn't pass

out. He's not hyperventilating. It's okay.

He edged a little closer, in case Noel did pass out. Every instinct screamed at him to reach out, to put his arms around him, to bring him back to here and now. Adam resisted. In New Orleans, touching had—*hot wind, black eyes, a woman's screams*—not gone well. Anyway, this was what they were here for. The past episodes had been frightening too, but Noel hadn't suffered any permanent damage.

So Adam waited. No touching. No talking. God, he wanted to talk. He wanted to know what was going on, what Noel was feeling and seeing. To know he was o... Adam cut the thought off. Noel had done this before. He had volunteered. He was *fine*.

So why was Adam's own heart beating a drumbeat in his ears?

"Noel?" He forced the word out.

For a split second, Noel's eyes met his, and Adam thought it was over. Then Noel made a garbled noise of pain and terror, turned on his heel, and ran.

Adam barely hesitated before pelting after him.

Maybe if he hadn't hesitated, he could have caught him before he was out of arm's reach. Or maybe if pigs flew down out of the sky, they could have caught Noel. Even before he hit the end of the block, before Adam's breathing grew labored at the unexpected sprint, he knew it was no good. When push came to shove, Adam was a desk jockey. Despite his laid-back attitude, Noel was an athlete.

Adam's breath came in gasps as he threw himself into the intersection after Noel, thanking every saint he could name there was no traffic. Noel was still pulling ahead, running flat-out half a block in front of him. Adam ignored the stitch threatening to form in his side and pushed harder despite the utter fucking futility of the exercise. Up ahead, the traffic gods were going to stop smiling on them.

"Noel!" It came out as a harsh exhalation of breath rather than the shout he intended. Adam blinked sweat out of his eyes as his brain calculated how far behind he would be before they hit the busy cross street. He stumbled to a halt, sucked in as much air as possible, and screamed. *"Noel Chandler!"*

He might as well have saved his energy and his breath. Noel hit the intersection without a second's pause.

The Tahoe crossing from the left slammed on its brakes. Adam started running again, as if it would matter…as if he could teleport into the intersection and fling himself between Noel and two tons of ugly white truck. In that moment, Adam didn't notice his breathing, the heat, his shoes pounding on the pavement. He was caught in glass—everything too quiet and too bright. Time moved forward one frame at a time—a series of small-town stills—impossibly blue sky, graceful old homes, oak limbs arching over the sidewalk. He felt caught, frozen in each frame, always impossibly far from Noel with the Tahoe impossibly close.

The screech of tires shattered the bubble of quiet. The world went from too still and quiet to too loud and fast. The back end of the Tahoe fishtailed wildly, and Adam lost sight of Noel as the driver made a desperate attempt at a turn rather than going straight across. The back end had other ideas. The Tahoe skidded in a drunken circle before jumping the curb and bouncing to a stop facing Adam. Somewhere behind it, more squealing tires sounded, punctuated by the blare of horns.

Adam dodged off the sidewalk and into the street

without slowing. In the intersection, two more cars had stopped, both at crazy angles dead in the middle of the street. He darted between them, eyes frantically searching the pavement, the sidewalk, the surrounding yards.

Distantly, he heard shouting. A hand landed on his shoulder, spinning him around. A face in front of him. Words he couldn't understand.

He jerked himself away, circled the cars, circled again.

More hands. More words.

Hey, man. He's gone, he's gone.

Chapter Twenty Two

The chair was uncomfortable.

Not nearly as uncomfortable as his thoughts.

It had taken over an hour before Noel was found. The police who responded to the near-misses in the intersection hadn't been interested in chasing down some guy on foot unless it was to cite him. Adam had finally called Jay, who didn't question his panicked cover story of "a PTSD episode." Together, they'd walked block after block, until Adam's phone had rung and the name of the local hospital flashed in the caller ID, ending their search. Adam could have saved himself the phone call, the awkward lie, and the even more awkward explanation he was going to have to give Noel later regarding anything he'd told Jason.

Right after the apology. The very sincere apology he would make from his knees. The apology and the promise they were never, *ever*, going to do anything like that again.

He'd made the same promise to a God he barely believed in a million times over the last twenty-four hours. Please let Noel be okay. I promise I'll take better care of him. I'll go to Mass every Sunday. I don't care about my job. I'll do anything. Please let Noel be okay.

He repeated the promises over again, sitting in the uncomfortable chair, holding Noel's hand. Promises to Noel. Promises to God. Promises to the devil if it would bring Noel back.

So far, no one had answered.

"Comatose," the doctors said. "No discernible physical trauma." Noel had been found by a mail carrier, curled in a ball under a hydrangea bush along his route. The tox screen was clean. Brain scans normal. Nothing had popped on the million other tests they had run, either. As far as Adam could tell, they didn't know shit.

He rested his head against the railing on the bed and rubbed his thumb along the back of Noel's hand. Only it didn't feel like Noel. Noel was warm and twitchy and larger than life. He smelled of expensive fabrics and luxe products and high-end gin.

The person in the bed was cool and still and smaller than Noel could possibly be. He smelled of cheap soap with a whiff of cheaper antiseptic. And Noel would never be caught dead wearing the ugly off-white gown with the faded matchstick print.

"Pretty sure that's a synthetic fabric," Adam whispered hoarsely. "You gotta wake up, papi chulo, before someone sees your hair like this."

Noel failed to twitch at the slur to his attire or his hair, which proved that things really were fucking sideways.

Twenty-four hours.

Noel's family should be here. Except the hospital hadn't called Noel's mother or sister. The ICE number in his phone had been Adam's. Maybe that was a matter of proximity. Even traveling for the show, Adam was usually closer to Noel than California. But the fact that after two months together Adam's was the *only* number not locked securely behind a passcode seemed... He shouldn't overthink this. And he should stop using it as an excuse. He couldn't imagine being in the hospital without his family coming to make sure he was okay. Noel deserved to have his family here, not just his emergency contact—the guy responsible for putting him here.

He reached for his phone. He'd looked up the number for The Chandler Foundation hours ago. It was the closest thing he had to a phone number for Noel's mother. After making his way through an endless voice-prompt system, he finally got a live person. He took a deep breath, "My name is Adam Morales. I'm trying to reach Ms. Astrid Chandler. It's about her son, Noel."

He was immediately dumped back into the voice prompts.

Adam stared at his phone, then tightened his lips and pressed 0, hoping to get back to a live person. The system informed him he had been returned to the main menu.

"Magnolias, not poppies."

He spun around at the sound of husky voice.

Noel's eyes were still closed but he kept talking. "Did I fall asleep? I don't remember going to bed. We were going to..." His eyes shot open, and he sat straight up, accusing gaze going straight to Adam. "Are you calling my *mother*?"

"I..." Adam grappled for a response, but his brain had latched on to the only important point. "You're awake."

"Hang up the phone, Adam." Noel's tone didn't brook any argument.

Adam hung up.

Noel nodded once. "Now we can discuss...we can..."

His voice petered off as he took in his surroundings. "Fuck."

Adam leapt to the side of the bed. "Just take it easy."

Noel batted at him. "Back off."

Adam backed. Because of course Noel didn't want him here. He swallowed hard. "Yeah. Sure. Of course. I'll leave. Just let me get the nurse."

"What?" Noel stared daggers at him, then pointed at the vacated chair. "Sit."

Adam sat.

Noel rearranged himself to sit cross-legged on the bed. He rubbed at the stubble on his chin and frowned around the room.

"The nurse..." Adam stopped when the frown turned to him.

"Okay," Noel said. "I'm in the hospital. How long was I out?"

Adam did the math in his head again, even though he'd been keeping a running count, "Twenty-six hours."

Noel stared at him. "It's tomorrow?"

Adam nodded. "We should call..."

"Nope." Noel looked down at his left hand, where an IV line still dripped fluids into his body, keeping him hydrated. He gave it a stiff yank, and it came free, tape and all. "I'm hungry. Let's go eat."

He managed to get the bedrail down and was in the process of swinging his legs over the side before Adam found his voice. "You're bleeding." Adam grabbed the first thing he saw, a washcloth that had been left on the bedside table, and mashed it against Noel's hand. "You've been passed out for over twenty-four hours. You are not leaving this room until someone looks you over."

Noel just stared at him. "My guess is they've already

looked."

"Yes, but…"

"Not my first rodeo. Where are my clothes?"

"Yes, but…"

Noel shook free of Adam's hold, though he did keep the washcloth pressed to the spot the IV had come from. He slid out of the bed, then turned to face Adam. "Hospital food sucks. Anyway, don't you want to know what I saw?"

Adam didn't really think it could be that easy. People didn't just get dressed and walk out of hospital rooms. If nothing else, there were bound to be forms. Lots of forms.

Noel didn't seem to be bound by any such considerations.

Fifteen minutes later, they were on the same deck, in the same restaurant on the river Jason had picked back in April. A hundred yards away, the Cane River sat still and silent, not even a breeze ruffling the surface. Noel was making his way through a rib eye like he hadn't eaten in weeks instead of a single day. He pointed his fork at Adam. "Aren't you going to ask?"

Adam put his coffee cup down. For once, he didn't feel like eating. No, he wasn't going to ask. Asking had put Noel in the hospital. "Do you want to head back to New Orleans tonight? Or we can stay here if you aren't up for the trip." *We can see a doctor either place*, he wanted to say. But he didn't dare push Noel. Not yet.

Noel polished off the last bite of steak and pushed the plate away. "We were wrong," he said. "They killed him."

They killed him. Either that, or Noel had lost his fucking mind. "I mean, normal people don't see ghosts, you know?"

If his non sequitur caught Adam off guard, he didn't let it show. "I think we're in fairly uncharted territory."

Adam's voice was polished, nonthreatening, as soothing as aloe gel on sunburn. Except right now, Noel wanted to feel every— "Wait. Aw fuck, you missed your flight. What happened with Annemarie?"

His lover might have rolled with the first leap of logic, but the question about Annemarie seemed to throw him. "I, uh, she... " He waved a hand like he wanted to brush the question away.

"You still have a job, right?"

"Yes, I still have a job." He gave the words individual emphasis, which only twigged Noel's radar harder. Not like Adam was lying, but Noel could tell the truth was longer than those six words.

Frustrated, he picked at the bandage covering the spot where his IV had been. "You still have to fly to LA?"

"We did a Zoom chat while you were, uh, out, and I'll talk to her again next week."

Noel should have been reassured. Adam sure wanted him to be reassured.

He absolutely wasn't.

For a little while there, he'd been convinced he could channel the spirit world, or specific spirits, anyway. He'd been so convinced of his own ability, he'd walked right into the path of one of those spirits. Or he'd triggered his own brand of crazy.

And whatever had happened had put him in the hospital, same as a psychotic break.

So, had he really proved anything?

He waved the waitress down and ordered a gin and tonic. Her name was Lacey, she had a pretty smile, and before she left, he'd upgraded his drink to a double.

She'd taken only a step or two toward the bar when Adam asked, "Are you sure?"

Noel snarled a response.

"I just...you were out for more than a day."

Clamping his jaw tight, Noel reminded himself that Adam had every right to be worried about him, and that under different circumstances he'd be glad to have someone who cared. *Jesus, try not to be a dick.*

But right now, the solicitous act had to stop, or he really was going to lose his mind.

"Okay, look." He spread his hands over the tabletop, palms down. "I'm going to have a cocktail or two, and then we're going to go someplace where I can tell you as much as I can remember." It would be like writing up a crime scene report, but without the hassle of typing. "We can't leave until I put this shit to bed."

Or until I lose it completely.

Adam sat silently while the waitress brought Noel's drink, and, except for a couple of stifled huffs, he kept his mouth shut until the last of the gin was gone. The alcohol hit Noel's system like a salve, quieting his nerves.

"Okay," he said, pushing aside the glass. "Let's do this."

Adam reached for his wallet. "Jason's expecting us."

Noel laughed at that, then laughed again out of simple relief at being able to laugh at all. "Of course he is."

Lacey with the pretty smile brought their tab, and while Adam was scanning it, Noel gave her a hundred-dollar bill and told her to keep the change. That earned him an exasperated snort. "So sue me."

Noel let Adam drive the Lexus again, because he didn't figure the combination of gin and ghosts made him safe to be behind the wheel. *Jason, Jason, Jason.* Noel eased into the leather seat, amused that Jason was now Not A Threat. *What a difference twenty-four hours of unconsciousness makes.* "Should I be jealous?"

"Nah, he knew you were in the hospital, and he said we could crash at his place if you needed to rest before we head back."

Noel hated being the weak link in the chain. "I mean, it's obvious why I couldn't stay on the force."

Adam gave him a sidelong glance. "Pardon?"

Non sequitur city, baby. Feel me. "The police force. My job. A detective can't be getting sidetracked by ghosties, you know?" Or by psychotic events.

What's it going to take to prove things one way the other? No easy answer came to mind.

They rode the rest of the way in silence, one born of exhaustion and a heavy meal more than anything else. When they arrived, Adam had his seat belt off and the door open before Noel even opened his eyes. He grabbed Adam's arm. "Hey."

Adam paused, one foot on the ground. "What?"

"We're a team, right?" Noel hated asking, but he had to know.

Reaching across the seat, Adam took hold of Noel's hand. "Yeah, papi. We're a team."

"Okay."

With that to fortify him, Noel followed Adam into

the house.

Jason met them at the door. "Hey man, you okay?" He tilted his head at Adam. "Is he okay?"

"Yes, Mom." Noel tried for a scowl, but his lips wouldn't cooperate. "Now come sit down. We're going to have story time."

"Wait." Adam elbowed Noel. "Him too?"

Noel snorted. "Why not? Let's make it a party." Without waiting to see their reaction, Noel strolled into the dining room. "Someone get paper or something. You might want to take notes."

He ignored their significant glances and didn't care if they whispered about him. This story, the events he'd experienced secondhand, filled him with pain and fear, and he needed nothing more than to let it out.

A chair scuffed across the floor behind him. "You ready?" he asked.

"Yup." It was Jason who answered. Adam was likely too agitated.

For a heartbeat, Noel felt bad about that, for putting his man through all this trauma, but then the words started to come. "They had a plan. I was, uh, Valsin was home. Waiting. Till four hours, five, after sunset. Then he'd go to the house in town where Marie worked. A cup of milk on the back stoop meant she'd left for their rendezvous."

Noel raked his hands through his hair. The line between him and Valsin was blurred. "But there were men. Two of them, on horseback. Brothers. She hadn't come directly to Valsin's house because of them. The younger one especially had tried to make mischief with her, and here they were. At my house... Talking about her. About her attempt to leave." Terror sent an electric surge through his nerves. "Somehow they knew, and I took off running."

He paused, facing the window, his back to the table. He'd run some two miles in the dark, knowing what he'd find. "I hoped they were wrong, but the cup was there." Desperation brought tears to his eyes. Not his despair. Valsin's. Noel realized that although he might be able to say the words, there was no way he could communicate the feelings. *Am I making it all up?*

He squashed that thought. There'd be time to wrangle with the truth later.

"We'd sworn to tell no one." Noel paused, confused over which memories were his and which were not. "I mean, Valsin and Marie had sworn themselves to secrecy, yet somehow the Basco brothers knew. Valsin had eluded them at first, but back in town, they got lucky. They'd seen him and ordered him to stop. When Valsin ignored them, they made a game of following him. Valsin ran, but they had horses. And hounds. He only had one real chance. The caves. He ran into the forest, leading danger away from Marie. Running took on a life of its own, a vicious race of desperation. The baying hounds echoed his terror. He had a stitch in his side and a sharper pain in his heart. Marie would wait for him. She had to."

Noel forced the words out through gritted teeth, sweat beading on his brow.

"The first gunshot came when he crossed a clearing. One of the dogs had clamped its jaw on his trouser cuff, slowing him. That first shot sailed overhead. The second one winged him. He paused long enough to kick the dog away, then ran. Slower this time, every footstep jarring his wounded arm. The bullet had hit him in the meat a few inches below his shoulder, and he clutched at it, ignoring the warm wetness seeping between his fingers." Noel grew light-headed, as if it was his own blood spilling out onto the forest floor.

"Valsin Ferrier knew this land as well as anyone, and he knew the shortest route to the cave. He kept moving by grit alone, so dizzy that when he reached the ravine, he damn near fell down the path to the bottom.."

"He needed a few more feet." Noel's arm throbbed, his pulse thudding in his ears. "Almost there."

This deep in the underbrush, there were only shades of darkness. He moved by memory, his vision blurred. Once inside, in the absolute darkness, he sank to the ground. The dogs bayed from the top of the ravine. His heartbeat slowed, and the dizziness dragged him under.

"Marie..."

His heart faltered, and all the lights went out.

"Hey." Someone shook him. Hard hands. Familiar hands.

Noel reached up and grabbed one. "Adam?" He blinked. He was crouched in the corner on the floor. "Adam?"

"I'm here, mi rey."

Adam encircled him in a hug, pulling him into his lap. Noel sighed and leaned his head on Adam's shoulder. "We're sitting on the floor."

"We are."

Noel heaved a tremulous sigh, his skin clammy, dizziness buzzing in his ears. "Are you impressed by my imaginary friends?"

Adam combed his fingers through Noel's hair. "Don't talk like that."

"You can't think any of that is true."

Jay cleared his throat. "Might be a way to tell."

Noel tried to turn his head in the direction of Jason's voice, but it was too much effort. "How?"

"I think I can take you to the cave."

Chapter Twenty Three

Jason drove, with Adam in the front seat and Noel in the Leaf's tiny back seat. On the way, Jason told stories about the cave. "The Spanish dug into the hills, looking for gold, and later, a gang of outlaws used the old caves as hideouts. I've heard there are still treasure hunters poking around out here, but the place I'm taking you is mostly the kind of place where kids party, or at least they used to. It's weird, though…"

"Weird how?" Adam asked.

Jason drummed on his steering wheel with his thumbs. "Nothing major. Just kids' stories and old legends. Same shit as you hear about the bigger site your crew did the segment on."

"We should have sent a team here instead," Adam said.

Jason chuckled. "Next time, man. And by the way"—Jason met Noel's gaze in the rearview mirror—"thank you for letting me hear your story, and for what it's worth, I don't think you're crazy."

"Thanks." Noel had to blink back a suspicious and annoying burst of wetness. "It's like they know I'll see them, and there are certain spots they can latch on to me." *Assuming the spirits were real.*

"There has to be a pattern," Adam said. "It can't be random."

Noel wished he shared Adam's confidence. Jason steered them from a highway to a road that hadn't been repaved in twenty years to a road that had never been paved at all. The trees grew in close, dense pines crowding around like they wanted to obstruct the car's forward progress.

He pulled onto an even narrower drive that disappeared into a tunnel of green. On the other side of the trees, they found a circle of flattened grass, apparently the parking lot for the trip to the cave.

"It's only about a quarter mile from here." After a false start, Jason led them to the trailhead at the top of a ravine. "Down here."

It couldn't be much past noon, and the sun poured unfiltered heat on them. The air was dense, humid, like walking into a jar of slime. Noel was sweating, and not just because of the heat and the heavy air.

Now that they were almost there, he was pretty much terrified of what they were going to find. "Okay, if we assume this spirit thing is real, then I've got a question for the academics in our club."

Adam, who'd been walking down the trail behind Noel, put a hand on his shoulder. "What?"

"Every time I tangle with a spirit, I end up collapsed in a heap. Like, what good is it to have a superpower if it utterly trashed me?"

Adam was slow in answering. "I don't know, mi rey. But you're not weak, and you're not alone. Like you said, we're a team. We'll figure it out together."

A team. The words bolstered his defenses. When Jason stopped in front of a blobby green shrub that looked just like all the other blobby green shrubs surrounding them, Noel didn't turn and run the other way.

"It's in here." Jason shoved some branches aside, revealing a gap in the green that didn't come to Noel's shoulder.

"That's it?" Noel had expected something...bigger. "It looks like the kind of thing bears hibernate in."

Jason grinned. "Maybe."

The cave—if you could call it that—was pretty much a black maw framed in green. "So there's more than one cave around here?" Noel asked. "What if this isn't the right one?" He tried to imagine trekking across the countryside, searching for the place he'd seen through Valsin's eyes.

"I can't make any promises," Jason said, "but when I was a kid, we used to dare each other to spend the night up here. This place has quite a reputation."

Noel caught Adam's eye and shrugged. "So do I, apparently."

"Nah, you're fine," Adam said. "Who wants to go in first?"

"Shoot. I should have grabbed the camp lantern from the trunk," Jay said. "You guys poke around, and I'll be right back."

He disappeared into the green, and for a moment, Noel and Adam stared at each other.

"I'll go first if you want." Adam saluted him with a flashlight.

Noel weighed his options. It wasn't as if they were going to find a 150-year-old body just lying on the ground. "I better go. If anything zings, I'll let you know."

Noel had to crouch to get under the lowest-hanging branch. He took a step inside the cave and stopped to let his eyes get used to the dimness. He hadn't brought a flashlight. His only role was to do his thing, whatever that meant.

He had a sense the space wasn't large. At the deepest point, though, he saw a dim light, as if someone had kept a candle burning for him. "Hey, Adam, squeeze on in here."

Hunched over, Adam joined him. There was just enough room for them to stand shoulder to shoulder.

"Do you see that?" Noel pointed at the light.

Adam flipped on his flashlight. "What?"

Waving away the artificial light, Noel pointed to the back of the cave. "Over there, to the right."

"What is? All I see is dark."

Shit. A special light that only Noel could see. How fucking perfect. Tension wrapped around his chest, making it harder to drag the heavy air into his lungs. *All right, Chandler. It's go time.*

Except, when Noel tried to take a step toward the light, he found his feet frozen to the ground.

"Damn it." He fought to lift one foot, then the other.

"What's going on?" Adam swung the flashlight around, catching Noel in the eyes.

Dread poured through him, replacing the marrow in his bones. If he went through with this, if he crossed the dirt floor with its layer of forest duff, he'd have an answer. They'd either find evidence of Valsin, or Noel would have his diagnosis.

And Noel really didn't want to know.

Funny thing, though. He couldn't make his feet move forward, but they moved back just fine. Without a word or a thought or a backward glance, he spun around and he ran.

He ran away from Adam and away from the cave with its damning secret. He didn't bother with the path. He just plunged into the trees, scrambling over downed branches, wicked shrubs lashing his bare arms and grabbing at his jeans.

The exertion didn't play well with his fragile state, and he hadn't gone far before he needed to pause, bent from the waist and gasping. The steak and the gin and the fear thrashed around in his belly, and before he could catch his breath, he started retching.

Everything came up, splashing onto the ground next to the stump of a fallen tree and leaving Noel weak and shivering. He wrapped his arms around himself as if he could hold in the shame and fear threatening to tear him apart. *I'm not a fucking loser. I'm not.*

Slowly, as if he'd aged fifty years in the space of a heartbeat, he straightened up. Still holding himself with both arms, he lifted one foot, and then the other. Because yes, either way the answer was terrifying, but the not-knowing would for sure drive him crazy.

When he got himself facing what he hoped was the direction of the cave, he saw Adam.

His lover. His teammate. Waiting for him just a few feet away, solid and strong and warm. Their gazes met, and although Noel wanted nothing more than to look away, to hide his humiliation, he forced himself to hold steady.

"You don't have to do this," Adam said.

Noel found a small smile. Adam wanted to finish Valsin's story more than any of them. That offer must have cost him. "I think I do, though."

They stood for another few heartbeats, then Adam held out his hand. "Then let's do it together."

Noel chuckled at that. "We're going to have to, because I have no fucking idea where the cave is from here."

Adam crossed the distance between them and pulled him close, and for just a moment, Noel clung to him. *Adam.* His counterbalance. His stability. Easing away,

Noel mustered up a real smile. "Let's do this."

The walk back to the cave was a lot briefer than he expected, and this time, Noel was able to enter without any drama. Jason had set up an LED lantern, and though Noel could no longer see the flickering light that first attracted his attention, he knew where they should dig.

Didn't take them long to find the bones.

Chapter Twenty Four

Adam sat on the same deck, in the same restaurant downtown. To his left, the Cane River lapped lazily against its banks. It was funny how things got passed along. Adam had never thought much about the Cane River. Louisiana had a lot of water, so one little river didn't much stand out. It had taken him a long time to realize that the full name of the water running through Natchitoches was the Cane River Lake. The "river" was really just a pretty little braid of the Red River that had been left behind when the main river changed course.

Just like the Marie and Valsin legend was a pretty little bit of almost-truth left behind when history changed course for the lovers over a hundred years ago.

Adam loved that story almost as much of the people of Natchitoches had. But now he was ready to stop fishing in the lake and see where the river took him. Maybe they would never know the full truth, but Valsin Ferrier deserved as much of it as they could find.

"Miss Cookie, I think you brought something with you?" He smiled gently at the woman across from him, Camille Cooke Williams. "Miss Cookie" to the thousands of kindergarteners who had been her students over the years even after she became Mrs. Williams.

Camille hesitated, and for a minute, he thought she'd changed her mind. Then she plunged her hands into the bag at her feet, like jumping quick into cold water before you lost your nerve.

Her hands were reverent as she brought the contents out, though. "This is the journal of my great-great-great-aunt Miss Emily Basco, and she may have been one of the last people to see Valsin alive on the night he was murdered."

Adam let her tell the story. It had been their deal. Mayhaw Days had gone ahead as planned for one more year. There had been no way to have the remains authenticated before then, even though he and Jay had no doubts they were Valsin's. Noel, who shouldn't have needed convincing at all, hadn't said a word until the results of the DNA tests had come back. The tests had confirmed that both Richard Lafont and Angela Davenport were a close family match for the remains in the cave.

Instead of celebrating, Noel had growled, "Figure out a way to explain this before you tell anyone," and refused to talk about it at all.

One of the cameramen stepped in, getting a close-up of the journal in real time, even though they would edit in a better shot later.

"Here is the entry where Miss Emily talks about hiring 'a girl from Magnolia' with fine needlework skills. Then Miss Emily says they were able to finish a few days early and she would send her home to her mistress if she could find someone to take her." Camille pointed to the date. "This is the last time either Valsin or Marie were seen. The next night, we know that

Marie's owner sent out a search party looking for her because she had not returned."

"This is the reason your family believes Miss Emily helped Marie and Valsin escape." Adam kept his tone encouraging.

Camille nodded. "She couldn't have written something like that down. I think she was establishing...what do they call it...plausible deniability? If someone asked why she didn't report Marie missing that next day, she could say she sent her home."

"That's a good theory." Adam made his voice sound skeptical. "But it's a little flimsy. Are there any other clues that Miss Emily knew Marie was leaving?"

"I never thought so," Camille said. "That's the part my aunt always showed me when I was a little girl. She knew I was obsessed with Marie and Valsin even then. I didn't get the full journal until she passed a few years back.

"But then Ms. Davenport showed up, and she knew all about Marie but not Valsin. After that, I remembered an entry in the journal that struck me as odd when I first read it."

Adam nodded for her to go on. On camera, he would have his "interested professor" face on. But inside, he felt a little of the tension ease out of his body. Camille was staying right on the script they'd discussed beforehand. Noel hadn't actually accused her of starting all the trouble in town, but he had pointed out that Harrison Whitney had to find out about Angela Davenport from *someone*, and it hadn't been Jay.

Camille carefully turned a few pages. "Here. Miss Emily says she received a letter from someone she only calls *A*. The length of lace she sent arrived, but the wool did not. The lace didn't suit A as well as she had thought, so she sent it along to a lady who could use it. If the wool ever arrived, she would let her know."

"And why did this strike you as unusual?"

"It always seemed out of place," Camille said, "but I never really thought much about it. Emily frequently refers to people in her journal by an initial, but she never mentioned A before or after. She never seems to care about the lost wool. If it was that unimportant, why mention it?

"It wasn't until you and Dr. Pham asked me to go back through the journal to see if there were any clues that I realized lace and wool might have been code for Marie and Valsin. Look." She pointed to the date. "Only ten days after they disappeared."

"Amazing. As a historian, you must be thrilled with this new evidence." Letting her take the spotlight didn't hurt too much. It wouldn't have been his discovery anyway; Noel had solved this mystery, not him. Miss Emily's journal provided an obvious reference once they knew what to look for.

This way made a lot of people happy. Angela Davenport had taken Valsin's remains to Pennsylvania, where they had been cremated and scattered on Marie's grave. At long last, they were reunited. Jay got an explanation for the "hunch" that the bones they discovered were Valsin's. Camille and the Historical Society got to take credit for "discovering" new facts about Marie and Valsin in Miss Emily's journal. The Merchant's Association had a whole year to come up with a new spin on the legend before next year's festival. Annemarie got a lot of shots of Adam being part of the team exhuming a century-old murder victim. Noel didn't get a single mention and kept himself away from the cameras.

None of it explained how they happened to be

exploring one of Murrell's caves with shovels when they discovered Valsin's bones.

Adam glanced over Camille's shoulder. Behind the camera crew, he caught a glimpse of Noel slouched against the wall, looking like movie star behind his designer shades. Next to him was a middle-aged woman with warm brown skin and short tight curls. At Adam's nod, she started toward him.

"Miss Cookie," Adam said. "I have a surprise for you. You've spent many years archiving the history of Marie and Valsin. I know you, like me, felt a personal connection with their story." He stood up as the newcomer approached their table, and Camille craned her head around to see what was happening. "I'd like you to meet Angela Davenport, Marie and Valsin's four-times-great-granddaughter."

Camille scrambled to her feet, almost knocking her chair over. She rushed forward, then stopped abruptly as if not sure how to greet the other woman. "Oh. Oh my goodness. Marie and Valsin's granddaughter. Goodness gracious. How wonderful."

Angela smiled. "Ms. Williams. I'm very glad to finally meet you." She nodded to the journal, still open on the table. "Without that journal, I might never have known my family history before Marie arrived in Pennsylvania. Would you mind sharing with me some of your research?"

It was exactly the right thing to say. As he had hoped, the women were soon sitting side by side at the table. Miss Cookie wanted every bit of family history Angela knew about what had happened to Marie after she left Natchitoches. The mics were still on and the cameras were rolling, but he motioned the crew to stay back a little bit so their presence wouldn't be intrusive. Adam sat back and let the ladies talk, only interrupting occasionally with a question or comment to keep the conversation flowing.

Angela hadn't brought the family Bible, but she had brought pictures showing the entries dating back to the birth of Marie's son. She also had pictures of dozens of cousins at family reunions. "It's gotten harder and harder as people spread out across the country. We've lost track of a few, like Uncle Richard, but we try to get together when we can. I think keeping a sense of family is important, don't you?"

"Oh yes," Camille exclaimed. "It's one of the reasons I've always loved keeping my own family history. Why, I can trace our roots in these parts to before the Louisiana Purchase on my mother's side. My father's family are what we call newcomers—they didn't get here until the mid-nineteenth century." She laughed a little at her own joke. "Our family tree has always given me a sense of connection. And I've tracked down so many stories. It's remarkable how many similarities crop up over the years in different people. I can see some of my own grandchildren following the same paths as their ancestors."

Angela nodded. "Yes, yes, exactly. So you understand why I had to come looking for the father of Marie's child."

"Oh, honey, you were right to come. Now that I've met you, I'm so glad you did. I don't mind telling you, when we first heard your story, it stirred up a bit of trouble."

"I'm sorry?" Angela looked puzzled

"I guess you know by now that Marie and Valsin are pretty famous around these parts. They were so romantic. That was a dark time in our history. A past like that can be hard to live with. To this day, a lot of folks don't want to talk about what went on. Marie and

Valsin's story was one we could be proud of. They showed us that even in dark times, love found a way. Now we know that Valsin didn't survive. A lot of people would have preferred to keep their happy ending."

Camille twisted her hands together on the table. Her lip trembled a little. "I guess I was one of those people. Around here, everyone has a story about how one of their ancestors helped Marie and Valsin. It's a way of saying they would have been on the right side of things, you understand? But me, I had proof."

A way of saying they would have been on the right side of things... Adam hadn't thought of it like that. More like all the sugar they put in their mayhaw jelly to disguise the tartness. And he couldn't believe Camille would say such a thing right after all that talk about how important knowing your family history was.

Maybe Angela was thinking the same thing. She stayed silent for a long minute. When she spoke, it wasn't about people being on the right side of things.

"Miss Cookie, your family history has been a great source of pride and comfort to you. I can tell how much you value all those old family stories.

"When I was a little girl, I could only trace my mother's ancestors back as far as the family Bible. It started with Marie about a hundred and fifty years ago. Just Marie, because she didn't record the name of her baby's father. And that was our family story down through the years—that Marie had been enslaved and escaped. That some man had gotten her pregnant, promised to help her, and then hadn't made the trip with her." Angela paused and gazed out at the river, clearly gathering her thoughts before she turned back to Camille.

"I guess that had an impact the women in our family. We've all always made sure we didn't have to rely on a man. I know I married late, maybe because that story made it hard for me to completely trust a man. Now you're telling me that Marie's man didn't abandon her, he was murdered. You're telling me he was a free man and his family has a history in this area. That I can trace my family tree back further than I ever dreamed.

"Miss Cookie, I'm sorry finding out the truth was hard for you, but I think Valsin deserved to have the truth told. I think our family deserved to know the real story of what happened. Thank you for your role in that."

Angela smiled at the woman next to her.

Camille burst into tears.

Angela threw a bewildered look at Adam. "What did I say? What's wrong?"

"You're right," Camille wailed. "You deserve to know the truth, and I haven't told you all of it. I was going to keep it from you." She dissolved into sobs so racking, she couldn't speak.

Adam shook his head. He knew Camille had been reluctant to accept the truth, but this seemed excessive. She was an old lady. Maybe he shouldn't have sprung Angela on her.

Angela seemed to share his concern. "Miss Cookie, calm down now. What do you mean?"

Camille dug a tissue out of her bag and dabbed at her eyes. Gradually, she got herself under control. When she could speak again, she kept her gaze on the tissue she still clutched in her hands.

"You both must have wondered why I never let Dr. Pham examine this journal and it was never on display at all until Charles convinced me to put it his is museum. I'm the president of the Historical Society, yet almost no one has seen it."

"I..." Angela seemed at a loss. "I didn't know that.

Why wouldn't you share the journal with your friends in the Historical Society?"

Camille's hand trembled as she reached for the journal again. She opened it back to the page about Miss Emily hiring Marie. She patted the page lovingly. Then, reluctantly, she turned a few more pages. She paused again at the lace and wool entry, then flipped two more pages. For a minute, she just looked at the page. Then she began to read.

"'How I wish J and C had stayed in Alexandria that week as planned. How I wish I had been as brave as M when they questioned me. Instead, I told them V would see M safe to Magnolia and they had left directly. If they hadn't tried to follow, all might have still been well. But J has always insisted on escorting M himself. When they returned late, drunk, and loud, I had my first misgivings. They could not have found M, I consoled myself. Later that night, I overheard V's name and talk of the cave. I have endeavored to put it all from my mind. The sleepless nights and dark dreams must be hysteria brought on by my own guilt—whether of the original deception or the misguided truth, I can't say. After A's letter, I can no longer ignore my misgivings. Tomorrow, I must know the truth.'"

Hand shaking, Camille turned the next page. "'If only I could return to ignorance. I went to the cave.'"

She looked up. Her eyes were red, but dry. She looked small and defeated as she echoed, *"If only I could return to ignorance.* J and C would be Miss Emily's brothers, Jeb and Charles. My great-great-great-grandfather, Charles Basco, murdered Valsin Ferrier."

Epilogue

Noel guided the Lexus down St. Charles Avenue, still grinning at the sour-lemon look the receptionist had given him when he said he was going to help his boyfriend move. "We can't all live in the twenty-first century," he mumbled.

That made him laugh out loud, mainly because he was alone in the car. Ever since The Nack, as he'd come to call the events of a couple of months ago, he talked to himself more often. "Because hey, can't ever tell when someone's listening, I guess."

Turning left on Phillip Street, he immediately started scanning for a place to park. New Orleans had turned up the heat to perma-sauna, and since they were moving Adam out of his apartment, Noel didn't want to haul boxes of stuff any farther than he had to.

Adam had taken a few days off so he could pack. The Miss Cookie episode had been a hit, which gave him a new enthusiasm for the show. He'd worked things out with Annemarie, and it had been a good few weeks since Noel had heard him mutter the words Twitter or tweet or viral.

Noel found a place to park within spitting distance of Adam's—*that's princess parking, Chandler*—and as he got out of the car, a blonde woman stepped out from behind the neighbor's overgrown azalea. A blonde woman Noel had seen before. He gave her a hard look, glad it was still light enough to justify wearing his shades.

"Noel? Noel Chandler?"

She came forward, her hand extended to shake, and he looked at her harder still. "That's me." He didn't immediately clasp her hand, letting her wait a half a dozen heartbeats while he tried to figure out how he knew her. "We've met before."

"We have!" She flashed her perfect white teeth, her eyes sparkling brighter than the diamonds on her ears. Her hand clasp was brief and surprisingly cold. "Last spring in Natchitoches. I'm Spring Whitney."

The Nack. He forced a smile, though the name of the town had hit him like a knee to the 'nads. "I remember now."

"I'm sure you do."

She reached for her sleek Coach purse, the bangles on her wrist rattling. They were the real thing too. Half a dozen gold bands, some with recessed stones, and a diamond tennis bracelet. Noel knew money when he saw it.

"I was just wondering"—she pulled out a small notebook—"if you could tell me how you did it."

Noel had that feeling, the one that sank into him right before he had to interview a suspect when he knew the guy was guilty. It was a heaviness, a weight that both calmed him and made him ready to run. "Did what?"

"Found the bones."

Everything around him stilled. "Not sure what you mean."

"Well, look, I'd been watching Jason Pham for

months, and while he's a cutie, he's not a think-outside-the-box kind of guy."

He crossed his arms but let her continue.

"And your snuggle bear Adam can't tell his ass from a hole in the ground without you to keep him straight." She smirked at him. "Though in your case, *organized* is probably a better word choice."

He gave her the gayest laugh possible. "You're wrong, girlfriend. I was just the extra muscle. One's a historian and the other's an anthropologist—"

"And you're an LA cop who left the force under some very interesting circumstances."

She raised her chin, more confident and poised than he would have expected from someone who didn't look any older than twenty-five. It was easy to underestimate petite blonde women, to treat them a little like children instead of potential barracudas.

"My work history is really none of your damn business."

She didn't shy away from the anger in his tone. In fact, she leaned into it. "What'd you do, Chandler? How'd you find Valsin's remains?"

He stuck his hand in his pocket and, for the first time in weeks, the gris gris gave him a weak electric shock. "Nice to see you again, Spring. I've got someplace I gotta be."

Without waiting for her reply, he pivoted and headed for Adam's house.

"We're not done, Chandler."

"Yeah we are," he responded without turning around. He didn't want to talk to her now and he might never want to talk to her again, but he wasn't stupid enough to think the events of last spring would stay in the past.

Still, he didn't need to deal with her or any other

awkwardness today. The driver's side door of an oversized pickup swung open as he passed, and Bergeron climbed out. "What's up with Carrie Underwood over there?"

Noel shrugged. "Asked for directions." He glanced over his shoulder. Spring stood typing on her phone next to an E-Class Mercedes that couldn't have been more than a year old. *She'll be back.* The certainty weighed on him.

Turning to Bergeron, he shifted gears and busted out laughing. "Put your tongue back in there, my dude. She's out of your league."

Bergeron jabbed him in the shoulder. "Outa your league too, but then you probably don't care much."

"Yup. I like the taste of dick better than fish."

Bergeron shook his head, laughing. "You are something else again. Let's go get your boyfriend moved."

They'd both knocked off work early on a Friday because Adam promised them food and bevs if they helped. On the way up the stairs to Adam's upper-floor unit, Noel caught sight of the guy who lived in the house across the alley. Sarasija Mishra, who called himself Sara and burned down houses as a hobby. For some reason, today he looked really rough. His house had been repaired, but he looked haggard. Before Noel could get too worried about him, the dreadlocked queen who lived there with him hollered something out an upstairs window, and the guy ducked behind the fence that separated their yard from the alley.

Odd, though he couldn't put a finger on why the guy's rough appearance bugged him. Then Adam opened the door at the top of the stairs, and Noel forgot all about Sara and his queen.

"Hey, you guys are earlier than I thought you'd be."

Adam hadn't shaved in long enough to have a full-on hipster beard. He had a sweaty bandana tied around his head and wore an old tee with the sleeves cut off, and shorts that hit his thighs at just the right place.

"How much is there to…" Bergeron's voice trailed off. The apartment had been furnished when Adam rented it, but now things were pushed against the walls, and in the center of the living room floor, he'd had made a small mountain of his belongings, mainly legal boxes filled with—

"Books." Noel walked around the stacked boxes. "You didn't tell us we were moving a damned library."

Adam cracked a smile. "You have been in here before, Noel. What did you think was in these?" He pointed at three sturdy bookcases lying on their sides.

"Babe." Noel shook his head.

"You gonna have space for all this stuff?" Bergeron asked Noel. Because yeah. That was the plan. Annemarie had run out of reasons for letting Adam keep an apartment in New Orleans, and they were "temporarily"—and Noel always used the air quotes when it crossed his mind—"temporarily" moving him into Noel's duplex.

"I'll do my best." Noel got an arm around his sweaty boyfriend and pulled him close. No, he had no intention of mentioning Spring Whitney until and unless he had to deal with her for real, and if Bergeron somehow brought her up, Noel would lie like a wall-to-wall carpet. Hell, he'd told Adam about that damned dream, right? Some two or three weeks ago, Marie and Valsin, holding hands, together in the mist. Noel shook his head. He didn't want to think about Natchitoches anymore.

Instead, he pulled his man in for a kiss, flipping Bergeron the bird to keep him quiet. No one would accuse Noel of being the perfect boyfriend, but he belonged to Adam. They were young, they were good together, and they were going home.

The End

Join Liv & Irene

Join Liv, Irene and other readers like you:
Facebook.com/groups/LivAndIrene/

Authors Note

From Liv...

This book, man. *This book.*

I took a look in our shared folder for Harrowed, and the oldest documents are from May 1, **2018**. That's not a typo. We started this book two years and five months ago. We worked on it sorta steadily and then set it aside while Irene took some time to reinvent herself. Because life, you know? I have an unending respect for the way she worked through some of the most challenging things a person can deal with, and I'm beyond thrilled that she had the energy to pick the story up again.

Look, girl! We did it! Book number 5!!!

As always, I'd like to thank Linda Ingmanson and Kate Rothwell for their excellent editing work, and I'd like to thank Kanaxa for the fabulous rebrand. We love the new cover for **Haunted** and we love love love the cover for **Harrowed**!

And Kent...wow. Your support means the world. Thank you for everything you do.

From Irene:

Honestly, I can't believe Liv stuck with me this long. There's a reason I call her St. Liv, and it's not just because when she lights one of her magic candles things get better. There is no doubt in my mind that this book wouldn't have happened if Liv hadn't gently coaxed me through the end.

Okay, at the end she might have used a cattle prod, but she got results!

In addition to the usual suspects, I'd like to thank D. Ann Williams of Tessera Editorial for her invaluable input. Until we were deep into *Harrowed*, I never realized how much ghost stories are a story within a story. There's a reason I don't normally write historical, but a search for a ghost took me down a fascinating research rabbit hole into the history of Natchitoches and the Cane River area.

Ultimately, Liv and I invented Marie and Valsin (as well as a Mayhaw festival), but the germ of the idea came from my research into Marie Thérèse "Coincoin" Metoyer. Marie Thérèse was an enslaved woman who gained her freedom and became a successful businesswoman. The empire she founded made the Metoyers one of the richest families in the state. Her story is fascinating and Valsin's cousins, the Rousseaus, are loosely based on the Metoyer family.

Finally, *dear readers*, thank you. It's been a long wait between books. I am deeply, deeply grateful for your patience.

And…if you love a good vampire romance, keep reading!

The Hours of the Night
Don't miss the series that started it all…

Vespers (Book 1)
115-year-old Catholic vampire. 22-year-old agnostic college student. A small error in hiring protocol.

Bonfire (Book 1.5)
Thaddeus and Sarasija spend their first Christmas together in the bayou, but mysterious lights in the swamp may overshadow the holiday festivities.

Nocturne (Book 2)
It's Mardi Gras, cher, but this year le bon temps kick off with murder…

Benedictus (3)
Coming in 2021

Change of Heart by Liv Rancourt
Preacher always said New Orleans was a den of sin, so of course Clarabelle had to see for herself. *Thaddeus Dupont makes a cameo appearance in this 1930s love story set in historic New Orleans.*

AVAILABLE NOW!

About the Authors

IRENE PRESTON HAS TO WRITE romances, after all she is living one. As a starving college student, she met her dream man who whisked her away on a romantic honeymoon across Europe. Today they live in the beautiful hill country outside of Austin, Texas where Dream Man is still working hard to make sure she never has to take off her rose-colored glasses.

Visit Irene at:

www.IrenePreston.com

LIV RANCOURT WRITES ROMANCE: M/F, m/m, and v/h, where the h is for human and the v is for vampire...or sometimes demon. She writes funny. She doesn't write angst. When not writing, Liv takes care of tiny premature babies or teenagers, depending on whether she's at work or at home. Her husband is a soul of patience, her dog is the cutest thing evah(!), and she's up to three ferrets.

Visit Liv at:

www.LivRancourt.com